Of Scots origin but largely educated in England, A. A. Gilbertsen is the pseudonym of a former chartered accountant and company director. He has dealt with several large companies and powerful businessmen, including negotiations with Mirror Group Newspapers, headed by Robert Maxwell, before its pension fund fraud was exposed.

After many years of business management in the UK and Continental Europe, the author established a consultancy, advising and financing smaller companies, including a very successful group, trading with Chinese manufacturers.

He and his Australian wife live in Buckinghamshire. Their three children have Italian, French and German spouses.

Pandora's Pension

A.A. GILBERTSEN

Pandora's Pension

Vanguard Press

ISBN 978 178465 087 2

Vanguard Press is an imprint of
Pegasus Elliot MacKenzie Publishers Ltd.
www.pegasuspublishers.com

First Published in 2015

Vanguard Press
Sheraton House Castle Park
Cambridge England

Printed & Bound in Great Britain by CMP (uk) Limited

For Gordon Williams, my guide to the world of literature.
And Robin, my ever-patient wife, who refrained from
interference.

To Dawn,

Our Golden Hostess.

Love from Robin
and Alastair.
("AA Gilbertson.")

Contents

INTRODUCTION

The author, A. A. Gilbertsen, is a former director of several companies, including two public companies. In one of those, he was instrumental in the sale of a subsidiary company to the Mirror Group plc. The negotiations involved in that, were largely conducted with members of the Maxwell family, including a 'completion meeting' with Robert Maxwell and his advisors, to finalise the acquisition by the Mirror Group on agreed terms.

The morning after signing-off the Heads of Terms at the evening meeting, Mr Maxwell unilaterally cancelled the agreement. Subsequently, he allegedly accused the author of 'screwing him'. Three months later, the sale was completed on the original agreed terms.

Two years after that acquisition by the Mirror Group, Robert Maxwell's body was discovered in the ocean, having apparently fallen from his yacht. Following a hasty burial in Israel, enormous misappropriations of cash from the companies' pension fund were revealed. The cash had been applied to reduce debts and bolster the share value of the Mirror Group, on the authorisation of Robert Maxwell.

A great deal of effort was made to try to redress the damage to the companies' pension fund but, Robert Maxwell's estate and those of his sons were insufficient to repay the missing funds.

Robert Maxwell was no stranger to illicit corporate dealings. In 1969, his control of the Pergamon Press Empire collapsed, when it was revealed that the profits had been grossly overstated by sales and purchases between subsidiary companies of his own group, at inflated prices.

The author retired from his post as chairmen of the group involved in the sale to the Mirror Group, and established his own management consultancy, dealing mainly with small and medium enterprises, or 'SMEs'. He invested personally in some of the client companies, including a small start-up group trading in electronic goods, mainly manufactured in China, and acted as 'hands-on' financial director and shareholder, building up a multi-million dollar enterprise.

Pandora's Pension is not a factual documentary, but a fictional mystery involving massive corporate fraud and the suspicious death of a powerful and ruthless man. The scenarios include international tax havens; Balkan civil war crimes, illicit arms trading and corrupt dealings in high value commodities between Africa and China.

The central characters, caught up in the mystery and dramatic events, sometimes involving investigation into obscure and boring details of corporate finances, are a former policeman from South Wales and a financial commodities trader from London.

1

An appointment in Liechtenstein

Riding in an old, tried and tested Mercedes taxi through the back roads of Geneva in the rain was not Andrew Tulloch's idea of international high living. The noise from four hard Michelin tyres slapping on thousands of even harder wet cobble stones made the journey no more comfortable than his EasyJet flight from Luton. It was much less than the business class and limousine journey that he had imagined and hoped for.

Not exactly luxurious but more… utilitarian, he thought. John Stuart Mill would have approved. So would any self-respecting misanthrope, such as a budding finance director of Scottish descent or his late father and mother. Not mean or penny-pinching. Just careful. The taxi drummed on, diesel engine throbbing in the rain, to the address given in the letter that Tulloch carried in his briefcase.

On arrival at a modestly conservative portico, fronting the offices of Bastarde et Fils, he suppressed a wry smile. If the head honcho was a 'bastarde', what did that make the 'fils'? he wondered. The classified advertisement in the *Financial Times* had been as small and reserved as the front entrance facing him. It had simply requested applications from suitably qualified finance officers, to be considered for a 'top level post in an international trading group'. Salary and other rewards were not even hinted at. Nor was location or any specific specialisation. Just the box number to which applications should be addressed.

After two years of increasing frustration in his middle management position at a large commodities distribution group, dealing with foodstuff and other basic supplies, Andrew was ready to consider any possibility of breaking away. Away from the restraining chains of an office and his repressive senior managers, who he considered were holding him down. His career to date in the group had been a continuous conflict between his own aggressive attitude to risk, following his instincts and forecasts of future commodity prices against the restricting and extremely defensive policy of his departmental manager.

Tulloch's approach to calculated risk taking had clashed with his manager's completely risk-averse stance almost every time that materials contracts were placed. The clashes were exacerbated by the two men's contrasting personalities. Without hesitation, or voicing the usual doubts about his boss's sub-zero IQ and complete lack of humour, he digested the appealing opportunity now advertised. It sounded like a long shot, but he promptly printed a succinct CV with a covering letter, and posted it to the box number and address in the advertisement.

The reply had been equally succinct giving the name and address of the Bastardes and a date for interview. No mention of travel arrangements or expenses. No details of the 'top level post' or the company's business. From the address, Andrew guessed that the Bastardes might have been engaged in commodities trading or financing. On the other hand, they might have been engaged in highway robbery for all he knew. Attempts to extract more information from the internet proved fruitless, and his discreet enquiries of friends and business contacts drew a similar blank response.

In fact, the Geneva-based firm, with a name from the wrong side of the blankets, was not engaged in trading of any commodity apart from the human variety. They were, what are labelled in the circles of aspiring upwardly mobile executives, 'head-hunters'. Very highly rewarded employment agents. As intermediaries, they could spread a small net in a big sea of business media and offer their catch to clients in the safe knowledge of reward without responsibility. A. Tulloch, Esq. was one of a half-dozen fish selected from a catch of hundreds, by age, qualification, experience, and apparent lack of dependant relatives or excessive moral scruples.

Being the last interviewee of the half-dozen likely lads on the shortlist (no likely lass having been considered), the reception afforded to Andrew was tired – almost jaded. If there was an M. Bastarde still living and working in the firm, he was not part of the process. Another director, M. Mathieu, looking weary after an unpromising series of interviews with five ambitious sprats of financial management, simply asked the latest interviewee to confirm his un-forged marital status and family independence. On reassurance of the stated facts, he allowed himself a soft sigh of relief and another cup of tea. After a sip, he also invited Andrew to have one.

The late afternoon light outside was beginning to fail, as was M. Mathieu's energy. Andrew accepted the tea, mentioning pointedly that it was his only refreshment since embarking on the journey. Mathieu accepted the blunt point without showing discomfort, suggesting suddenly that Mr Tulloch might like to stay overnight at their, or rather their client's, expense. They could reconvene in the morning, when he – Mathieu – would go into more detail.

As Mathieu had not entered any detail at all so far, his offer was accepted, although not without a show of resignation and enquiry as to the overnight accommodation and its quality. If they were going to piss him about, they could at least provide a good bed and a meal. More importantly, they could pay for it. Before leaving the Bastardes' office, he mentioned his travelling expenses, doubling his estimate of the costs incurred, on the basis that he could and should have flown first class and been received by a chauffeur with a stretched limousine.

Five minutes in yet another Mercedes taxi brought Tulloch to the Hotel de Lac and the comfort of a quiet, well furnished room. As the name suggested, the hotel overlooked Lac Leman, as Lake Geneva was referred to locally, from the rising north-western bank. His bedroom window faced east, so he would get the morning light, if only a glimpse of the evening lakeside. However, the dining room had a splendid view across the calm water and on to France and Mont Blanc, silhouetted against the cool evening moon.

Dinner was better than expected – grilled lake trout and pan-fried veal, digested with a rather bland red wine from vineyards on the same hillside as the hotel's restaurant.

Andrew mellowed with the meal plus a cognac in his room. And then – a sound night's sleep. Morning would bring its own surprises.

Fresh from his pristine hotel and relaxing overnight rest, a typical Swiss breakfast inside him and a raw wet sky outside, Andrew Tulloch taxied back to the Bastardes' offices at eight thirty a.m. Mathieu was waiting and working, as he had been for an hour and a half. A tray, with two cups and a pot of tea, sat beside a thick file on his desk.

"Good morning, Mr, uh Toollock, is it not? I hope you slept well." Brushing aside the mumbled affirmation and nod, he continued. "I will explain in detail, what we... our client... is and does. And I will tell you what we require for you to work for us... them." Andrew sat silent and impatient, waiting for the most important part.

"Our client company is P.O. Holdings Incorporated. It is incorporated in the State of Delaware, USA, and operates in several countries, controlled from a head office in Vaduz, Liechtenstein. The main business is trading in commodities such as oil, copper and other minerals, but it can and does trade in... other items too." Andrew wondered what 'other items' included but remained silent, except for a grunt to register his vague understanding of the vague information.

Mathieu resumed. "We require a CFO. That is, the chief financial officer, experienced in all forms of currency exchange and financial control plus a sound working knowledge of contractual exposure and funding. The group treasurer and the controllers in each of the operating divisions will report to the CFO, who will in turn report directly to the group chairman and chief executive." From the dull drone in his voice, he could have been reading the Old Testament or one of his pre-written 'Sits vac' advertisements.

The interviewee swallowed and reached for his teacup to hide his excitement. "And, who," he asked, "is that please?"

"His name is Patrick Klevic." (Mathieu emphasised the Slavonic pronunciation as Clay-vitch.) "His address is stated as Vaduz in the website but he has other residences in Andorra, Monaco and on a small Greek island called Lenios. You, if you are appointed, will also be based in Vaduz but expected to travel extensively to other offices of the group. The contract offered will be for a term of three years, with six months' notice either side."

Then, despite a fleeting inward observation of the recurring low-tax status of each location mentioned, came the most important part in the Tulloch enquiring mind.

"Remuneration is negotiable but should be in excess of quarter of a million US Dollars p.a. plus discretionary bonus and stock options. Your travel and relocation costs will be paid, but Mr Klevic does not appreciate excess spending – unless it is for himself. He laughed. "No, I'm joking, of course. You English…"

"Scottish actually."

"Yes. You English, you like the good jokes, don't you." This was a statement, not a question.

We don't joke about money, thought Andrew. But, he nodded again and forced a silent smirk to mollify the Swiss agent. "Right. That all sounds perfectly straightforward. What's the next step?"

"The next step, Mr... uh, how do you pronounce your name? Ah. Mr Toollack, that's right, is it? The next step is for you to say whether you wish to take that step and if so, we will drive to Vaduz for a meeting with the chairman and the CFO."

"I thought you were offering the post of CFO to me. Aren't you?"

"Yes, but..." – he sighed – "the present CFO has to, uh, retire very soon. There will be much for him to explain to you before he retires."

"He's getting on then? Very old, is he?"

"No. Not very old but not very healthy. He has a cancer – a tumour in his head – and expects to die within the next six months. We should go now if you are agreeable." Once more, M. Mathieu did not expect demurral from his candidate.

Without waiting for a response, Mathieu spoke sharply to the receptionist and beckoned Tulloch to follow him to the front door. A dull black BMW 750 was already outside with its engine humming. A chauffeur, also in black, opened the rear doors for the two travellers. Once safely seated behind tinted windows and secured by the seat belts, the motor party departed from Switzerland and sped across the mountainous borders to Liechtenstein.

During the drive from Geneva, Mathieu agreed to supply Andrew with various glossy publications, including full financial statements as published to the world. It looked impressive, with photographs of metal ingots trying to look interesting, and pages of detailed accounts and statistics. Far too much for anyone to swallow in one afternoon but just enough for a prospective chief financial officer to dive into what he considered to be vital.

Mathieu was not an expert in corporate finances, but he knew where to find the wealthiest clients, who would pay enormous fees for his procurement of the right person for the job. The high-level employment agent of Bastarde et Fils presented his own thumbnail sketch of his client's business.

The P.O. Group, he explained, consisted of several semi-autonomous companies, in which P.O. Holdings Inc. owned a majority share. Each company traded as if it were independent, sometimes selling commodities or traded options to each other.

He continued in a monotone, suggesting a well-rehearsed speech. Trading, he said, was conducted by the individual companies' executives. Cash was borrowed from and returned to the holding company as required. Profits were paid as dividends to P.O. Holdings Inc. and to the minority shareholders of each subsidiary company, who were mainly senior trading executives of those companies. Mathieu's voice started to sound like a solicitor reading a very long will.

Although not entirely disinterested in Mathieu's droning, what was uppermost in Tulloch's priority list at this stage was to see the audited financial statements. Once Mathieu had produced a copy, like a magician taking a rabbit out of his top hat, Tulloch grasped it and turned to the section marked 'Group Balance Sheet'.

The Balance Sheet, as certified by one of the 'Big Four' firms of registered auditors, showed that P.O. Holdings Inc. had assets worth more than most. In fact, more than all but the top hundred companies in the Dow Jones or FTSE lists. Included in the assets, was an item of 'Cash and cash equivalents' in excess of one billion US Dollars.

"That should be enough to pay the rent for a few weeks," observed Tulloch. All other details could wait until he could obtain a contract and get his feet under the proverbial new desk. Assuming, of course, that he did get the job.

Although not familiar with the P.O. Holdings Group of companies, Tulloch had a fairly good idea of the massive personality at its head. The reported reputation of Patrick Klevic was not always supported by facts, but sufficient to display an image of a dynamic and sometimes bullying battering ram; the victor of several mergers and acquisitions, often conducted in acrimonious negotiations.

After an uneventful journey through the dark mountain roads, the BMW arrived smoothly at a stone-faced office building, probably designed and built well before the First World War. The chauffeur helped the two men from the car and then stepped forward quickly to open the front doors of the building. Behind the doors, a smartly dressed woman welcomed Mathieu and conducted him and his charge – which he hoped would result in a very large charge – to a richly decorated room furnished in the style of a Hapsburg palace.

Andrew was introduced to an older man with pale, drawn features. The smart woman ushered Mathieu and Tulloch to meet the incumbent and await the messiah of industry. She then withdrew whilst they shook hands and discussed nothing in particular. After a few minutes of journey times and weather, the door opened again and a large, strongly built man entered the room, which descended into hushed silence broken by a grunted greeting from the entrant and polite mumblings from the rest.

All four men sat around an elaborate Louis XVI style table. Coffee was offered by the conductress but declined by all, and then what was described as 'meaningful discussions', ninety percent of which were dictated by the dominant latest arrival, commenced. Apart from Tulloch's careful but positive answers to any meaningful questions, the other occupants spent most of the time looking blankly at their shoelaces or just looking.

Before the sun would set, but after three hours of hurried talks with P.O. Holdings Inc.'s brusque chairman and a tired and nervous retiring chief finance officer named Anton Vanstraat, Andrew Tulloch would have been offered a new job; Mathieu would have charged a large fee and the P.O. Holdings Group would have appointed a new CFO.

But, not all of the many whose lives had been touched by the chairman and chief operating officer of P.O. Holdings Inc. would be satisfied.

2

A CRY FROM THE EMPTY COFFERS

The newly if unofficially appointed chief finance officer had absorbed as much as he could during the three hour discussion. Almost two and three-quarters of the three hours had been driven by Patrick Klevic, down a one-way street, mainly with details of the P.O. Holdings Inc. group structure and the importance of controlling risky operations to gain maximum reward. What little time was available for others to contribute was given to the ailing retiree's worried emphasis of what he considered to be the most important features of his past employment.

Of these, for a reason beyond Tulloch's comprehension, the finances involved in group pension arrangements appeared to occupy top billing.

Probably worried about his own, was the new-boy's uncharitable conclusion. But, he then remembered that this overly concerned retiree would probably not live to enjoy more than a tiny fraction of it.

Throughout the questions and answers, the concerns and assurances, Chairman Klevic remained stoical. In sharp contrast to Tulloch's current employer, the big man continuously emphasised that their business involved a great deal of risk management. His sole topic of discussion seemed to be centred around the constant need to calculate, and then to take, some element of risk matched to anticipated reward when dealing in forward contracts. After that, his own questions were short and hard. Either Tulloch could do the job or he could not. He précised his management ethic:

"There are always several ways to – how you say – skin the cat. But, we ensure that we all do it the same way here. That is: my way. Just like in the song, eh?"

More like Capt. Queeg in The Caine Mutiny, mused Tulloch. But, he nodded and smiled. Consensus, at this stage, was obligatory. In any case, he was fed up with the years of arguments with his current boss. Those had also ended 'his way' but destroyed departmental co-operation and efficiency. The man before him now appeared to welcome trade involving an element of risk and to be able to control it.

Mathieu had confined his contribution to a few confirmations and nods of approval, all of which were ignored by the others. Eventually, with the exhausted and retiring financial officer's glance of approval to his chairman, and a returned tight-lipped nod, Klevic turned to Andrew Tulloch and commanded him to start work immediately.

Before anyone could point out that the newly appointed one would have to return, not only to Geneva but to his home and his existing employer, Klevic strode heavily from the room, leaving the other three men to pick up the pieces of employment laws, terms and contracts.

Tulloch decided that this, right now, this was the time for him to set the pace and establish his position on firm ground.

"Right, gentlemen. If you would kindly give me a copy of your proposed contract, I will take it back to my lawyers" – not that he had any to take it to – "and make arrangements to join P.O. Holdings Inc. That is, assuming that we can agree all the other terms and that my employers can agree when to release me."

(*Tomorrow would do nicely*, he said to himself, with a mental pat on his own back.)

Mathieu leapt in with a thick, bound document from the file he was clutching. It contained a draft contract of employment. It also contained a copy of his own contract as agent, carrying a fee as thick as the file. Letters of polite and condescending rejection had already been posted to the five failed candidates preceding Tulloch, and now he was not going to let this big fish with his big fee slip away.

Both contracts were safely stowed away, respectively in the briefcases of Mathieu and the new CFO. Before the meeting concluded, the weary Vanstraat summoned up one more sally into his main concern. "Can I have a talk with you in private, Mr…"

"Andrew, please. Just Andrew, Mr Vanstraat."

"Thank you, Andrew. I want to tell you… advise you further, about the immediate currency arrangements. I'm sure you will be in a better position to control the treasury in future by having a little more detail now." He looked as though he was frightened, in case he did not survive until the new officer started on board. At the same time, he did not want to frighten the man before he actually signed the contract and burned his existing employment boats behind him. Time and careful diplomacy were both of the essence.

Anton Vanstraat had tried hard to appear relaxed, but his tired eyes adopted a slightly nervous flicker, as he went into more detail of the various banking arrangements and location of cash 'and cash equivalents' around the group. He often mentioned the subject of pensions, and whenever he touched upon it, the flicker turned into a decided twitch.

Pension arrangements were not uppermost in the Tulloch objectives. Like many ambitious young thrusters, he considered that they were boring, until retirement loomed on the career horizon. But he supposed that they would have to be specified and agreed before he would sign the contract.

They appeared to be very much at the top end of Mr Anton Vanstraat's interests, however. Before he parted with his retiring predecessor, Andrew Tulloch made a mental vow to explore that area and the group's actual cash balances in more detail, before turning his attention to other features of P.O. Holdings Inc.

Vanstraat was even more open and direct in his closing delivery. "You must look after the group's pension scheme. It is the key to the security of the employees and of the company. After all," he smiled reassuringly, "it guards the door to the long-term prosperity for us all. Cash flow too. That is another key. The coffers must be filled to keep the business going at all times, don't you think?"

Age and ill health, Tulloch thought, were probably the root causes of distress and concern. But, not withstanding the extremely good financial health displayed in the audited financial statements, the older man's repeated emphasis on cash and pension schemes made Andrew think very hard about liquidity. An old cliché came back to him, which he expressed to return his concurrence of Vanstraat's concerns.

"Turnover," he recited, "is vanity. Profit is sanity. But, cash flow is real money."

Almost exhausted by now, Vanstraat offered a smile of relief. His successor appeared to have got the thinly disguised message. "Cash flow is indeed," he agreed, "real money."

3

FLIGHT OF THE CASH-FLOW

After a more relaxed and quiet four hours' drive back to Geneva, Mathieu put the seal on his agent's fee, confirming the afternoon meeting in hard copy, with a letter and fee note for an outrageous sum of money based on the proposed salary to be paid to Tulloch over the next three years. That done, he offered his human charge, the alternative of another cup of tea or a taxi to Geneva airport and home.

Andrew accepted both, subject to a pre-flight overnight stay in the lakeside hotel. The following morning, he was winging his way to the doubtful splendours of Luton Airport and a train to central London, contract in briefcase and briefcase in hand. He was wondering how he could obtain early release from his existing employment without losing anything due to him.

A phone call to, and returned call from a friend, whom he had collected from a past business negotiation, followed. The friend supplied the name and number of a solicitor specialising in employment law. The next day, a meeting was arranged and Andrew learned the basic rules of the game he was about to play. The solicitor, one of five ladies in the sixteen partner practice, approved the new contract from P.O. Holdings Inc.

after a cursory glance, asking only that it should be subject to English Law, rather than that of the United States or Liechtenstein.

To get the best from one's current employer, she explained, the employee should be dismissed, preferably unfairly in the eyes of the law. That would obviate three months' notice and offer possible compensation. Not very ethical, perhaps, but entirely legal. Tulloch was very impressed with such clear and practical advice – especially from someone as attractive as she was intelligent. He made a note to follow the advice and to try to follow-up their consultation with a more social one involving food and drink, and hopefully some rather more personal counsel.

Even before he had fired-up the computer on his office desk and opened the waiting e-mails, the Tulloch mind was fermenting tactics. His first aim was to generate the desired exit from boredom and frustration, with some closing reward, and then to start earning the rewards of his new job as soon as possible. The second target in his mind, which was now quietly brewing delightful thoughts of flirtation leading to mutual passion, involved the legal body that he hoped would offer much more than usually involved with the practice of solicitors. In this situation, he considered that practice and perfection should be closely allied and that she might select him as her own preferred choice of partner – sleeping and active.

His humourless manager was also hoping to be selected as replacement of another, one more senior in the pecking order. He was aspiring to succeed the retiring director and treasurer, no less. To achieve that aim, the cautious manager would have to demonstrate commercial risk skill, which was alas, as absent as his sense of humour. Andrew felt sure that he could help himself and his nemesis at the same time, although he was not anticipating a vote of thanks for his labours.

Grim faced as ever, his departmental manager had issued strict orders limiting options on currency movements, which at the same time limited any possible advantage from them. This had always irritated Andrew, who knew that he could take forward options on exchange rates and fix the company's exposure to currency fluctuations. Even if it didn't result in a gain, it would prevent any substantial loss on currency fluctuations.

Taking forward options would cost a small amount but if the exchange rate at which the currency was fixed was better than that calculated in the trading contracts, it might also achieve a substantial additional gain for the company. The same principle applied to markets in other commodities, particularly metals and fuel, as well as the basic foodstuffs. Even though his approach appeared to be adventurous, the experience gained over recent years had given him an amalgam of security to blend with his youthful confidence.

A substantial entry into the forbidden land of forward options was planned. Before putting it into action, he e-mailed the retiring director, whose job was coveted by the failed comedian managing Tulloch's department, warning him of impending possible catastrophe if currency and commodity costs in future contracts were not safely secured against forecast inflation. He added 'cc. departmental manager' to the body of the mailing, without actually sending it to him, and deliberately misspelled his e-mail details in the address box to ensure that he would not see it – not yet.

The incumbent director and pending retiree, was more interested in securing his own pension and 'golden goodbye' payments than in the details of the storm warning. He immediately concurred and instructed Tulloch by "reply all" (although there was no other actual address listed) to make the required arrangements.

Soon, Andrew's plan was put into effect, fixing forward currency options for fifty million US dollars, and forward price options for about a hundred million dollars of oil and foodstuffs at prices only fractionally higher that the spot prices of the day. He then resent the original e-mail, addressed correctly this time to his dour, promotion-hungry manager.

Within an hour, Andrew's computer glowed white hot with a furious reply from his boss, known amongst his staff as The Grim Reaper. Not knowing that it had already been approved at top level, he demanded that Tulloch should *not*, under any circumstances, take the suggested action on pain of dismissal. The demand, already too late to be executed, was studiously ignored.

Mr Tulloch went to town and to his newly appointed lawyer. A hard copy of the furious e-mail threat was printed for possible display in court or at least to be pinned on a dartboard for target practice. Other copied documents included the earlier concurring reply from the retiring director and some external reports and recommendations on future market prices. These had been circulated regularly to several

33

members of his department but treated by his miserable manager with the same ignoring distain as that shown to Andrew.

Over the following ten days, a series of bewildering discussions took place – some heated with rage from the foaming mouth of his manager – others warm with congratulation from the otherwise disinterested retiring director. Whilst executives in his employers' offices argued about Tulloch's actions, and lawyers in London and Vaduz argued over minor points in the contract from P.O. Holdings Inc., many of the international currency and commodities prices inflated gently, triggering sharper rises in quotes on the futures markets.

Soon, with sharp orders from Klevic, legal niceties were settled in Vaduz and A. Tulloch, Esq. was ready to sign on with P.O. Holdings Inc. Time then for him to burn an old boat or two at his existing employers and with them his miserable manager's ears.

First, a back-dated copy of a previously unsent e-mail, defying the managerial demand for inaction and thinly veiled threat of dismissal. Then, a verbal slanging match, carefully stage-managed to ensure an audience nearby, including the retiring director. Finally, an equally theatrical exit, to the well-worn lines ending with, "I'll see you in court!"

Apologising to the perplexed retiring director for the noise, Andrew explained briefly that he appeared to have been dismissed for the crime of doing his job too well. He added that he would now have to throw himself upon the mercy of the legal eagles and attendant vultures of employment law.

Lawrence Olivier could not have delivered a better performance.

Before counting the un-hatched chickens of compensation, there was the matter of Mr Vanstraat's cash flow concerns at P.O. Holdings Inc. to determine. Another EasyJet ticket was booked, this time flying as near to Vaduz as possible, together with a room in a small hotel near to P.O. Holdings Inc.'s office, and a day's discussion with the ageing, retiring CFO. Vanstraat's greeting was warm but without losing the tired air of concern often associated with dying men seeking absolution.

"Come on, Andrew. We have a lot to discuss and not a great deal of time, I fear."

Tulloch had a list of questions prepared, starting with names and functions of the company's extensive cast.

Vanstraat moved to answer as fast as his health permitted, or probably faster. Absolute management control, he repeated, was exercised by Klevic, the company's co-founder. (The other had been a cousin who was no longer involved in the business.) There was also Madam Klevic, who acted as Klevic's PA and controlled all public announcements and press releases. Financial management and staff would be in Tulloch's domain, although he could enlist some help from Madam Klevic if required and from Vanstraat, "If" – sigh – "if available."

As Mathieu had outlined during their earlier car journey from Geneva to Vaduz, all of the traders operated from various locations, communicating by online computer with the offices of Klevic and of the CFO. Each trading office controlled their own staff and local facilities subject to occasional and very rare involvement from Klevic. "Very rare but absolutely final," he emphasised again.

Delving deeper into the arena of assets and liabilities, Tulloch prepared to take on board details of properties, materials and commodities. They were of relatively small value, although they had been growing progressively in recent months. Nearly all of the other items were also of modest value for the size of the businesses of the group. But one much less modest area, 'Cash or cash equivalents', which appeared in the audited statements to have been extremely healthy at the company's year-end, still shouted out to him from its place on the balance sheet.

All this was bread and butter to the two financial chiefs, if sometimes bewildering, and nearly always boring to the majority of braves. They were too busy fighting their daily commercial wars against the aggressive cowboys in their markets. Tulloch was impressed by the scope of such a large operation, controlled from such a small command centre.

Vanstraat warmed to his task and the apparent enthusiasm of his successor. Further explanations followed. International trading in oil and related products – sources and supplies of metals and minerals for industrial production, many of which had featured in Tulloch's exit plan from previous commercial slavery – all were explained in bewildering detail.

Going in the opposite direction, he continued, were trades in manufactured goods purchased in Eastern Europe or China and supplied to Africa and central America. Much of those were straightforward purchases and sales, but a large part of the profits were from commissions on supplies to third parties.

Then, just as Tulloch was beginning to relax in the mechanics of company troops fighting in the trenches, the primed and short-fused artillery ordinance was fired. The latest situation was exposed to his scrutiny. Compared to the audited financial statements at the year-end, the current picture differed startlingly.

Most of the asset values varied only with seasonal or cyclical movements but one glaring protrusion from the balance sheet was now showing, in the words of Monty Python, 'something completely different'.

'Cash, etc.' was now nowhere near as large as before, and composed largely of the 'etc.' part, such as bonds or notes. No mention was made of the source of the bonds and notes. Most of the actual cash flow had somehow flown away.

"But, to where?" asked Tulloch.

Vanstraat sighed again. More softly this time. Like a man who had reached the easy chair of life after a long hard walk. But still slightly nervous.

"We have to present the published accounts in the proper light for the shareholders and the other interested parties, don't we? Well, fortunately we have favourable arrangements with our associated organisations, to place some of their assets where they will give the most assurance to those parties. Then, by the same token, as you say, we simply return the favour to our associates."

"So… You borrow cash overnight and return it the next day?"

"Not quite. Yes, we do borrow cash as short-term loans, but it is returned in stages over a few weeks. Priority is given to associates who have to close their own accounts shortly after ours. It's all secured on our fixed assets such as the properties and personal guarantees from Mr Klevic and his business associates."

"Who are the companies or people who lend it, and who are Mr K's other associates?"

"The first category includes banks and insurance companies. They are usually supportive for about fifteen percent of the short-term cash advances. The rest comes from… uh… more directly associated sources."

"Are we talking about the directors? How can they afford that sort of money?"

"Those who are involved raise it from their shares or interests in savings and similar funds. That provides a small amount. The rest is advanced by other associated funds."

"You don't mean pension funds, do you?"

"Pension funds are sometimes involved."

"Well, as long as they are independent and it doesn't include the group pension fund."

"The group pension fund has been involved. That is where most of the cash balance at the financial year-end came from, and that is where it has since been returned to."

I thought that a preposition was something which you should never end a sentence with, Tulloch muttered to himself, feeling slightly dizzy. Taking a deeper breath, he sat back in his chair without knowing what to say next. He remembered the old Tom Hopkins training video and, sales pitch advice: 'At the crucial point of negotiation, the first one to speak loses the game'.

After what seemed like a very long twenty seconds, Vanstraat lost the game. "It has to be managed very, very carefully. Very carefully," he repeated softly.

Tulloch's voice was not so soft. "Carefully? I'll say so. More than carefully, I would think. It must be either illegal or not exactly acceptable, depending on which country's regulations apply to the funds."

The softer voice resumed. Calmly. "I have a list of all of them. I will give it to you now so you can judge for yourself, but it must be absolutely confidential. Some of the other associates – those close to Mr Klevic – are very powerful people. They would not, and do not, accept any form of mislaid information."

Tulloch gave a tiny, almost imperceptible, gulp but remained silent. He was not going to lose this game and he was definitely not going to mislay any of the information.

In London, another form of cash flow was taking place. One which had Tulloch's complete approval. His erstwhile employment contract was deemed, by lawyers on both sides, to have been breached unfairly. The embarrassed retiring director of his former employer was happy with the result of the forward options established by Tulloch. But, he was very unhappy with the apparent slap in the face dealt to Tulloch as reward.

He invited Tulloch's miserable manager – by now an even grimmer reaper – to consider two options: a generous payment in lieu of notice to Tulloch or a much less generous one to himself for the same reason.

After the briefest moment's consideration, the hapless man agreed to the former option.

Three months' notice, a period of boredom and hard slog for Tulloch, was suddenly replaced by a staggering eighteen months' salary plus the value of other benefits and a glowing letter of reference. By the end of the month, Tulloch's personal bank balance went from a painful burning red to a cool and comfortable black.

Andrew was relieved that his exit strategy had been so successful. He was also very careful to ask for full details of his own pension entitlement to be set out by the actuaries acting for his former employers, together with the name of an expert in pension fund law with whom he could consult at any time.

He was going to need a great deal of added expertise in that subject to handle his new employer, not to mention his 'very powerful' associates. An involuntary shudder spread through his neck and shoulders at the thought.

4

COCKY LLOYD'S ASCENDANCY

Port Talbot Grammar School had produced some very fine rugby players in its time. One of its very worthy alumni and former star of the rugby field had become a famous actor – a film star of worldly acclaim. Dicky Jenkins was to become one of Britain and Hollywood's highest paid actors, and no less than two of Elizabeth Taylor's multiple husbands. He never forgot his passion for rugby football, and the school, whose master's name he adopted on stage and screen, never forgot him.

But of all the muscular forces in the school team pack and the twinkling feet of half-backs and three-quarters, none were as highly regarded by themselves and as confident of future Welsh national and World Cup selection as young Llewellyn Lancelot Lloyd. His disdain for would-be tacklers, and many of his team-mates, plus boasts of his adolescent sexual prowess, had earned him the dubious accolade and nickname of 'Cocky'.

The young Lloyd's father had been a steel worker in the huge Margam works that dominated the South Wales skyline by day and illuminated it by night. The rush of searing heat and light as the blast furnace opened was still a wonder to the population of all, from Neath to Aberavon. But it was not sufficiently wonderful for the prancing inside centre and schoolboy international to accept employment in its hot and dusty environment. No. An ascending superstar of the school rugby field was destined to rise far beyond such menial, manual tasks.

Leaving school with only a few O Level passes and an unflattering final report, making particular emphasis on the level of confidence waiting for academic ability to catch up, presented no barrier to future success. Whatever the field of activity chosen by Lloyd to conquer, it would be witness to the same level of brilliance seen on the playing fields of Port Talbot Grammar. The schoolboy may have shed his satchel, but his glowing confidence outshone even his own shining morning face.

His first objective would be the Welsh Development Agency. They would probably want to employ him, even at sixteen years of age, as a senior manager of something or other.

Disappointment, disillusion, despair. None of these words sprang to mind over the next three months, as his applications to potential employers drifted from the civil service to the regional bankers' association.

Quite a few of the targeted organisations invited Cocky to attend an interview. As usual, his initial self-assurance created a good impression. Sadly, the initial impression quickly dissolved as the interviews continued and correct answers to their questions were conspicuous by their absence.

All were impressed by his record as a schoolboy international, although one interviewer had unkindly suggested that adult Welshmen who had *not* been schoolboy international rugby players were as rare as middle-aged Frenchmen who had not resisted the German army. Time bore an increasingly close resemblance to an ever-rolling stream as the weeks and months collected more cares to be passed away.

After a worrying four months of applications to, and polite demurral from a series of would be welcoming employers, an envelope bearing the more promising warning, 'strictly private and confidential' flopped gently through the Lloyd family letterbox and into the tender care of its addressee, Mr L. L. Lloyd.

With what remained of his standard swagger, a relatively anxious Cocky cut the top of the envelope and extracted what he secretly feared would be another decline if not fall, in his proposed career path. The letter was from the Glamorgan division of the South Wales Police and invited Mr L. L. Lloyd to attend another interview. Secret fears turned to open hopes of joy. Visions of Detective Inspector Lloyd of the Yard floated before his imagination and he treated his worried parents to a breakfast smile.

Cocky's second interview was surprisingly relaxed. Reference to his rugby prowess was made – and more than once. As a relatively large schoolboy who could run, tackle and, most importantly, side-step his opponents, Cocky was well endowed in more than one sense. His six feet frame and upper body strength might even have made him a candidate for 'going North' to a rugby league club, but that was considered infra dig for an ex-grammar school rugby union star.

At the end of the interview, a friendly detective sergeant smiled and said that they would contact him shortly. Within two days, another letter arrived at the Lloyd household, informing young Cocky that he had been accepted for training at the South Wales Police Academy. Smiles and kisses from his mother, and a warm if relieved handshake from Mr Lloyd Senior, told Cocky that his window of opportunity was now wide open and that he should be careful not to close it or break it.

Life at the training academy was a lot harder than expected. Constant written tests, interspersed with hours of lectures and revision, reminded trainee Lloyd that he might have made adult life a little easier had he applied himself rather more to his maths and English studies at Port Talbot Grammar. But the physical training and rugby games were, as he put it to his pals, 'a doddle'. After six months and a shaky final exam series, PC Lloyd was declared fit for duty and assigned to a station in Bridgend.

Despite the relative boredom of routine work at the police station, Cocky was pleased to be on the road to what he assumed would be an exciting and heroic career. He made himself slightly unpopular with the station sergeant by asking about detective work and terms of appointment. He became even more irritating when he talked about his self-anointed place in the imagined Rugby Hall of Fame. Then, out of the blue, or rather out of the blue lamp came the opportunity for which he had waited and expected.

South Wales Police Rugby Football Club had a fearsome reputation amongst the constabulary and an even more fearsome one amongst competing clubs. At more than one stage in their history, the club had received informal warnings of disciplinary action following play that was admitted to be robust but claimed by others to be dirty, illegal and downright dangerous. Some of their more mature players had been advised to adopt a more avuncular role, such as training instructor. Others had been advised to join another club or take up a different pastime – anything from bull fighting to knitting their own chain-mail armour.

With enforced changes to their squad, the club sought new blood to replace that of their players and many of their opponents, and to repair their hard shed reputation. The large, young schoolboy international from Port Talbot would fit the Old Bill's bill nicely. After a brief phone call to Bridgend cop-shop, PC Lloyd was recruited and told to turn up for training at six thirty p.m. on the following evening. He arrived at the clubhouse, complete with over-confidence, playing kit, tracksuit and training boots, some forty-five minutes early.

Recognition of his playing ability confirmed the trainee's opinion of his own potential in sporting and policing careers. Reporting for duty the following morning, he had walked with what could only be described as a swagger. Confidence oozed from his pores and, ignoring the duty sergeant's scowl, he decided to apply for detective work immediately. To the duty sergeant's amazement and dismay, PC Lloyd was accepted for further training as a possible detective constable.

It had not escaped the notice of the other uniformed staff at Bridgend that Lloyd's probable promotion coincided with the re-organisation enforced upon SWP RFC and their desperate need for new players. However, Cocky simply took it as his rightful place in life and entered the detective training course like a mature mallard on a calm lake. Enthusiasm for the job was projected as much as self-confidence. Admonition shrugged off as part of the toughening up process.

On completion of the course, he accepted his promotion as taken for granted, reporting to a new post and station in Mumbles. At first, the cases to which he was assigned appeared to be trivial. Petty theft and the occasional mugging were laced with indecent exposure, which turned out to be nothing more serious than a pensioner urinating on the grass in his vegetable allotment.

Then something almost foreign to the little station squad: a complaint from the owner of a small dental supplies business in the nearby trading estate. Complaints of illicit transactions and puzzling discrepancies in the books. The majority of the station staff viewed any form of fraudulent activity with dismay and horror at the thought of investigating bookkeeping records. After all, they were not accountants. Those who were, they knew to be subhuman zombies who probably produced children by computer calculation and took their holidays in a bank vault.

DC Lloyd was equally unenthusiastic, until someone mentioned that the dental supplies' bookkeeper was a stunning girl with a reputation of, what they described as, 'an all round sport'. Lloyd of the Yard announced that he was, "On the case like the proverbial flea on a stray bitch." *Perhaps,* he thought, *he should think of another analogy.* A quick call to the owner of the business, and a lift from one of his uniformed colleagues in a borrowed Ford Escort, took Cocky to the dental supplies warehouse and Gladys the glamorous bookkeeper.

Introductions were completed in seconds, before the strange case of the receding dental supplies and cavities in the bank account was opened wide for examination. All too soon for the budding detective, the facts, but not the bookkeeper's obvious attractions, were laid bare. The suspicious owner had been warned by the warehouse manager that Gladys might have been manipulating the entries to cover her tracks.

On further questioning from the warehouse manager, came an embarrassed admission and tale of unrequited lust. He mentioned with unbecoming modesty that he had naturally assumed that the girl would fancy him, due to his good looks, managerial position and new Vauxhall Victor. He added darkly that instead of carousing with him, she spent her lunch breaks in a nearby café with another man, taking some of her work with her. This, he suggested, was evidence of a conspiracy.

Lloyd's maths at school may not have been to the highest standard but he did know how to add up. After an hour and a half checking the cash book, he found a couple of simple little errors but not enough to account for the reported cash shortage. He also discovered from his police colleague, who lived locally and knew most of the young men and women in the village, that the alleged lady fraudster was actually the daughter of the café owner, where the conspiracy was supposed to have been hatched.

Glamorous Gladys was one of millions of girls and boys who were embarrassed when wearing spectacles. Without them, her eyesight was confused, if not particularly poor. She subscribed to the misapprehension voiced by Dorothy Parker concerning girls who wear glasses and boys who don't make passes. The refusal to be seen wearing them was a significant contributor to the insignificant errors in the cash book.

With Cocky's discoveries and correction of Gladys' mistakes and reluctant use of spectacles, an understanding quickly developed between them. That, and the identity of the café owner, put paid to the accusations of conspiracy. It should squash the gossip of criminal masterminds and painless financial extractions.

After applying her specs and correcting the cash-book entries, the inexperienced bookkeeper satisfied her boss and the detective that no cash had been mislaid. However, on reporting back to his station, Cocky discovered that the warehouse, often full of valuable dental materials and equipment, had been under investigation before following an earlier request from the company's owner. A return visit was arranged hastily.

This time it was more productive. The would-be womanising warehouse manager had been observed extracting – not cash – but a bulging briefcase. Even without her spectacles, Gladys had noticed that it usually occurred straight after his impromptu inspections of the inventory. That might not have been unusual if he had exited by the normal front door. But slipping out through the fire exit before the alarm had been set was another matter. Lloyd made arrangements with his Ford Escort driving friend to follow the manager's

Vauxhall after a furtive tip-off from the appreciative lady bookkeeper.

After a brief passage of time, the contents of the briefcase also passed from the warehouse manager to a scrap dealer. The scrap merchant was well known to Lloyd's colleagues as having 'previous' for receiving stolen property. Soon, thief and receiver were arrested and charged. Being 'bang to rights' as they accepted, both the warehouse manager and the scrap dealer made rapid and signed confessions.

The scrap merchant placed all of the blame on the warehouse manager, who followed suit by confessing his part and returning the compliment and the entire blame on the receiver. Each culprit ensured the conviction of the other in a mutual parting of their joint and several partnerships of crime.

Lloyd of the Yard had cracked his first case. But a later case would crack his career.

5

SELL-U LLOYD'S FALL

Life seemed to be following the desired upward path as far as Cocky could see. Promotion, of a sort, was awarded gradually by the police force. He was assigned to cases that were slightly more dramatic, although his initial success with the dental supplies fraud had become a double-edged sword as any case involving suspected fraud was dumped on his desk.

Still, there had been one consolation. The glamorous, if slightly myopic, bookkeeper had become appreciative not only of his detective work but of his company outside of office hours. She had agreed to accompany him to any form of entertainment short of the cold touchline support and post-match boredom at rugby matches. Spectacles were considered to be an option at the cinema or theatre but discretely tucked away at other times.

Social life for the two became comfortably more affectionate, if not particularly passionate. This was not without several attempts by Cocky to live up to his nickname. After one visit to a romantic play and an equally romantic restaurant, DC Lloyd persuaded Gladys to spend the night with him in a smart little hotel in Langland Bay.

He had taken the precaution of buying a replica rugby shirt in the national colours and emblem of Wales to act as temporary nightshirt. This failed miserably to arouse Gladys to sexual excitement, who pretended to gasp in awe when he donned it over his naked body. Even without her glasses, she recognised the significance of the red shirt and ostrich feathered motif of a Welsh international and recalled an old international joke:

"Oh, Cocky! I am impressed," she mocked. "You didn't tell me you shagged for Wales!"

Rugby continued to boost his standing in the police force. After a half-season of success with the second team, Lloyd had been picked as reserve for the SWP first team. Inevitably, the home games were attended by the initial selection. But, on the occasion of a far-away, away match, which was subject to sudden excuses for absence from the more complacent poseurs in the team, Cocky found himself promoted off the bench and ready and willing to display his unbounded talents.

And display them he did – with a series of dazzling runs and bewildering sidesteps, resulting in two tries for his close supporting team-mates and one for himself. With an unexpected away win against a more fancied opposition, Cocky Lloyd became slightly more cocky and his place in the first XV became slightly more secure. For the remaining fixtures of that season, L. L. Lloyd was the regular first choice and star three-quarter.

As one season followed another, and the years of robbery and petty fraud followed suit, further promotion came with success and the authority borne of experience and self-belief.

Detective Constable Lloyd became Detective Sergeant Lloyd and started to wonder when he would assume his rightful mantle of Detective Inspector Lloyd. A transfer to the main station in Swansea allowed him to take charge of some larger forms of social disturbance, including two suspected murders and a bank robbery. But still, the legacy of his first fraud case stuck to his reputation like a limpet mine. And like that weapon, it was to be the source of disaster and of his fall from grace.

Hard-won convictions, including that of a violent criminal accused of murder – resulting from DS Lloyd's persistent and gruelling pursuit of the prime suspect – followed similar successes in over fifty percent of less serious crime investigations. Despite these triumphs, one apparently minor complaint was to strike the Detective Sergeant's Achilles heel and inflict grievous bodily harm to his police career. It also hampered his rugby career, having taken time away from the level of training required of a serious player. The damage was to be lasting and physical as well as professional.

In the middle of a busy week at the Swansea Central Police Station, a smartly dressed middle-aged man visited the front desk and asked to see an officer regarding a possible complaint. The desk sergeant naturally asked him to supply some details of the nature of the complaint. This only resulted in a reluctance to divulge details until he had the ear of 'an authoritative detective, as the matter might involve fraud'.

The word 'fraud' was a signal for the sergeant to call for the station specialist and hero of the dental supplies case.

"One moment, sir. I'll just have a word with the detective with whom I believe you need to consult."

DS Lloyd was busy with a series of minor breaking and entering crimes. They had occupied too much of his time and were driving his bored mind to distraction. The smart businessman with a possible fresh case to solve provided just such a distraction for the jaded detective.

With two cups of hot tea from the canteen and a quiet room, the two men sat to discuss the fresh case. First to speak was the businessman, whose name was also Lloyd, and who was now the employer of Cocky's girlfriend, glamorous Gladys Watkins, the former bookkeeper of dental supplies fraud fame. Businessman Lloyd spoke first:

"It appears, Inspector…"

"Detective sergeant, actually but, carry on, sir."

"Oh, sorry Inspect—Sergeant."

"No problem. What's troubling you, Mr Lloyd?"

Businessman Lloyd then explained to Detective Lloyd that he had no more than a gut feeling, although that had often been proved correct in the past that something was not right in his business. Cocky tried to be patient but, his curiosity aroused, he couldn't resist pressing his new client to put, as he himself put it, 'some meat on the bone'. The meat was literally a large part of the problem and became somewhat distasteful, if only to Cocky's ears.

Businessman Lloyd's business was wholesale butchery – supplying retail shops and restaurants. He had been in the meat trade for twenty-five years and knew just what the supplies should fetch in sales and gross profits without checking the accounts. At least, he thought that he knew.

For the last five months, receipts from sales of the meat that his business had bought, had been for much less than he would expect or almost guarantee. It would leave his business with a net loss unless the situation was corrected. His problem was how to identify the source of the suspected shortfall and to establish whether it was due to theft, fraud or error. That was police work, he suggested.

Without confirming or denying responsibility for an investigation, Cocky asked for details of location, function and names of those involved in running the business. He gave a slight inward start when Butcher Lloyd named Gladys Watkins as the assistant accountant responsible for invoicing sales to customers. Memories of previous allegations against her, and her refusal to wear spectacles, flooded back over him in a tide of mild panic. He was sure that she would expect him to protect her at all costs – and it would certainly cost him – more than he could imagine.

Cocky had been told that Gladys had taken a new job recently but the name of her new employer had gone in one ear and out of the other. His immediate thought was to try to clear her and the case before another body started trying to incriminate her. Unfortunately, he was already too late. Other parties had asked questions too.

Yet more Lloyds appeared on the crime scene. The bank of the same name was the custodian of Butcher Lloyd's overdraft. And that red debit balance had been increasing in recent months. The local branch manager, infuriatingly also named

Lloyd, had compiled a thinly veiled threat in an enquiring letter to Butcher Lloyd.

The meat purveyor had then consulted one of the partners in the firm of accountants, who included Lloyd's butchers in their clientele. Alarm bells were about to ring.

Cocky then made one of the two worst decisions in his erstwhile star struck career. He called Gladys to ask what she knew and warned her not to tell anyone of anything that might incriminate her. He then told Butcher Lloyd not to mention their discussion until he, D S Lloyd, could investigate the situation.

Fearful of losing his chance of enhanced love-life and anticipated sexual gratification, he tried to disguise the possible source of the problem without first establishing the facts. The attempted cover-up soon became a complete cock-up.

Gladys had applied for the post of assistant accountant without mentioning her father's position as a customer of Lloyd's butchers. What she had proudly mentioned was that she had recently completed a course in computerised accounting. That, she explained, would increase efficiency in the Lloyd's Butchers' accounting system.

Her work involved invoicing customers for meat supplied. The invoices were produced with the aid of a new computer program, charging the quantities supplied, at set prices, graded by quality and current market costs. Each type and quality of meat was entered into the program as a pre-set unit at the current price for that cut and weight of meat. For six months she had satisfied herself that an overall check on total units sold and invoiced confirmed that she had counted them all in, and counted them all out again.

Before Cocky could attempt to investigate what he knew would be largely foreign to him, a hurried visit by a newly qualified member of the auditor's firm started a more professional investigation than Cocky could ever complete. The auditor was, like Gladys, conversant with computers and accounting software. Unlike Gladys, he was equipped with, and wearing reading glasses, and he knew what he was doing.

Very soon, he spotted a simple, fateful error. The computer had been incorrectly programmed to charge all of the pre-packed cuts of meat as if they were all the same smaller size and cost.

That little 'one size fits all' error was magnified to a near catastrophic level by the powerful machine. The program was not the responsibility of Gladys, but it reduced the value of her invoices and destroyed Butcher Lloyd's profits. Had the meat been wrongly charged at higher prices, every customer would have complained, but when getting their meat supplies at half-price, it had somehow escaped their notice.

The bespectacled auditor swiftly corrected the program, observing cheerfully, "To err is human. For a complete cock-up, you need a computer." Butcher Lloyd was less cheerful. He realised that his lost revenue would never be recovered. Nor, as it happened, would the reputations of Gladys and her detective friend.

Unfortunately, all previous attempts to glean an explanation from glamorous Gladys had been met with blank looks and a stony refusal to discuss it, "because Detective Lloyd has told me not to." This had puzzled the young auditor, who could only report the findings to his senior partner. In turn, the senior partner reported it to Butcher Lloyd, who reported it to the bank and to the Police Complaints Commission.

Gladys and DS Lloyd were now subject to an official investigation of a much more serious nature. Butcher Lloyd was agreeable to continue employing Gladys, who would intensify her internal checking with a new procedure introduced by the auditor – a new pair of spectacles – and a revised computer program. But the PCC were not agreeable to continuing DS Lloyd's rank – or perhaps – not even his employment.

To make matters worse, Gladys and her father had not avoided the curse of gossip this time, which was suggesting that the Watkins café had been receiving stolen meat. Cocky was no longer on a promise of anything warmer than a cup of cold police canteen tea.

Worse punishment to Cocky's physical well-being was yet to come. In his rugby games as the star three-quarter of SWP RFC, he had developed a penchant for selling a dummy pass to his opponents on the field. With his well-balanced running and reputation for the baffling side-step, the dummy was usually purchased gratefully by exhausted defenders even though it made them look flat-footed. After a season of success with the dummy pass, Cocky became well-known for his salesman's skill, so often bought by even the more intelligent defenders. Unfortunately, rugby football was not confined to the intelligentsia.

In only the first fifteen minutes of a game, against an opposition even more robust and physical than the South Wales Police, Cocky pretended to throw an outrageously long pass to where his wing man should have been. The defenders included two very muscular gentlemen in the back row of the scrum, whose sole purpose of playing appeared to be the pursuit of murder and mayhem. As Cocky pretended to pass, but then withdrew his hands with ball intact, a combined thirty-four stone of man-eating flank forwards drove his ribs into their cage and his shin-bones into the accident and emergency ward of Bridgend General Hospital.

A singular absence of sympathy greeted him as he recovered from the anaesthetic, with plaster casts on his ribs and one leg, plus metal staples in the other leg. A leering ex-player had watched the game until the GBH had occurred. Then, out of morbid curiosity rather than empathy, the spectator had accompanied the shattered player to hospital. He greeted Cocky with words of distinctly cold comfort:

"Well, you won't be playin' again, boyho. At least, not rugby. Not this year, nor the next, will you?" Doan' know why you keep tryin' to sell dummies to thick sods like them. You know they doan' know what a dummy is unless it's the chap playin' against them. We could all see right through you from the touchline when you tried that. Right through you." Cocky was too tired and too devastated by his injuries to demur. The Job's comforter continued gleefully.

"We'll 'ave to change your name, from Cocky Lloyd, to *Sell-You* Lloyd. Get it? Celluloid. They seen right through you!" Something between a chortle and a sneer erupted from his throat and ran like a dew-drop down his nose. Something between a shotgun blast and a flame-thrower emitted from Cocky's eyes. But he was still too tired to even spit at the smirking oaf and too sore to care.

On his eventual return to the police station, DS Lloyd was summoned into his chief's office. The PCC had recommended dismissal and possible criminal charges. The chief inspector had, however, pleaded with the assistant chief constable, to mitigate the near disaster to his force, on the grounds that Lloyd had been trying 'to prevent premature revelation of information, pending further investigation'.

He might as well have pleaded insanity as far as the ACC was concerned. Following several distasteful accusations and investigations into local police misdemeanours, the ACC had been appointed to clean up their act. The force was under pressure to dispel any taint of corruption, no matter how trivial. Lloyd would have to go. It was up to his chief to arrange it, quickly and quietly, to avoid unwanted publicity.

The chief's first port of call was the HR department, to calculate Cocky's length of service and pension entitlement. Despite his relatively young age, Cocky had started his career early and had served most of it at a fairly good rank. The HR officer tried to explain the pension entitlement, which was beyond the understanding of Cocky and his chief and, if truth be told, beyond the HR officer too.

However, they all understood that Cocky was moving out of a job and into a very early retirement. That should provide him with ample time to digest the mysteries of his pension calculation – if not how to live on its meagre income.

6

The former and suddenly retired DS Lloyd realised that he would have to act very quickly to retain any vestige of respect or income. No longer on the South Wales Police payroll or rugby team-sheet, and with the prospect of waiting many years before he could draw any of his anticipated police pension entitlement, he would just have to start again on his career path. For the last few weeks before his downfall, he had thought of little else – apart, perhaps, from his thoughts of the sexual charms of Gladys, which were drifting from his grasp as fast as his police career.

In order to appear to be continuing in the area of security services, Lloyd applied for various jobs with private security companies and even considered recruitment to the armed forces. But the damage to his ribs and legs put a physical barrier between him and regular army or RAF service, and there was no way he was going to sea.

Private security work was available overseas in less than delightful locations, such as Nigeria or Saddam Hussein's Iraq, none of which would attract him unless his injuries spread to the brain. One overseas opportunity seemed to be still open and fairly attractive, however. The Hong Kong police required a small number of experienced officers to support their Criminal Investigation Dept. in the run-up to the colony's return to the Peoples Republic of China, which would be within a few years.

Despite his faux pas with Lloyd the wholesale butcher, he was officially retired from the South Wales Police and was not disqualified from further employment with another force. Cocky's demeanour moved a little closer to his nickname as he sent a confident application to the recruitment agency acting for the Hong Kong police force. His confidence was strengthened when a promising reply flopped onto his doormat.

After another verbal contact and interviews with the agency and a representative of the former Colonial Office, the ex-DS Lloyd was appointed, again with the rank of DS. Travel arrangements were soon in place and he was instructed to report to Hong Kong. Police work in the colony should be very exciting compared to that completed in Glamorgan.

Life there was busy to the point of frenetic. Life for most of the five million inhabitants was also cheap, unless you were an ex-pat business resident – a gweilo or round-eye with white skin, an expense account and the accepted protection of a large corporation. By day, Lloyd's work moved at the pace of the endless stream of red and cream taxis along Gloucester Road and the Star Ferries crossing from Hong Kong island to Kowloon. Taxis for bankers and trading house managers in Central, and ferries for the milling shopkeepers and tourists in and around Nathan Road.

By night, he witnessed another life and – occasionally death – as the clubs and drinking haunts buzzed with drunken executives and hostesses, competing for sexual gratification and cash. Competing with each other and with the pimps and mommas who watched the scene – waiting for the lion's share of passing money. Night or day, the scene changed but the pace never slackened. Recruitment of Europeans to the police force ceased in 1994 and Cocky was fortunate to avoid injury or worse in the thirty-six months before the colony was to be amputated from the British Empire, after a hundred frantic years.

He was suitably rewarded in financial and social terms, with enough pay to fund a tiny apartment in Aberdeen and regular outings to restaurants on Lama Island and Stanley. These usually started with a drink in the bar below the Imperial Hotel. Initially, his social companions there were limited to colleagues in, or associated with, the police force. But he soon met men and women from other backgrounds, including some very pleasant Cantonese, as well as the alcohol-saturated ex-pats and civil servants. It occurred to him that he might try to stay on after reunion with the PRC, although that would be dependent on the attitude of the new administration.

As the state handover approached, it became apparent that continued employment with the Hong Kong police was not going to be on the cards. Time to take stock of what *was* on the cards and look around for the next step in his very sporadic success story. Amongst his other qualities, he had developed his strong physical presence to a level of natural authority. This authority had been augmented by other skills, including a few involving small weapons and a mental anticipation of impending danger.

In considering his future involvement in the colony or ex-colony, Lloyd was conscious of his improving social life in Hong Kong and of the lost contacts in Wales. Glamorous Gladys had promised to wait for him when he departed to South China and, so she did. Sadly, her waiting time shrank to six months after she met and consorted with an ex-Halifax Bank assistant manager, who had also developed a new career selling the dreaded 'PPI'.

Lloyd had suspected the inevitable outcome, and his own prospects of love-life had brightened with introductions to semi-attached or semi-detached ladies. Most of these were British – divorcees of ex-pat workers or unmarried career girls. There were also some very attractive Chinese girls: dark local Cantonese and taller, pale-skinned immigrant northerners. After two years of playing the field, one considerably softer and sweeter than those of the rugby clubs in Glamorgan and Carmarthen, a mutual understanding developed between Cocky and Miss Betty T'Sang.

Betty had moved to Hong Kong to take a job with a freight forwarding company near the harbour. Her immediate family lived in Shanghai but originated from a largely Muslim province hundreds of miles north of Beijing, close to the border with Mongolia. Like Cocky and the vast majority of Hong Kong's resident population, they were considered to be foreigners amongst other foreigners.

For more than two years before Governor Chris Patten officially handed the colony to the PRC, an atmosphere of nervous civic apprehension developed. Many of the British administrators felt immune, as they knew that they would either be retained as consultants or returned to employment and a comfortable retirement in the UK. The future was likely to be much more interesting for the indigenous Chinese and immigrants from other countries in Asia. And 'interesting times', formed the core of one of China's oldest and bleakest proverbial threats.

In the event, the actual handover was much less dramatic than imagined. The natural adaptability of those working in one of the world's busiest trading ports ensured a minimum of disruption to business as usual. Government attitudes in Beijing had been adapting to capitalism for years, ever since Deng Xiaoping had driven a pragmatic coach and dragons through the maniacal dogma of Chairman Mao and his retrograde cultural revolution, which had spread chaos throughout the PRC.

Superficially, the most common evidence of change was often the subtle transposition of adopted English (or American) first names on business cards and company reports, to be placed in parentheses after the bearer's full Chinese name. Even Betty T'Sang became, 'T'Sang Xi Lao (Betty)' according to the ubiquitous business cards in her purse.

In her inner social circle, however, she remained as the freshly promoted DI Lloyd's particularly close lady friend and confidante. Confidences and friendship became even closer and warmer in their shared bed. Some joked crudely that Betty was Cocky's rock and Lloyd was Betty's cock. Joke or not, Betty was to provide the firmest foundation for Cocky's future development in love, life, and the pursuit of business prospects.

Betty the rock was an equally reliable assistant to her employer – the proprietor of the freight forwarder and shipping agency based near Hong Kong's intensely busy commercial harbour. The freight forwarder also had offices and warehousing in the industrial area of Guangzhou, less than a hundred kilometres from Hong Kong. Betty was familiar with both the regional geography and government officials who controlled most of the business development and regulations applied to her employer's operations. Contacts bred contacts.

One of the local officials had dropped a hint that his own business development plan included trade with an international group based in Continental Europe. Later, he had heard that his trading partner was seeking a new personal security officer with experience in China and Europe, as well as contacts with police forces in Hong Kong. Betty immediately made the mental link between a prospective appointee and her particular friend.

Freight forwarding was a perpetual series of tight deadlines and shipping dates and times. They had to be observed meticulously, for as the clients reminded the forwarders and the forwarders reminded their staff constantly: 'Time and tide, wait for no man'. That applied to women as well but Betty T'Sang was well up to the task. When she heard of the security officer requirement, she did not wait for anyone. After some quick checks on the source of the search, she then gave Lloyd's phone number to her employer.

On her return to their shared flat in Aberdeen, Betty told Lloyd of the appointment.

"I have looked into the background of the man who says he is trying to find the right candidate, Cocky. He is not the sort of man that I would like to do business with, but he is only the agent. His client may be more reliable. I don't know.

"But, you should take your own precautions before agreeing anything. And everything should be agreed in writing – preferably with a witness."

"You think this chap's not straight? I thought that you said your boss was very well thought of."

"My boss is all right. He's quite straight. Not all of the people that we serve are quite as straight. That's all. I know you'll be careful, won't you?"

Outwardly, Lloyd remained confident – inwardly diligent, overtly cautious. Had he been armed with foresight, he might have abandoned the display of confidence.

7

ENTER THE DRAGON

A few days later, DI Lloyd received a call from a middle-aged Cantonese man who advised him of a possible employment contract for an experienced security official to operate between Europe and China. The man asked him if he knew anyone who might be suitable and who would not require a work permit in the European Union.

Lloyd thanked the caller and said that he would make enquiries. That was, of course, provided that he could have a ton and a half of further details and the legal qualifications of both the employer and the caller on the other end of the line.

Profuse verbal assurances were offered, but Lloyd insisted that full transparency, including hard copies of appropriate documents, would be the sole source of satisfaction for him to pursue the matter any further. The verbal assurances only became more profuse, coupled with an invitation to dinner, where turkey might be talked as well as eaten.

Jokingly, Lloyd suggested the Jockey Club as a suitable venue. The suggestion was not taken as a joke. The Jockey Club lounge and dining room it would be.

Before flying to the tender mercies and service with the Hong Kong police, Lloyd had been advised of the real forces of power in the colony. For many years they were the Hong Kong & Shanghai Bank, Jardine Matheson & Co. and The Jockey Club of Hong Kong. Of these, the Taipan of Taipans was The Jockey Club. Until relatively recently, no Chinese national had been admitted to the club and it had maintained a bastion of British wealth and exclusivity.

Times had changed, however. The Hong Kong & Shanghai Bank purchased the Midland Bank to become Britain's largest bank; Jardines moved their head office to Bermuda, and in Hong Kong more Chinese were promoted from the public stand in Happy Valley Racecourse to the Members' Stand and hallowed carpet of the Jockey Club premises. These had expanded to include a still-exclusive, but not entirely British and private, dining room and lounge for members and guests in a more politically-correct environment.

Lloyd had often fancied himself as a member but, as he had ruefully observed, his nickname was, and was likely to remain, Cocky, not Jockey. Nevertheless, the invitation to dine was not to be ignored. Nor was it likely to be repeated often. Ignoring the temptation to familiarise himself with the horses running that week at Happy Valley, Lloyd donned his best lounge suit and took a taxi from Central Station to his familiar watering hole beneath the Excelsior, where he was met by a smart blue Mercedes and ferried to the Jockey Club.

The driver stopped the car, which was greeted by a vaguely familiar face beneath the entrance canopy. The face was connected to someone whom Cocky had seen several times on his weekend visits to Stanley and the occasional round of golf. That face had been involved more in rounds of drinks than rounds of golf. However, Lloyd looked forward to his share of the face's generosity. At the same time, he was wary of just how acceptable the face of business entertaining would be.

With a welcoming smirk that had to pass for a warm smile, the face conducted Cocky to a couple of clubman armchairs beside a low table. Highland Park Scotch, with water but not ice, and a small dry Martini were delivered to the table, without a request from either of the men. A sheaf of papers was proffered by the face, including some printed dossiers from one of the other two Taipans of Hong Kong power. They were commenting on a corporation called P.O. Holdings Inc. In a lightly sealed envelope, Lloyd found a 'strictly private and confidential' copy of a brief job description.

8

FROM CHARLIE CHAN...

As an agent seeking the confidence of a target for recruitment, the face introduced himself with the mandatory exchange of calling cards. His card carried the name *Chou Li Chan (Joseph)* and title: *President, Chan Industrial Corporation.* There was an address in Repulse Bay printed beneath the title. The golf club in Stanley was obviously his local, if very exclusive, pub and networking haunt.

Their present venue – The Jockey Club – was Chan's very, very, exclusive club. Downing only a token sip of martini, he tried to stun Cocky into amazed wonder at the importance and status of the post on offer. The situation vacant was 'not less than that of Personal Security Officer (Asia) to the chairman and CEO of the giant P. O. Holdings Inc. group'.

Showing due deference to the impressive world standing of the international captain of industry opposite him, Cocky raised half an eyebrow and the utmost respect.

"Who's he?" he asked, before raising the whisky glass to his mouth. The face's smile turned slightly sour with disappointment but retained just a smidgeon of composure.

"His name is Patrick Klevic. He is one of the most powerful industrial commodity traders in the world. He has interests all

70

over the place and a personal security officer in Europe. Now, he wants a counterpart to conduct security operations covering Asia – particularly in China.

"Now, let us cut the carp, as you might say. Do you want to be considered for the job or shall we just have another drink, some nice dinner and enjoy the evening. Perhaps with some nice lady friends of mine – who knows?"

Cut the carp? thought Cocky. *Is that what we're having for dinner?* He smiled back at the face. "Right ho, Mr Chan. Let's, as you say, cut the crap. I'll accept that it might interest me. Naturally, it depends on the conditions."

"The conditions, as you call them, start with one hundred thousand US dollars a year and lots of, uh, other benefits."

Another smirk left Cocky slightly uneasy at the thought of this right Charlie Chan's idea of benefits. Might be monkey brains on toast. He was beginning to feel like a meal-free evening. "Well, that's not going to put me off." He tried not to show excessive interest in the salary offered or excessive distain to the offering party. "What are the other conditions?"

Relief spread like tepid soup over Chan's face. "I shall explain them after we take a short walk – a very short one – into the dining room and dinner." He brightened as he said it and rose from his chair without finishing the martini. "After that, I can make arrangements for you to discuss it with the man himself. He will be visiting our offices in Guangzhou next week and you can come over to see us and talk to him then. Don't worry about travel. I will take care of the visa and everything like that."

Cocky relaxed a little more and settled back to some delicious lobster thermidor and cold Sancerre. Betty would be pleased to see him later that evening and the pleasure would be extremely mutual.

When he had said, 'Don't worry about travel', Joseph Chan was slightly optimistic. The Lloyd sleep was limited to post-coital catnaps on Betty's breasts and the inevitable dropping off just before the alarm shouted at him to rise and get washed and dressed. A car was waiting for him when he eventually stumbled to the front of his apartment building. From there, he was whisked smartly to the hydrofoil terminal, at which Chan took his passport and disappeared to another building. He returned a few minutes later with the passport and another small document.

"Your visa," he explained.

Forty-five minutes on the smooth ride over the harbour and on southwards gave Lloyd another chance to catnap. He just heard Chan mention that nearby Macao was about to overtake Las Vegas in gambling revenue, before the noisy hydrofoil cut its engines and floated gently against the jetty. At the entry port to the PRC, Chan handed both men's passports and visas to a stone-faced official wearing a ridiculously large peaked hat. Lloyd noticed that his own passport had been fattened by a small fold of banknotes. Peaked Hat took the documents without comment, turning to take a rubber stamp from the desk behind him and whack the open page of each one.

During the half-second turn, the fold of money had mysteriously vanished. *Nothing up his sleeves, either,* mused a sleepy, droopy, Cocky. *Unless he has a snake up there.* Another car carried them on their next journey, past dark green trees, which reminded him of Norfolk Island Pines, and deeply dirty canals, one of which was in process of discharging the body of a road accident victim. A little knot of onlookers looked on while two policemen supervised the human fishing party.

The saturated corpse had until very recently been a young woman, recruited from a rural village in the far northwest of China to work for three years in a factory and workers' residential complex near Guangzhou. The factory processed low-cost computer chips. Their occidental customers often joked about their products being 'as cheap as chips', a joke that was lost to the factory workers, happy to have a daily supplement of rice.

Before travelling the hundreds of miles to Guangzhou, the woman had never seen a concrete road or traffic lights. She had never seen any level of motorised traffic. And, she had never seen the speeding white van that struck her from behind, propelling her lifeless body onto the bank of the canal, from which it rolled into the dark mixture of algae, oil and water. Life there, like the factory output, was definitely as cheap as chips – or even cheaper.

The visitors' car continued on the part-completed concrete highway, strewn with travellers and detritus of all shapes and sizes. Cyclists and donkey-carts mixed with fast taxis and open trucks carrying chairs and chicken cages, some of which flew off the trucks to become mixtures of chopstick splinters and feathered chop choi as other vehicles struck them.

After another forty-five minutes, alternatively on newly constructed highways and unmade roads, they entered a square surrounded by very new buildings with tinted glass and garish signs in Chinese characters. Twenty minutes more, at a quieter pace, saw the car in the basement of a new and smart office block. "Here we are," announced Chan. Wherever 'here' was.

Cocky became much more alert when he saw the large European figure awaiting them. Chan was waved towards a conference table and some hard chairs. The meeting was 'compact', in Chan's words. Seventy percent of the talking had been restricted to the powerful voice of international magnate Klevic and twenty-five percent was taken by Lloyd's confirmation of everything asked of him by the big man. Chan and his Chinese customers there with Klevic were limited to the remaining five percent – asking for coffee or tea and answering their own questions.

In common with most of Klevic's business meetings, the recurring subject had been the management of risk, but in this case the risk was to human life and well-being rather than to profits. The dangers to be resisted included natural perils such as typhoons and less natural perils from any person or persons unknown, particularly those from the former Soviet Union.

Lloyd felt the cold air of apprehension in the meeting room. In less than an hour, Lloyd and the now silent Chan were on their way back to the hydrofoil and home. The taxi ride back to the seaport and the noisy ferry to Hong Kong were punctuated by glances at the accompanying traffic and passengers. Anything of a faintly threatening appearance.

Rather than simply returning to the apartment in Aberdeen, Chan suggested a drink and dinner at The Peninsular – Hong Kong's iconic old hotel in Kowloon. "Klevic," he added, "would be staying there for a few days, starting tomorrow." Cocky couldn't sum up enough energy to object. He was thirsty and he liked the atmosphere of the old colonial hotel, as long as he wasn't paying.

Chan said, "Call me Joe – it sounds the same as my Chinese name anyway." He ordered beers and some stuffed olives, whilst the stately waiter brought the menu cards to their table. The beer was delicious and the olives helped to remove the strange taste and smell of the mainland highway and canal from Lloyd's mouth. Chan sipped his own beer and then cleared his throat to offer a quiet word of encouragement.

"You impressed Mr Klevic. I can tell, you know. He has already approved your appointment and all you have to do is sign up – I will arrange the contract tomorrow. One other thing, while we are here… uh, you should get a few new suits and shirts. We can fix that tomorrow too." Cocky was too tired to take offence at the suggestion of shabby appearance but made a mental note to order the most expensive wine with dinner – once more at Chan's expense.

Chan continued, "Mr Klevic will take some new suits tomorrow too, before his other contacts arrive. They will be delivered here by his tailors. The suits, that is, not the contacts. He laughed. "They keep his measurements and favourite materials ready for him. You can get suits and shirts made up in a couple of days – no hurry. I'll phone my tailors in Nathan Road – only a few minutes from here. You can drop in there any time tomorrow and chose materials while they measure your, uh…"

"I know. My inside leg measurements. Hope their hands are warmer than the last one to do that." Returning his attention to the menu, Cocky looked for the most expensive dish to go with the Chateau Petrus, which he hoped to set his sights on ordering. Petrus was not on the standard wine list, so he had to settle for a young Chateau Palmer and medallions of grilled duck. That night, Betty would be able to sleep soundly as well.

In Kowloon the next morning, Nathan Road was as busy as ever. Tourist groups almost blocked the road traffic and traders' touts weaved though them, sensing the serious buyers from the 'only looking', and waving them towards their principal's shops in the alleyways behind the main road. Chan's tailor was situated in such an establishment – a cramped room full of bales of wool worsted or mohair fabrics and poplin or silk linings. The cutter took great care measuring Cocky and displayed some lengths of fine worsted. "Best woolsted woorens from Hooddelsfeerd." He even mispronounced the town's name with a Yorkshire accent.

The fabrics certainly were of the best quality. Cocky wondered how many miles had been covered by the wool since it left the Merino sheep's back in Victoria or New South Wales. By the time that Klevic or whoever takes his new suit to Europe, he thought, it will have covered about twenty-five thousand miles. From Melbourne to Huddersfield, then from England to Hong Kong, then back to Europe or wherever.

Quite a journey for a sheep's clothing – with or without the wolf inside it.

He selected three models: a dark blue mid-weight wool worsted, a grey striped lightweight linen and a lighter grey and understated (according to the tailor) red striped wool and mohair blend. With six poplin shirts, he felt like Swansea's answer to Beau Brummel. All went on Chan's account, to be increased by fifty percent and re-charged to P.O. Holdings Inc.

The new security officer made a mental note to check the expenses claims charged by Chan and to approve only those related to himself.

9

After a deeply emotional discussion with Betty, Inspector Lloyd prepared to retire once more from police service. He said his goodbyes to his old friend and superior, Chief Inspector James 'Elementary' Watson, and reported for duty with P.O. Holdings Inc.

Using Chan's Hong Kong office to communicate with P.O.'s business activities in Guangzhou, Cocky soon constructed a picture of the nature and venues of the various contacts that Klevic and his executive used and the lines of communication between the parties involved. Those lines were often convoluted and sometimes disappeared altogether, only to emerge elsewhere later. The commodities and finances were a complete mystery to him, but he remembered their names and who appeared to be dealing with them.

A flying visit to the head office in Vaduz was arranged, where a very smartly suited Mr L. L. Lloyd met the central characters in the P.O. Holdings Inc. group hub of control. On the first day, Lloyd was introduced to the new CFO, Mr Andrew Tulloch, who Madam K confidently suggested would be welcomed as a fellow Brit.

In fact, Cocky was almost dismayed to find that this senior expatriate officer was a boring bean counter. He could not expect a grey-brained financial zombie to be interesting or interested in his own more important security work as a commercial version of James Bond. In the event, his expectations were justified and his instant distain reciprocated by the cold financial calculator.

The initial and unenthusiastic meeting of the two expatriates was disturbed by a call to Tulloch, demanding his presence and attention in the boardroom. There, he found a gaggle of commercial and financial spear-carriers awaiting the entrance of the chief gladiator. A knot of strangers from a prospective supplier, who had been approached with an offer to buy their business, were already seated and whispering last-minute tactics. They appeared to be weary but possibly desperate to conclude the negotiations on the terms already agreed with Tulloch's colleagues and approved by him and Patrick Klevic.

Almost at the sound of a curtain call, Klevic entered the room. His presence and aura sounding a call to arms, which the attendant support heeded instantly. They were accustomed to a mental click of the heels and silence, awaiting a signal to sit or to effect introductions between visitors and the axis of corporate power.

After brief and totally insincere mumblings of greeting, the entire party took their seats and resumed subservient attention. Klevic eyed the gathering and stared at the prospective selling party, as Genghis Khan might have viewed a stray herdsman on his steppe. For once, Tulloch detected a relative lack of interest in the detail of the proposed contract for negotiation. Klevic's mind seemed to be less than one hundred percent focussed on the job at hand.

In less than two minutes, the sole voice in the room delivered the final terms, which would be acceptable. The voice rose steadily and ended with the financial consideration – the price for their business.

"We agree to pay a total price for your… rather modest business… of ten and a half million Euros," There was stunned silence. The visiting party looked surprised. The attending executives, accustomed to confirming whatever the CEO said, looked blank or simply stared at the floor – "and, not a red cent more!" (No reaction from the vendors – or from anyone else.)

"Well, gentlemen" – a look of control, demanding instant submission – "I suggest that we break for ten minutes, after which you can agree or we can part company without parting our friendship." This was a well tried and tested closing broadside. "I will leave you to discuss it amongst yourselves. My colleagues will be available to put the finishing touches to the contract after that – *if* you agree. It is, of course, entirely up to you but we will not accept any further delay or changes of any sort."

Tulloch could not believe his ears. He desperately re-read the proposed heads of agreement on the table before him. Before he could think of what to say, Klevic rose and left the room. From there, he paced swiftly in the direction of his car, which was waiting impatiently outside the front entrance. Lord Genghis had spoken. The world could sleep.

Running after the striding CEO, Tulloch was just in time to see the car racing away towards the airport, where he knew that Klevic was about to board a plane and fly to Greece. Back in the anteroom, he faced the residue of his colleagues at the meeting.

"What on earth did he mean? Ten and a half million *euros*? Has he lost it?"

The only other who had realised the error of his master's voice remained bashful and silent. Tulloch continued. "It's ten and a half million *US dollars! Not euros!* That'll cost us four million dollars more! What's going on?"

A nervous voice bleated from the back of the small anteroom. "Well, we can't just tell them" – pointing his head towards the board room of puzzled would-be vendors – "that Klevic made a mistake. We'll have to leave it for now as it is. I'll tell them that we have to check some other details with the investment bank and auditors and confirm in the morning.

"Then we can say we've found some hidden problem in their business and that they have broken the underlying terms of sale. With luck, they'll go tits-up in two or three months after we pull out and we can pick up the pieces of their business for next to nothing."

Tulloch almost vomited. He knew that there was no underlying problem. Just lying underlings.

Away from the blundering and Machiavellian squirming in and around the boardroom meeting, most of Cocky's time in the Vaduz head office had been spent under the watchful eye of Madam Klevic, who guarded Klevic's time and movements so tightly that Lloyd wondered why a security officer was necessary. On the next morning, wandering past an open office, he thought that he saw Klevic – alone but with his back to the open doorway. But Klevic had already flown to Greece with Madam K.

As the figure turned and left the office, he realised that he might be mistaken, although he was sure that there had been a strong physical likeness to the chairman and CEO. If not Klevic, he thought, perhaps it might have been Petric, the elusive European security officer.

He continued along the corridor to find Tulloch, without mentioning the man in the other office. After one more day, with still no obvious introduction to his European counterpart, he said his goodbyes and flew back to a steamy Hong Kong – to Betty and more familiar territory.

The burly figure that Lloyd had seen briefly in Vaduz also said his goodbyes and flew to other climes. As did two others – two slightly more sinister characters from the former Soviet Socialist Republics, who just happened to be visiting Vaduz on that day. They all travelled separately but they all travelled east – towards Greece.

10

FROM THE ISLAND

Pathos Paramides felt, as he put it to his drinking friends in the harbour café bar, like burnt shit. His entire one hundred and five kilos of flesh and flab throbbed with the residue of half a litre of raki and several more of the cheapest local wines. They had been consumed during his attempts to impress tourists and friends with his entertaining skills. Sadly, the quality of his anecdotes and antique jokes usually matched those of the drinks.

"You see those fine houses? I built them all. Do they call me 'Pathos the Builder?' No!" This was delivered with an exaggerated spit to the café floor. "And those boats I sailed around these islands. Do they call me 'Pathos the Navigator?' No!" He spat again.

"One sheep… I shagged one sheep…" There was a brief pause, followed by his own roars of laughter; a shocked gasp from a more delicate American maiden and some forced chuckles from the tougher tourists.

"So, what d'ya call yo'self now, honey? Mutton Jeff?" Hard toned, from a hard-faced Texan lady. She had travelled the world, heard it all before and knew too well what was likely to follow. Before Pathos could answer and claim a reward, she had summoned the po-faced waiter and ordered a flask of the cheapest raki in the house, and then made her escape, together with most of the other visitors.

When she had left the café, Pathos tried to decide whether 'Mutton Jeff' was a compliment or an insult. Taking the easy path, he settled on the more favourable former option. He had heard the coarse expression 'Mutton dagger', which he supposed would refer to his manhood. Not that he had seen much of that recently below his bulging belly. He pondered on the thought of his chances of survival after stabbing his dagger into the softer part of the leathery lady from Dallas – if she ever had a softer part.

Sprawled now, on a low wall beside the harbour in the weak dawn light, Pathos felt a strong trembling in his head and stomach, which he assumed to be the after-effects of his previous night's toxic consumption and performance. Taking a slightly deeper breath, his head cleared enough to realise that a large launch was approaching through an indigo-grey mist that married early morning sea and sky. As the throbbing from the twin diesels intensified and synchronised with his hangover, he could just make out thirty metres of Sun seekers marine luxury, gliding to rest at the jetty's blunt end, another thirty metres from the harbour wall.

Two large men, supporting a stretcher bearing an equally large but covered body, walked quickly out of the launch and onto the jetty towards a black ambulance vehicle by the harbour wall. A smartly dressed woman and another man, who appeared to be businessmen of some sort, followed. Pathos shambled across to try to see the body.

All he could see was the blanket and one bare arm, which had a smashed Vacheron Constantin wristwatch and a small sepia tattoo; a thin crescent and five-point star halfway up the forearm. Below the smashed remains of a very expensive wristwatch, Pathos could not fail to notice the bloody hand, with four fingernails almost torn from their limp digits.

A cold shudder, too strong to be accounted by excess alcohol, reminded the sickly fisherman of tales passed down by his elderly relatives. Accounts of victims of Turkish captors in the First World War and of Gestapo interrogators in the Second. Extraction of fingernails was often applied by them then – whether information was extracted or not.

In less than two minutes, stretcher, corpse, and four live humans were in the back of the ambulance. With the rear door shut firmly by the driver, the entire entourage departed at speed, leaving the launch in the care of three crewmen. The natural curiosity of the island layabouts drove Pathos and a couple of onlookers to the stationary launch. With no more than boredom to bridge their morning inactivity, conversation became a series of staccato mumblings.

"Who was that?" demanded one grubby fisherman. "Where are they off to?"

The crew stood silent and sullen. One sailor broke the silence. "Our boss – in the villa on Lenios. They're taking his body to the airfield."

"Taking his body? To the airfield? Why?" From another bystander.

After a moment's silence, the obvious curt answer was delivered from the tight mouth of the launch's skipper: "Because he's dead, of course."

The fishermen shrugged off the cold sarcasm with a resigned frown, shuffling back towards their own boats on the beach. Pathos was less sanguine – about the snub or the intrigue appearing in the usual dullness of the morning. Through the alcoholic haze, which threatened to cut off his sight and thought altogether, he summoned up enough composure to pursue his curiosity further.

He was aware, as all the villagers were, that someone with a lot of money and political power had bought the tiny island of Lenios and its old mansion some years earlier. He was also aware the he had not received any benefit from the fortune spent since then, expanding and converting the old mansion into a modern palace. "And a rather vulgar one," he had suggested, to hide his disappointment.

It might be time to obtain some recompense, for that lack of respect and income. The rich pickings in Lenios had been effectively out of bounds since the palace was completed. But now, the proverbial mountain – or its wealthy owner – had come to Mohammed, albeit as a corpse.

"I'm a senior member of this village council. Kindly tell me, what happened to him?" That seemed to be a reasonable request and a civil starting point.

As far as the launch's skipper was concerned, it was also the finishing point. He did not have a cap to doff – not even a forelock to tug, in order to register subservience. Clearing his throat of nicotine flavoured mucus with a strangulated cough, he expressed due respect for the dead body and for the near-dead busybody before him.

"Mind your own fucking business!"

However, Pathos Paramides was made of sterner stuff than the skipper might have assumed and too incapable of straight walking to march away. Time for a show of authority.

"It is my business!" A stronger tone in the wobbling voice. "I repeat. I am a senior member of the village council and you should show some respect and co-operation or—"

"Or what?" There was a slight sneer in the skipper's challenge but not as hard as before.

"Or... or you could find your boat in custody of the village council. And another thing... I can inform the authorities at the airfield that they cannot allow those people to take the body from here. Not until we have a proper coroner's report."

The skipper heaved a huge sigh of resignation. Not only had he seen his newly found and future employment probably drive away with the corpse, but now this fat pratt was threatening him with untold hassle and removal of the only means of return to his residence and personal belongings in Lenios.

In death there might be life but this life was indeed a bitch.

"OK. I can only tell you the little that I know and all of that will have to be in strictest confidence. Otherwise," he added darkly, "you may have some very unfortunate consequences." He hoped that the last bit would shut Pathos up.

Pathos warmed to the thought of strictest confidence, which he was about as capable of keeping as he was of flying to the moon. The immediate warmth from his pretended

87

authority quickly cooled, with an inward shudder at the prospect of unfortunate consequences. He had suffered enough of those over the past years, he thought. His joke concerning sex and sheep had become less of a joke after some of the women in the village and the local shepherd had taken it seriously.

No matter. What could he deduce and embellish later, from the little that the skipper was about to reveal? His dry mouth wanted to salivate at the prospect of being the village café society centre of attention for the foreseeable future. It remained dry but not dry enough to stop him adding to his irritating interrogation.

"As a senior member of the village council," came the pompous words from a sandpaper throat, "strictest confidence applies to all information in my keeping. That goes without saying." And, he hoped, he wouldn't have to do much more saying until he had downed his morning half-litre of recovery in the café.

"OK. This is all I can tell you." The skipper wondered how quickly he could fob off the annoying impediment before him. "The boss is... or was... the head of a huge international business. A multi-multi-millionaire. He had an accident sometime last night and has died. They're taking him back to somewhere for burial with his family... his ancestors. You know what I mean."

"Which business is that? What's his name, anyway?"

"His company or group is called something like P.O. Holdings Inc.. Nothing to do with the shipping company. I've never met him before and don't know any more about his business but his name is… or was, Patrick or, Prek, or Perparim, Klevic. You've heard of him, of course."

"Of course," lied Pathos. How could he find out more without the others in the village knowing? Perhaps one of the boys in the village could show him how to look up things on his computer, although that was also a complete mystery to him. On the other hand, it would be a mystery to the others in the café, who were all well past the age of education, let alone computing.

"How did he die?"

"I told you. He had an accident. Seems to have fallen and hit his head on the side of the pool. That's all there is to it. Now, I have to get these lads back to Lenios before they send a gunboat out after me."

"Right. Of course. Well, that will do for now but I… we… may have some more questions for you later."

No bloody chance of asking this bully any more, I suspect, thought Pathos.

No bloody chance of me giving this fat sod any more answers, thought the skipper.

Within a minute, skipper and launch were throbbing their way back through the misty haze of horizon and on towards the tiny island and huge palace on Lenios. He knew that very few locals would ever visit Lenios Island, even if invited, because of its sombre history.

Pathos gulped in some more morning air to his dehydrated throat, making his way slowly to where the village nerds congregated, with laptops and desktops and top-tops or whatever they called them. What passed for an internet café was occupied by only one young lad. Fortunately for Pathos, the lad had no connection with sheep on the island and no interest in the raucous jokes from the cheap raki and wine emporium. He looked up at the flabby picture of bad health before him.

The village nerd expected to receive demands for access to internet porn sites, but instead of taking the conversation along that route, he thought better of it, mainly due to the forty-five kilo discrepancy in the weights of the two. A more gentle level of insult would suffice, to maintain his superior computing power and avoid Pathos's superior muscle power.

"Hello. What are you doing here? Don't tell me – you're starting a computer instruction course."

Pathos treated the lad's sarcasm with the same distain as that shown by the fishermen to the launch's crew and reciprocated by the sailors.

"I need some important information. Very confidential and, you must keep it quiet, but it is required by law and the village council." He wondered what else, if anything, he could add to try to get a result without it being spread all over the village.

A disturbing silence greeted him in response. Trying to stand completely upright, Pathos adopted a more authoritative manner.

"I… uh… have to have all the information you can get from your computer system about a business called P.O. Inc. or something and a man called Klevic."

"Is that all?" The boy ran his deft fingers over the keyboard of his laptop and peered at the little screen. Pathos tried to peer too but his peering ability was limited to a hazy moving fuzz around the screen frame. "Here we are. There's a P.O. Holdings Inc. with a head office in… Vaduz? Where the hell's that? Oh, it's in Leichtenstein, wherever that is. There's a list of company big-wigs and bankers and accountants and—"

"OK, OK. Just tell me what they do and what you can tell me about Mr Klevic."

"They have companies in lots of countries, dealing in lots of things. It's called a commodities trading conglomerate. And Mr Klevic is in Liechtenstein too. Or, at least that's his address, according to this website bullshit."

"A congromal… whatever. Yes, I know that." Lies came from the village gossip's mouth like flies from the bar's lavatory. "I'll make a note of that place in whatever-it's-called too. That's all for now, thank you. And, don't forget – this is official business, so keep your trap shut."

A smirking grin washed across the young nerd's face to confirm receipt of the raki-scented order and the empty threat.

Pathos wondered what he could do to glean more fuel for his dream of impressive storytelling and enraptured audiences for several years to come. Perhaps he could dig deeper at the little airfield, which lay on a flat plain two kilometres behind the village.

Perhaps the body was being examined there before any aircraft could remove it from his nosey prodding forever. Not enough time or energy for a walk. The rusty bicycle, parked outside the nerd's paradise, would have to bear his weight and that of the village council's authority.

11

FLIGHT TO NECROPOLIS

Even such a short journey, as he now attempted on the creaking bicycle, proved to be a laborious and sweaty task. But, to the flab-laden Pathos, it was a labour of love. As he approached a thin wire perimeter fence and entrance gate, his heart sagged. A four seat Cessna 172, engine throttled well back, made its first and final approach, touching down on the grass landing strip with a near-silent bump. A single passenger, wearing a dark business suit and carrying a small leather bag, emerged from the right-hand seat leaving the pilot at the controls.

Please don't take the body yet, Pathos pleaded silently. He pedalled and puffed the remaining few metres towards the back door of the shed, which served as passenger terminal and customs point, where he could eavesdrop for all, or rather more, than he was worth.

The dark suit moved quickly from beneath the overhead wing straight into the customs point building. Not that they had a proper customs officer but one could be enlisted if needed, they had been told. With some desperate last-gasp pedalling, the sweaty T-shirt and soiled jeans tried to reach his listening point. By the time he had reached it, the suit was already talking rapidly to the well-dressed woman and one of her accomplices in the shed.

The suit was in fact a medical authority of some sort, as far as Pathos could ascertain from a distance. After a five-minute discussion, the suit removed his jacket and opened the leather bag, extracting a few shiny instruments and a torch. Moving over to the body on the stretcher, he peeled back the blanket, revealing a ghastly mess of blood and bone where the face should be.

As he peered down at the corpse, he took a deep breath and recoiled slightly but distinctly. Only a mash of bruised tissue could be seen on the front of the head, with pieces of shattered bone poking out from the skull. Hardly any trace of skin remained on the fingers of either hand. What remained of the fingernails pointed loosely at ninety degrees from the tattered flesh and bones.

"How on earth did this happen?" gasped the shocked suit. "There's no need for me to guess the main cause of death, by the look of it. What about drowning? Any obvious sign of water in the lungs?"

"You're the doctor. You tell me. And get a move on. The plane will be here soon to take him... us... away." This from the woman – pale faced and red-eyed – more concerned with her own timetable than with any medical evidence or certainty.

The doctor resumed his cursory examination, squeezing the body's chest and solar plexus. A small trickle of water and mucus oozed from a gap in the mangled face. "Not much to go on there. I'll have to say the cause of death was brain damage, coupled with asphyxiation from water. That'll have to do."

"Right. Get him cleaned up as much as possible before the aircraft lands." Orders snapped out from the woman and the men snapped to attention accordingly. Little or no sign of sadness, let alone grief or mourning. Only the nervous signs of people in great haste.

The doctor's next objective was cleaning his instruments and ensuring that his shirt and trousers were unsullied by the detritus on the corpse. He reluctantly waved a swab over the wet body parts, spread a form of adhesive bandage over the face and hands and washed his own hands vigorously, before donning his jacket again and stuffing an envelope of paper money into its inside pocket.

As the jacket resumed its rightful place on his shoulders, another larger aircraft approached: a Beechcraft King Air, with twin propellers driven by gas-turbine engines, its undercarriage audibly thumping on the grass. Taxiing to the side of the building, without cutting power, a door opened from the broader fuselage but nobody left the craft.

Within the building, the only available airfield official, who ran the local ships' chandlers business between the normal bi-weekly aircraft arrivals, hurried over to the doctor with a batch of forms to be completed and signed. Only the most cursory inspection of the forms was given, followed by some rapid scribbling and signatures, before the body resumed its place under the blanket and on the stretcher.

The two large bearers bore it towards the waiting aircraft. Keeping a careful eye on the corpse, they reached the little

Cessna and appeared to consider entering with the stretcher. They were met by, and rewarded with, a curse in English from the pilot. "Not there, you bloody imbeciles! Get round to the back door of the big plane."

Pathos had quite a broad grasp of English, but he was not sure of 'imbeciles'. He had only heard that once before, levied at himself when he had tried to barge forward into an unlocked door for a visiting English town's mayor instead of pulling it open. The stretcher-bearers understood it all too well and moved smartly around the little Cessna and into the open doorway of the larger twin-engined aircraft.

Stretcher and corpse safely installed in the waiting air-ambulance, the rest of the party joined them, whilst the doctor stood waiting for it to leave. After another agitated shout from the woman, who was now the principal passenger, the two turbo-prop engines screamed up to twenty thousand rpm, driving propellers and aircraft westward and upward, into a watery blue morning departure. At three thousand feet altitude, it banked ninety degrees right and continued climbing northwards until Pathos and the remaining men on the airfield lost sight of it.

The doctor returned to his lesser airborne vehicle, clambering back into the right-hand seat next to the pilot. Throttle open, the little high-wing followed its recently departed fellow, climbing slowly to a more modest altitude, before reciprocating and continuing east towards the mainland. As the black ambulance, now deprived of its passengers, drove slowly through the airfield gate, Pathos grabbed his chance to steal whatever was left of the remaining information.

Entering the building, he resumed his role as village busybody. "I am representing the village council today," he explained to the chandler-cum-air traffic controller. "I need to report the movement of people through this island and, in particular, through the airfield."

The official, who rejoiced in the name of Cyrus Constantiou, eyed him with a mixture of suspicion and contempt. "What do you want now?" he groaned.

"Nothing much, Cyrus. Just names and destinations of travellers. Oh, and whatever that man in the dark suit was doing here. Oh, the body from the ambulance. The one on the stretcher. Include him and, of course, the cause of death."

"You wouldn't like a letter from the archbishop and one from the prime minister as well, would you?"

This was going to be harder than bullshitting the skipper of the launch.

"All right." The official had to get back to his shop and more importantly, to his breakfast. "I'll make out a list of passenger names and the last bit of the doctor's report and let you know later. That's more than you deserve. OK?"

"Don't forget the aircraft's destination."

"I won't forget. But I won't tell you either. That's none of the council's business and certainly none of yours."

Pathos pretended to be put out. In reality, he was over the moon at this treasure trove of juicy gossip. He complimented himself at his powers of detection. His mouth moistened slightly at the thought of his self-esteem being reflected by customers and staff of his dingy second home. By the time he had embellished it, the story could run and run. So, he hoped, could the free drinks.

"Very well. If you won't tell me, I will just have to report that and, of course, your involvement in this to the council."

"That's my life in shreds then. Now, bugger off. I'm late for my breakfast."

The two men departed from the airfield gate. Cyrus the part-time official to his chandler's shop and breakfast, Pathos the full-time gossip to his harbour café refuge and a small but well-earned hair, or perhaps two, of the previous evening's rather large dog.

During all of that time, the two aircraft continued their flights – one containing the black suit and his wad of folding money to the mainland and his surgery, the other, with the destroyed body and attendant mourners, to a larger commercial airport and refuelling point in another country.

By the time that the hastily appointed pathologist had reached the safety of his surgery on the mainland and filed his copy of the brief autopsy with the island's records of births, deaths and marriages, the airborne mourners had radioed well ahead of their first landfall. Their message had been forwarded to a burial site that catered for those who had departed this life at short notice and with even shorter reports of the cause of their sudden departure.

All of the corpses interred there were, or had been assumed to be, ethnic Muslims, mainly of European origin and mainly with severe wounds. However, following decades of tyrannical Socialist repression rivalling the dictatorships of Orwell's *1984* or Kim Il Sung's North Korea, any religious attention was, as they say, purely coincidental.

The barren necropolis amongst the mountains was managed by people who understood that they were there to answer questions rather than ask them and to obey orders rather than even think of issuing them. Orders had been received from some very powerful members of the ruling party and controllers of several national industrial enterprises. They would be obeyed without question or hesitation. The orders were to receive and bury the corpse of an important man, who would arrive within a few hours and be interred within a few minutes of arrival. Obedience was instant and coldly efficient.

Having refuelled at its first point of landfall, the twin-engined King Air and its almost silent funeral cortege flew on towards a former military airfield at the foot of some small mountains guarding the rocky cemetery. Very little activity disturbed its daily round of maintenance and local traffic control. The aerial cortege would be its first and only arrival on that day.

By the time that the funereal aircraft touched down on the stone and tarmac runway, yet another ambulance and a large black Vim limousine were parked, ready to accept its contents and deliver them to the waiting cemetery. Throughout the flights and motor vehicle journeys, a pall of silence accompanied the corpse and all of the attendant mourners, except for the woman issuing the orders.

At the cemetery, the corpse was hurried to a basic uncluttered coffin and from there transported within it to an open grave. As the coffin was lowered, without ceremony, into the little gaping gash in the land, one of the grey officials muttered some words whilst raising his open palms before his eyes.

The mourners stood beside the open grave, impassive and silent, until earth and stones had been deposited on top of the coffin and formed a low mound above it. Then, looking grim and resigned, they repaired to the limousine and went back to the airfield with their aircraft without comment.

Three of the figures entered the King Air and the King Air entered the sky again.

12

THE FUNERAL PARTY

After another equally jolly series of aircraft and car travels, the far-from merry mourners arrived later the same day at the village on the island. Pathos was already dining, or rather drinking, at the harbour café's tables and at its customers' expense. As he embellished his accounts of death and distraction, the stories moved location between the Lenios palace, the island's airfield and back again.

Pathos was too occupied with his versions of events, actual or imagined, to bother looking at the little party of dismal mourners alighting from their car and re-joining the waiting launch by the jetty. He was too busy drinking and talking to realise that only three of the four alive who had flown from the island had returned. Anyway, he was too engrossed in his performance to care.

However, one person, who had studiously avoided the café bar that evening, had noticed. The island's customs officer-cum-chandler refreshed with breakfast, lunch and a little light wine to wash down a plate of olives and fried fish. Later that day, in the airfield office, he glanced at the record of passenger numbers, when the aircraft returned and discharged its payload. There was one less than the outbound number.

Like Sherlock Holmes' 'curious incident of the dog in the night-time', the absence of one person puzzled the customs officer only slightly, but sufficiently to be retained in his memory as a nagging, unanswered question. The missing link could have remained at any of the aircraft's destinations, but his earlier impression had been that the compact funeral party from Lenios was a party of some adhesion and unlikely to fragment.

There had been no mention or suggestion of anything other than a return trip for all except the dead man on the stretcher. The outward flight was destined to land first in Montenegro and none of those on board appeared to have any direct connection with that country. On the other hand, they didn't appear to have any connection with the village either, other than their travel to and from and brief stays in Lenios.

As the remaining three of the mourners' party boarded the launch, the harbour-side onlookers observed an even more stoic expression on the woman's face and almost a grimace on those of the two men with her. The two men were virtually expressionless and had only appeared to have been interested in a seat and a drink on board.

Twin marine diesel engines started to throb as the launch moved smoothly from the jetty. Launch, skipper and the two crew conveyed three tired travellers into a dark meld of coastline, sea and sky. Back to the empty palace and its blood-stained swimming pool.

As Cyrus later observed, it was not his affair. Sherlock Holmes was probably on holiday and he was off-duty. However, he made a mental note to re-visit the passenger list from the outbound flight and to try to work out which of the party had failed to return. He had little or no idea of what he would do with his conclusion, if he ever reached one, but it would possibly satisfy his own idle curiosity.

It might, just might, avoid any awkward questions later from airport higher authorities or whoever. At least he could take a look at the list and compare it with whatever information he could get about the returning party. He would try to get that from local sources – except for that bloody nuisance in the café.

The following day would see the bi-weekly airmail delivery. Occasionally, it would be accompanied by a passenger or trainee pilot but usually just the small Cessna, a bag of airmail and its regular driver. Perhaps he would know who had returned in the larger aircraft, or perhaps he knew somebody who did.

Either way, he had to be at the airfield. As soon as he reached his desk in the airfield shed, he opened the log record of the previous day's passengers and tried to work out which one matched the picture in his memory of the group around the corpse. The list was understandably short.

Doctor Aristotle Panalides. That was easy. The dark suited ersatz pathologist who arrived and returned in the Cessna. He lived in one of the mainland's coastal towns, somewhere near the main ferry to and from the other end of the island. Not one of the mourners. In fact almost a celebrant, judging by the thickness of the payment envelope.

Madam Rosa Klevic. Also easy. The only woman there. Probably the grieving widow. Although she seemed to be grieving for her own situation rather than for the faceless corpse on the stretcher.

Mr Dmitri Petric. No idea which one he was. Any relation to Klevic?

Mr Ostal Klevic. Brother? Hard to say if there was any family likeness, given the state of the corpse.

Athos Carolides. Must be local-ish. Probably one of the stretcher-bearers.

Now, which one could have been the missing mourner? He was fairly sure that one of the bearers – the local man – had returned and was completely certain that Madam What's-her-name was with them. That leaves the other Klevic or, Petric. They were both of similar build and even had similar, and irritatingly forgettable, faces.

They also were of similar stature to the corpse but his face had been horribly unforgettable. He would have to ask the pilot if he could add any clues to their identity. Unfortunately, today's pilot was not the pilot of yesterday's twin-engined Beechcraft. Fortunately, he knew a man who was.

After a week or two, quietly putting scraps of information into his identity jigsaw puzzle, the chandler concluded that Mr Dmitri Petric might be the late tycoon's butler or minder and personal manservant. It might have been kinder to refer to him as a personal secretary, but his qualities of literacy were subordinate to qualities of loyalty and devotion to breaking people's legs.

His ample bulk was usually enhanced by an underarm holster containing a loaded Makarov PM automatic pistol, and he was supposed to be prepared to 'take a bullet' for his employer if needs be. Was it the burly subservient Mr Petric who had flown away but not yet completed the return journey?

It had also occurred to the chandler that the live 'Mr Klevic' may not have borne the weight of the stretcher. That duty must more likely have been executed by the faithful Mr Petric. The true function of the living Klevic was completely unknown. Like many people in the Balkans, it appeared that he spoke Greek as well as Serbo-Croat and Albanian. He was also reasonably fluent in English, judging by his reading of some air safety documents in the airfield shed. All of the documents produced for the flights had been inspected by him and there was no evidence of manual labour on his hands.

Thinking back to the hurried pre-flight departure, the chandler recalled that the brown envelope of money for the brief medical inspection and report had been handed to the doctor by the man assumed to be the live Mr Klevic. Perhaps he was the travelling family bank manager? Perhaps he was the one who had not returned. Perhaps not.

The one man who he assumed to be a local Greek was Athos Carolides. The chandler was fairly sure that he had seen him in the village, near the harbour. Not so much of a mystery man. More likely another servant or sailor in the hire of the Lenios villa group. He certainly did have evidence of manual work. Big shoulders, big hands and the tan of someone who worked outside most of the time. Like Mr Petric, he appeared to be used to taking orders rather than giving them.

Unlike Athos Carolides, Mr Petric had a previous, and quite different, identity.

13

THE UN-MOURNED DEAD

Apart from acting as a 'minder' to Klevic himself when he was visiting business contacts in Asia, Security Officer Lloyd was not sure exactly what he was supposed to be securing. So, he started to create a list of theoretical 'what if?' situations, which might require investigation and/or correction. The one situation not on his list occurred even before he could complete what he considered to be his first tour of duty.

Within a few weeks of Lloyd's visit to Vaduz, a telephone call to Chan's office in Hong Kong came from Madam Klevic. It delivered a thunderbolt, more dramatic than those lighting the skies in the typhoon now blowing over the South China Sea. "Mr Klevic," she said, "has been killed in an accident by the swimming pool of his villa on a small island in the Mediterranean."

What followed was way beyond the control or knowledge of the former detective. Madam Klevic told Chan and Lloyd, that the funeral arrangements had been made without delay or fuss, apart from curt announcements in the business media, and Mr Klevic had already been interred near his family homeland. Lloyd and Chan should inform all other staff and associates in Asia and then make their way immediately to

Vaduz, reporting to her and the new chief financial officer of P. O. Holdings Inc., Mr A. Tulloch.

Back again in Vaduz, the two Hong Kong representatives of P.O. Holdings Inc. were met by Madam Klevic, together with Mr Tulloch and his predecessor, Mr Vanstraat. Several other executives from devolved operations came and went but appeared uncertain of whether to continue their business as before until they had received further instruction and advice from Vaduz.

There was a small gap in the list of those present who had been close to Klevic over the years – at least one of whom had apparently attended the funeral but could not or would not be traced. Neither Dmitri Petric, the European security officer and minder-cum-manservant, nor Patrick Klevic's cousin and co-founder, Ostal Klevic, appeared in the Vaduz offices.

Lloyd and the newly appointed CFO Tulloch were not overly concerned. They had never met either of them anyway. There may have been very good reasons for their absence from the head office, and the two new boys in the organisation might not be expected to know of the absentees' usual locations. However, the unanswered questions remained doggedly at the back of their minds.

To say the least, Lloyd had not taken an instant liking to Tulloch. On the other hand, he had no real reason to dislike him either. It was simply a matter of common interests between the two Brits. Other than language and UK passports, they shared none. None, that is, until their recent appointments and the sudden concerns for their future employment. Without the company's founder and dominant driving force, what would happen to the vast sprawl of trading businesses?

No obvious successor was apparent to lead the group and maintain anything like the rapid corporate growth, achieved under the Klevic rule. The handful of non-executive directors had been tagged by institutional investors as 'nodding donkeys'. That was due, not to their familiarity with oil extraction but to their subservient concurrence with Klevic at every board meeting. The chances of them independently sourcing a suitable chairman and CEO were described in the words of boxer Mohammed Ali describing his opponents: 'They got two chances – fat chance an' no chance!'

In circumstances such as these, a company board tends to take a step back and consult the elder statesmen of corporate governance. This frequently involved retired senior executives of large companies who might give them opinion and possibly direction to close such a gap in the company leadership. Klevic had left a gap of Grand Canyon proportions and it would take someone of similar experience and stature to fill it. Lloyd knew little or nothing of such matters but Tulloch, despite his limited number of years scrambling through the corporate jungles of previous employment, instinctively headed for his first port of call.

Madam Klevic knew all of the board but also knew that they would revolve around each other's seats for guidance before offering any. Without waiting to talk to her, Tulloch acted. He put in a brief telephone call to his predecessor, Anton Vanstraat. The older man's health had deteriorated further since they had last met but he was strong enough to meet Tulloch at the Vanstraat residence. A widower since his wife's death from breast cancer some ten years earlier, he was very willing to relieve himself of as much of his burden of stored information as he could before his own anticipated demise.

Vanstraat's initial outpouring was not, as Tulloch had expected, one of grief at his late master's sudden death but puzzlement at the circumstances. He had known Patrick Klevic for years, he said. Klevic was not just one of nature's survivors but one of the world's leading exponents in it. Taking an extended deep breath, he continued without being asked to explain further. The early years of the Klevic rule had been somewhere between dynamic and desperate, with risk being the rule rather than the exception.

With his cousin and co-founder of P.O. Holdings Inc., Klevic had bought large quantities of commodities at the lowest market prices and he was prepared to sell them before full settlement was due if prices rose or let the business collapse if they fell. Cousin Ostal had been widely respected as a skilful financier who would ensure that any credit offered by suppliers to the company could be guaranteed. Patrick, on the other hand, would abuse that credit and respect to the limit of trading suppliers' patience and beyond.

Eventually, the two cousins had fallen out over several matters not always connected to the business. They had gone their separate ways and Patrick Klevic had continued to trade with his share of the wealth generated with the aid of his cousin's reputation and skills. At that juncture, the tiring ex-CFO added, Madam Klevic became the company's safety valve, hoping to restrain Klevic from his more outrageous transactions. Tulloch's curiosity increased at the thought of outrageous transactions.

He asked his new mentor to elucidate. "What sort of transactions were they?"

"Dangerous ones." The soft tone was subdued. Almost to a low whisper, without appearing to be over-dramatic. "Not usually involving quoted commodities or industrial goods."

There was a brief pause, with neither man wishing to talk next. Eventually, Vanstraat realised that he had opened a channel of discussion that had to be completed. Another soft sigh of weak breathing, then: "You remember the fighting in Kosovo and surrounding areas? Of course you do. Djackovica was the worst of it... the very worst. How do you think that the Albanian Kosovans got their weapons? Or, should have got them..." he added soulfully.

"Klevic liked to say that he would trade with his partners on a fifty-fifty basis, except that his allocations were fifty-fifty-fifty, with two of the three fifties going to himself. He organised the supply of weapons to be sent from Chechnya. Mainly standard AK47s but with some grenades and small mortars as well, even a few rocket launchers. He took half of the money due from the Kosovans and paid the Chechens half of that.

He then took the other half paid by the Kosovans and sent half of the arms to them just as the Serbs were rounding up their young men. They didn't have much chance of fighting their way to freedom but by then the Serbs had some good excuses for mass murder. Not that they needed much in the way of excuses.

Klevic kept the rest of the money until the coast was relatively clear in Kosovo. By then, most of the Chechens had been killed too – by the Russians. Then, he sent a small sum to the survivors there to appear as a benefactor. After that, he said that he didn't deal with either of them – in Kosovo or Chechnya. Nice business, wasn't it?

"The other half of the arms, meant for Kosovo, went to unofficial private armies in Montenegro and Albania. He sold those weapons at low prices to keep his new customers happy and asking no questions. Deals like that financed his more orthodox trading, although they also generated other more severe risks."

It was Tulloch's turn to draw a deep breath. His erstwhile new boss was formerly a gunrunner – an arms dealer dealing with and double-crossing vulnerable, desperate victims of ethnic cleansing warlords. No wonder he needed a second security officer. It made him a little more curious about the circumstances of the ex-gun runner's death, and of his other 'powerful associates', to whom Vanstraat had alluded at their earlier meetings.

His mind returned to the leaderless company and its current management vacuum. "Who," he asked, "would you think could be considered to replace Klevic now?" Such a direct question requires careful thought, and Vanstraat was a past master at careful thinking. He was also perhaps the only man to have a detailed knowledge of the company's business areas that required the strongest management control. An even longer pause followed, whilst Vanstraat developed strength and breath enough to offer an answer.

"The trading divisions can continue as they are, but only if they receive strategic control and sufficient finance from the centre. To a great extent, that's now your job. In answer to your question of an operational replacement for Klevic, there's no one in the trading divisions who could do that. In any case, the appointment of any man from there would weaken his own trading business and might cause friction amongst the others. It will probably have to be someone completely new – someone from another company – possibly from another industry.

"It's no use expecting the non-execs to find one. They couldn't find their own arses in the dark. Possibly your head-hunter colleague Mathieu in Geneva might find someone good enough to hold the fort, as you English say. Then, either a better one will be found or the company might be gobbled up by another. Or" – he sighed again – "the group might just fall apart." The thought of that seemed to relieve him of some of his fears rather than exacerbate them. "If you don't get the cash flow sorted out quickly, that is just what might happen anyway."

On the taxi ride back to his room at the Bar Brasserie Burg, facing one of Vaduz's cobbled streets, the new CFO realised that there were more than two missing mourners for the late Patrick Klevic. There were probably hundreds who didn't mourn one iota, including the ailing Vanstraat, who would be more concerned with his own life's impending failure.

Tulloch also realised that he had a very urgent task ahead if his new employment was to continue. His attitude to risk suddenly switched from aggressive growth to defensive survival. Cash flow, the real money and company's lifeblood, had to resume its inward flow very soon.

That objective would be shared by all of the employees and directors of P.O. Holdings Inc. It was not shared, however, by some of the late chairman's 'other associates'. They were determined to maintain the status quo. Determined and, as Vanstraat had warned, dangerous.

14

DEBTORS AND PENSIONERS

Thoughts of another career cut short by disaster occupied Cocky Lloyd's mind throughout his second stay in the company's head office. In the absence of his late boss, he sought someone to whom he could report and obtain directions. A kindred spirit or at least an empathetic shoulder. Back in Hong Kong, he might tag on to Joseph Chan but Chan wasn't even an employee of the company. Legally, Chan was an agent and a pretty shifty one too. The only people whom he knew to be close to the nerve centre were Tulloch and Madam Klevic.

Madam K, as she was known in the group HQ, scared the stuffing out of Lloyd most of the time, but she appeared to have moved closer to Tulloch since Klevic's fatal accident and seemed to have softened slightly when in his company. There was no doubt that she knew who was who and what was where. And she still controlled people's lives in the company. She hadn't moved an inch from that position.

A man-to-man chat with Tulloch – Andrew (or would it be 'Andy' now?) That should be the first item on the Lloyd shopping list. The second item would be in a glass. Cold beer or scotch, he didn't mind which. Perhaps both. Even better.

Better than a cold stare and hard words from Madam K. And definitely, better than doing nothing.

Cocky shuddered at the thought of an icy stare and sharp questions and answers from Madam K. (What the devil was her first name, anyway?) She was quite young – about the same age as him. Quite good looking too. Pity she was as hard as nails and so bossy with it. Pity that he would have to take orders from her until further notice. His home thoughts turned to a warm Hong Kong and an even warmer Betty.

Recovering to blood temperature, he looked up Tulloch's internal office phone number and dialled it from the reception area of the office. In the absence of a human voice, he listened and then spoke to the telephone answering machine, leaving an invitation to 'share a drink at the Lloyd hotel bar'. The response was an instantaneous, human, and quite encouraging return call.

"Yes. I could just do with that. What time? OK. See you there at seven." *Better get back to the hotel and a wash and brush up*, he thought. *Then, down to the bar. Hope there's a couple of seats with a vacant table near the quiet end of the room.*

There were several of the desired chairs and tables in the bar lounge. Despite the dramatic news of the P.O. Holdings Inc. chairman's death, a tide of visiting mourners and business friends was not exactly in full flood, much to the hotel owner's disappointment. Occupancy rate had not even passed the halfway mark. Cocky ensured he was in the lounge and parked at a comfortable table near to a handsome Vienna Regulator clock on the lounge wall before the appointed hour struck in it.

Andrew Tulloch entered a couple of minutes later, as Cocky tried to look as if he had been waiting for some time but was quite relaxed about it. A firm shake of hands and an order for two beers and two small glasses of Talisker scotch met absolutely no resistance. Muttered grunts, sounding to the barmen's ears like 'Yaki da' and 'Slange va', slipped from the Celtic mouths as the glasses of refreshment rose to the occasion. Neither men spoke for a few seconds but they both had the same subject in mind.

Cocky spoke first. "What d'you think is going to happen now, then?"

Tulloch knew exactly what he meant but, to allow more time, he asked, "What? D'you mean, what's going to happen with the company?"

"Yes. Of course. Don't know about you, but I come 'ere to see who's going to be my new boss – if anyone is – and what, if anything, I'm supposed to do. So far, I don't even know if I still 'ave a job. That Madam Klevic, she scares the shit out of me, like most of us. But she 'asn't said who's in charge now or what we 'ave to do."

Tulloch said nothing but nodded as he sipped his beer. Then, as he was about to say something, he changed his mind and sipped the scotch instead. The beer and scotch warmed its way down his gullet. He relaxed a little and decided to let some of his own thoughts out.

"I don't really know any more than you at this stage, Mr Lloyd, but I have my own job to do and have to get a decision from someone on that too." Getting no more than continued silence from Lloyd, he thought he should elaborate on that.

"I'll probably get straight to the point with Madam K tomorrow morning and, if she can't tell me anything, I'll make my own decision and discuss it with some of the other directors. I agree. It's not at all satisfactory and we must do something to get organised at once."

"Oh. All right then. Can you find out what I'm supposed to do? And call me Cocky – everyone does. It's a nickname from when I was in school – back in Wales. Don't ask me why – just ask the girls."

"I'll try to find out but can't be sure of a clear cut answer. Tell you what" – Tulloch felt that he had to do something to help the man who had just supplied him with the traditional wee half and half – "why don't we meet in the conference room, at eleven a.m. for a coffee, and I'll let you know what I can then. I should be able to pin down Madam K by then – figuratively speaking, of course." Then he added, as a muttered aside, "Cocky, eh? That's interesting. But I won't mention that to Madam K – not yet."

Both men laughed softly, although Tulloch had to admit to himself that he wouldn't mind pinning Madam K down, physically as well as figuratively, if only she wasn't so formal and downright scary.

They ordered another wee half and half and followed them with two more beers without the second 'half'. By ten thirty p.m. they both felt like a good night's sleep, before the battle of wits ahead of them in the morning. At seven a.m. they had both ducked any thoughts of serious breakfast, apart from coffee and a croissant. They wound their way into P.O. Holdings Inc. offices, arriving at seven thirty.

Tulloch went straight to an anxious and tense Madam Klevic and asked her to sit down and listen to him before she could start laying down the law and issuing orders. She was shaken to be addressed in such an unfamiliar manner but sat down as ordered and prepared to listen. Almost as if she wanted to. And, like the blonde girl's bathing suit in the old song, her dry composure never got wet.

He continued his advance. "I've been assessing the financial position of the group and I've also taken advice from someone who is very well positioned to give it. Unless you have a plan or proposal regarding the top management of the group, we have to call an immediate emergency board meeting at which I – and you if you wish to – can propose a plan of action." He paused, waiting for reaction, recalling the Tom Hopkins sales tactic. Almost immediately, she lost the game, though not with anything to add.

"That's fine... fine. I was going to suggest that anyway. What time should we call it?" She was strangely receptive to the straight talking and plan of action, without trying to pull the rank that she didn't possess but usually assumed. At this stage, she would accept advice and instructions from the new CFO, if not orders. Again, it was almost as if she wanted to.

Despite the distances between locations of the non-execs on the board, and that of the central office, Madam Klevic's call to arms was obeyed within hours, including one elderly director who offered to join the others by video conferencing. The emergency board meeting would be held at eight thirty a.m. the following day.

An outline agenda was drafted by Tulloch. Madam K, who was officially assistant company secretary, converted that draft agenda into a formal one. She then scanned it to the senior company secretary, who was used to doing what she said. The first item on it was not as the others assumed, the replacement chairman and CEO. That was the second item. The first, to be reported by Tulloch, would be the group's current cash flow.

Coffee with Lloyd became a short and simple event. The new CFO told the new Asian security officer of the forthcoming board meeting and suggested that they repeat the previous evening's social gathering in the hotel bar lounge at 19.00 hours. By then, he hoped that both men might have some more information to share, or hide, from each other. For the rest of the day, Lloyd tried to find out more about the role and whereabouts of Petric, the European security officer, and Tulloch tried to find out more about the whereabouts of the group's cash and pension fund.

After seven months of service in P.O. Holdings Inc., Andrew Tulloch had felt reasonably pleased with himself, despite the initial shock on hearing from Vanstraat about the cavalier manner of Klevic's use of company and pension fund cash. It was true that enormous sums had been transferred to and from the two organisations but so far most, if not all, of the cash from pension fund sources appeared to have been returned.

With Klevic's heavy hand behind each new trading opportunity, profit margins had been above industry standard levels and rewards had justified risk. At the time of his death, however, the latest high-risk venture had absorbed an abnormally high level of cash, as well as high exposure to market price fluctuations in currencies and commodities. Tulloch called the chief pension fund trustee in the Cayman Islands to assess their position and get confirmation of cover, before addressing the board meeting.

The trustee was relaxed, but his information on the enormous amounts advanced by the pension fund and of those still outstanding did not tally exactly with the figures given to Andrew by the group's treasury department in Vaduz. In fact, they were about *a quarter of a billion* US dollars different – a little matter of some two hundred and forty-six million dollars, not including accrued interest and not returned to the pension fund.

To say that Tulloch was surprised would have been an understatement of a size similar to the sums involved. He had seen the reports of each of the transfers over the past year. All sums borrowed from the group pension fund except for the latest one of about forty-five million dollars, had been returned to the fund in full – or so it was reported in the company accounts. They had chapter and verse of each transaction, supported by their own bank accounts and authorised receipts.

The latest trading venture had received the outstanding forty-five million or so from the pension fund but was not due to generate the promised returns for six more months. In the meantime, other divisions were profitable but needed short-term cash too. The group's bank facilities were overdrawn and there was not more than the two 'fat-chance and no-chance' possibilities of further advances from the pension fund.

With the enormous discrepancy between their accounts and those of the group, there had to be some sort of simple error in the pension fund figures. Apart from that, and the loss of Klevic's driving force in the group, everything in the corporate garden was absolutely wonderful. Another call to the chief pension fund trustee soon established the extent to which everything was wonderful.

Being a Delaware registered company, P.O. Holdings Inc. enjoyed a considerable degree of liberty from high taxation and restrictive regulations. Several of the trading operations were based in countries such as Liechtenstein or Switzerland, giving access to the group's bankers and also enjoying relatively uninhibited freedom to trade. The broad outlines of those operations were public knowledge, although the public only knew the details published and filed with the regulatory authorities, such as Companies House in Britain and the Internal Revenue Service in America.

By contrast, the group's pension fund was a very private affair. It was registered in the Cayman Islands, with trustees based there, hand-picked by Klevic for their firm adherence to his instructions. In the words of one literary wit, they qualified for the description: 'They stoop to concur'. Nevertheless, they were trusted by the numerous employees whose future retirement benefits were supposedly guarded and invested on their behalf.

The potential retirees of the P.O. Holdings Inc. group numbered over one thousand four hundred. Many had less than ten years' service so had not built up a vast amount of pension entitlement. There were, however, nearly four hundred who would expect to retire and receive a generous income within the next five years. Most of those were too old to anticipate alternative employment before retirement age, so were completely reliant on the group-sponsored fund – for income in retirement – for them and their dependants.

According to the last published pension fund accounts, total net assets of the fund amounted to just over five hundred million US dollars – double the size of the apparent 'black hole' in their cash reserves but not so much more that they could gloss over the deficit.

Unless the unaccounted discrepancy could be corrected, the pension fund would itself become a black hole in the financial futures of hundreds of long serving employees. And unless the company's cash flow position could be alleviated very soon, P.O. Holdings Inc. could disappear into apocalyptic history. The hunt for a new chairman and CEO might be obviated or reduced to a game of hunt the financial slipper.

It was a very pensive Andrew Tulloch who sipped his beer in the hotel bar lounge with Lloyd that evening. He might be able to offer the Asia security officer more employment than he expected, if there was any money left to pay him. He certainly wouldn't suggest participating in the group pension scheme, however. Not yet, anyway.

Compared to the startling revelations unearthed by Tulloch, Security Officer Lloyd's detective work had been miserably free of detection. He had almost, in cricketing terms, failed to trouble the scorer. The search for his counterpart, the European security officer, had only unearthed a report that Dmitri Petric had spent most of the last six months at the Klevic island palace in the Mediterranean. Someone had also heard that Mr Petric had flown with his boss' corpse to its final resting place in the Albanian mountains. But that was all.

Even that report had not been verified, although Madam K might confirm it. Nothing further was known of his location or occupation. Petric had been employed by Klevic personally, before the company had been formed. He was now, however, a full-time employee of the company and, for what it was worth, a long-time member of the pension scheme.

Not worth very much, I'm afraid, thought Andrew.

Tomorrow's board meeting was going to start like a large firework on Bonfire Night. Time to light blue touchpaper and retire to bed. Two large glasses of touchpaper were ordered and, having warmed their troubled minds, the two tired men retired.

15

THE MISSING MILLIONS

Board meetings at the headquarters of P.O. Holdings Inc. had traditionally been a one-sided affair – the side of Patrick Klevic. Until now, it had consisted of Klevic himself, as chairman and chief executive officer, plus half a dozen hand-picked bankers and representatives of institutional shareholders, including a consultant actuary. Like the pension fund trustees, their primary qualification was to give full support to Klevic's decisions. It wouldn't have made much difference if they had not given their support, as most of the CEO's decisions had already been implemented.

Madam K usually recorded the minutes but she did so before the meeting had even started. A copy of her drafted minutes was given to the senior company secretary after the meeting for him to sign and date for company records. The signed copies were then circulated to the board directors.

In the unlikely event of dissent or another opinion being offered during a meeting, Madam K would politely point out that it was not in the agenda – by which she meant her pre-ordained minutes of the unfinished meeting. As she explained later to one of the directorial sheep, it did avoid any conflict of interest – meaning Klevic's interest. It would also, she told them, save the directors much of their valuable time, for which she would not charge them.

Today's meeting would be different. Today would see the company ship, not only with a more muted guiding rudder of Madam K, but without the captain to dictate progress. In the absence of the late skipper, Andrew Tulloch took the wheel for the first, and possibly the last time. His previous day's succinct discussion with Madam K had paved the way for him to put the facts of company life before the weak flock of non-executives and the senior, and even weaker company secretary.

Tulloch began to speak to the small assembly. For once, Madam K had not printed the prescribed minutes of what they were about to receive. The rest of the board stopped chattering and wondered what the first emergency was. They could and should listen, for the information which Tulloch was about to divulge might destroy their own status in the corporate and financial universe, as well as that of P.O. Holdings Inc. The only noise in the few seconds before he started speaking was a light tinkling from the senior company secretary's coffee cup and saucer, held tightly between his trembling fingers.

In the absence of any items on a written agenda, the new CFO outlined a verbal list of one.

"Gentlemen, we – the board – the company – stand on the edge of a proverbial financial volcano. Unless we can effect an immediate remedy, the company faces shutdown and one of the biggest scandals in corporate history."

That should get their undivided attention, he thought.

He was absolutely correct. The tinkle of cup and saucer developed into a rattle and, the company secretary excused himself as he fled to the executive washroom, leaving the cup and saucer, and a distinct trail of uncontrolled bodily wind, reaching from his chair to the washroom door. Nobody else made the slightest sound.

"Despite the attentions of the company's internal auditors and those of the group pension fund's trustees, a huge amount of cash – hundreds of millions of dollars appears to have been, at best, misplaced, at worst, misappropriated and subjected to fraud and embezzlement. This information has only been made available to me within the last twenty-four hours. It is imperative that we all provide everything in our resources to clarify the situation and to restore the cash shortfall to the pension fund in the shortest possible time. I will now give you the few details I have obtained and my proposed initial plan of action."

Nobody seated in the conference chamber felt like joking or saying anything. There was nothing remotely amusing, other than the company secretary's sudden attack of flatulence, to supply material for comedy. It could be said, perhaps, that more than one of the non-executive directors might consider the old music hall question and answer of: 'What steps do you intend to take?' followed by the inevitable 'bloody great big ones!'

Unfortunately for them, there was nowhere for them to hide. No haven of refuge and safety. Nowhere for them to take those bloody great big steps. Privately, they realised that they were trapped in a mess, if not of their own making then of their passive support to the master mess-maker. All they could offer now was their allegiance and possible active support to the bearer of bad tidings. The new CFO.

Eventually, Rudolph Goldsmit, the former consultant actuary, spoke. "I can assure you, Mr Tulloch, that I will give you all the support that I can, to investigate and remedy this – what you call – a volcano. But, in order to do so, please let us have some details and your proposals, including what you would like us to do." He looked around the table to check if all the others were indulging in their usual nodding agreement. The nods and grunts were restrained but unanimous. They couldn't escape at this stage.

Andrew took stock of his captive audience. He took a deep breath and then presented his limited details of fact and less limited guesswork and opinion.

"It was brought to my attention some months ago that the group has been receiving short-term loans from associated organisations, which have been supplied to trading divisions for their commodity trades. These loans should have been repaid with interest within one to six months. Generally, the trading positions have been favourable. That is, we appear to have made good profits. More profits than losses, by a large margin. Unfortunately, I have now discovered two major problems:

a)   The lenders have included the group's pension fund, or their bankers and,

b)   A very large amount of the borrowed cash, which our records state as repaid, have not been received by the lending parties or the pension fund."

After a short pause for effect and another deep breath, he continued to turn the knife.

"As far as the lending bankers, some of whom are represented here today, are concerned, these loans remain due, although not overdue as yet. Their positions have been advised to the pension fund trustees, who are now liable to lose any underpayment. I am investigating further, as a matter of the utmost urgency, our company's records and the trading positions of the divisions involved.

"The approximate shortfall, even if the trades are entirely profitable, would amount to over two hundred million US dollars. If unable to repay that shortfall, the group pension fund would be reduced accordingly. It would have to sue the company – P.O. Holdings Inc., which could and probably would be declared bankrupt."

A shorter pause, followed by a deeper tone:

"I have to tell you, as you might realise, that there is no way that the company could repay that amount without further bank facilities. Our facilities from the banks are already stretched and it would be most unlikely that fresh capital would be forthcoming in these circumstances.

"There is, in addition, another two hundred million dollars owing to personal associates of the late Mr Klevic. They were also guaranteed by the group pension fund. I don't know these associates personally but have reason to believe that they are unlikely to be satisfied with anything less than complete repayment immediately. The pension fund trustees have advised me that they are now obliged to start repayments of these loans."

The bankers' representatives at the board table blanched. Some of them knew who those of Klevic's associates were and did not wish or intend to be within a million miles of them in the event of default by the pension fund. The consultant actuary seemed to be about to burst into tears. He had built up the pension scheme and fund over the last twenty years and now it appeared to be about to collapse with over a thousand bereft members.

One other board member was even more frightened. He was an international corporate lawyer, with a large and well-known practice based in Bern, the Swiss capital. He knew the penalties, both legal and moral, of any illicit movements of cash. Those penalties would in his case be both severe and personal. He would be lucky to escape jail and, bearing in mind the type of associate personally associated with Klevic in the past, perhaps lucky to escape with his life.

Then there were over a thousand employees to face, whose financial futures would be ruined by the pension fund collapse. They would be even more frightening than Klevic's associates. Noise levels in the conference room reduced to a hushed whisper. Only the combined cup and saucer rattling and flatulence increased, as more directors harmonised with the terrified company secretary.

Madam K was silent. She looked pale and weary to the point of collapse. Summoning up remarkable reserves of inner strength, she interrupted the speaker and CFO with a surprising and calm observation. "If you will excuse me for interrupting, gentlemen, I would point out that the company has to appoint a chairman, even if he or she is a temporary appointee."

Tulloch was surprised at her direct intervention at this stage. He almost marvelled at her composure – impressed by her striking appearance under such duress. A shrinking violet she had never been, but he would have expected to see a mourning woman in 'widow's weeds', rather than the smartly dressed picture of dynamic control before him. He should try to emulate this stance before she took over the whole show.

But before he or any of the other men could say anything, she continued. "Bearing in mind the extreme urgency of the financial situation, it would appear to be an obvious solution to the chairman's vacancy, to appoint Mr Tulloch as acting chairman whilst he investigates and reports back with recommendations – hopefully solutions."

"Hopefully," the board echoed under their breath. "Please, God, make them solutions."

First to speak of the non-execs was Jacob Carlsen, the investment banker. "I'm sure we would all support that and of course support the acting chairman in his, uh, further actions. Are we agreed, gentlemen?"

The others were not sure that the title of gentlemen befitted them after what they had heard but nodded and grunted in relief and gratitude for some of the responsibility being eased from their narrow shoulders – at least for now. The senior company secretary even stopped rattling his coffee cup and asked eagerly, to no one in particular, "Shall I record a motion passed to that effect?" After his uncontrolled flatulence, some of the others were concerned at the thought of any sort of motion being passed by him but the nodding donkey spirit rose and fell again. Dissent was unlikely to be aired. Nor was it.

Tulloch was still slightly puzzled at Madam K's intervention, although it had resulted in what he was about to suggest. He couldn't see much alternative. It would take ages to get the auditors to mount an investigation, and that would almost certainly not be concluded before the entire group of companies had been declared bankrupt. He simply accepted the recommendation, the motion, and the appointment, in one single sentence. It was coupled with an outline plan of further investigation and a provisional date for his next report.

The board meeting ended in gloomy silence. The drained non-execs took their leave of Tulloch and Madam K with light handshakes and grim resignation. In fact, resignation – from the board – would have been uppermost in their minds had it not been for the assumed blame that would accompany it. As they left the room, Madam K turned to Tulloch with a semblance of a thin smile. He thought that he should have felt honoured at this rare show of approval, until he realised that she was smiling at her own show of force – rather than at his.

A list of the dates and amounts advanced to the company, from the group pension fund or its bankers, was already in his file. Attached to that was another list of the repayments claimed and recorded in the company's financial records. A third list, much smaller than the first two, contained the details in the group pension fund accounts of repayments received. The differences between the second and third lists were startling in their simplicity, as well as in the sheer volumes of cash involved.

To his disappointment, any additional common thread linking the various transactions was conspicuous by its absence. Only the late chairman's name appeared regularly against the payments in and out of the company's trading divisions. Only the pension fund's principal trustee's name featured on each of the very few sums received by it. The traditional route for an investigation was to 'follow the money'. In this case, that only led to a series of trading divisions and a series of blind alleys.

To get more details and a background knowledge of the characters who were, or might be, involved would need the dedicated work of others. At this stage, he decided to enlist the only people who he thought could offer real help: his ailing predecessor, retired ex-CFO Vanstraat; his newfound drinking companion and colleague, Asian security officer Lloyd and his promoter at the board meeting, Madam K.

Trust did not enter his thoughts at this stage. The only trust he could accept was in his own judgement.

16

Even before he could take the three potential assistants into his confidence and put their tasks to them, the shattering secrets of the board meeting soon destroyed any of the confidence in which they had been revealed to the board members. The now distraught senior company secretary, whose uncontrolled hold over his coffee cup or his bowel movements had been a source of either mild amusement or nasal offence to the others, returned to his office and promptly suffered what was described later as a coronary malfunction. Not instantly fatal, he had enough time to scream in pain and start blurting out cries of doom and disaster worthy of a Greek tragedy, which was, someone remarked later, strangely appropriate.

It was also the spark that ignited a series of rumours, some of which turned out to be absolutely true. Rumours developed into management questions and demands to and from trading divisions, followed by further questions and demands from banks and employee organisations. By close of business for the day, most of the business appeared to be in danger of closing permanently.

Within the time difference between central Europe and the Eastern seaboard of the USA, lawyers acting for the company in the state of Delaware acted very quickly. A statement was issued to the financial authorities announcing the filing of a plea to be protected under Chapter 11 of US company bankruptcy law, pending recovery or full bankruptcy proceedings under Chapter 7 of the same laws. It added that trading operations would be suspended 'until further notice'.

In European and Asian offices, notices were issued to employees, suspending employment whilst asking for their patience until trading could (hopefully) be resumed. No mention was made at that juncture of the employees' perilous financial position in retirement. More rumours quickly developed. Hastily convened meetings with union and staff association representatives divulged nothing more than further questions without answers.

As the fourteen hundred or so employees involved in the group pension scheme were spread across several relatively small offices, very few of those meetings were dramatic enough to inspire reports of riot or civil commotion. But, they were sufficiently dramatic for those involved to create more rumours and to attract the attention of journalists and legal authorities. According to the reports and opinions flying around between media and employees, the entire business empire of the late Patrick Klevic appeared to have died with him.

Acting Chairman Tulloch now faced one of the shortest CEO careers in corporate history. He was, however, the only one available with the experience and resource to do anything about it. After telephone conferences between Vaduz and

Delaware, his practical role was quickly confirmed by the company's legal representatives. In turn, Tulloch asked for his proposed team of three to be formally appointed as investigating assistants in the company's administration, reporting to the authorities via the legal eagles and corporate vultures.

Under Chapter 11, the company was then allowed to continue its existence and business for the time being in order to try to recover without the threat of immediate closure by its creditors. There was just enough cash in one or other of the bank facilities provided and renewed by the senior banker on the board for the investigating team to proceed with their work. That would cost his bank less than the appointment of external investigators and much, much less than an instant and complete bankruptcy under the more final Chapter 7. Tulloch and his three financial musketeers would be likely to produce a lot more, for much less cost, than any professional liquidators. It was the best of a very bad job.

Without the tasks of managing the daily trading business, investigations could occupy all of Tulloch's and the team of three's available time and resources. Before starting that occupation, he had to decide on their modus operandi. And the best place to start making that decision, he said, was back in the hotel bar lounge.

At first, he thought to ask Madam K to join him with Lloyd, but on reflection, a nagging doubt held him back. He simply asked her to ask Vanstraat whether he could be consulted soon and for her to meet him again in the conference room on the morrow. As usual, Madam K showed no emotion in agreeing to the following day's meeting. Nor did she pose any further questions.

She understands much more about this than anyone, I suspect, Tulloch thought. *But I have to get Lloyd completely on-side before trying to get more out of her.* That ran through his mind as he wished Madam K a good evening and wandered back to his hotel. Then, *A good hot shower before a good cold think* ran into and stayed firmly in his mind.

Lloyd was waiting for him in the bar lounge when he descended – refreshed on the outside and prepared for similar treatment internally. The order to the steward had already been given for some snacks and cold beer with Glenfiddich chasers. Lloyd had also ordered a small bottle of spring water. *Just in case we need to wash,* reflected the latter-day Sherlock Holmes. No mention of the corporate task in hand was made until the more immediate personal tasks: the snacks and the drinks had been tackled

"I 'ave to tell you, Andrew, I don't understand much of this at all. I have been involved in some fraud cases before but they were tiny compared to this. Tiny businesses and tiny amounts. Where do I start with this one?" He sat back, drink in hand, and waited in hope for an answer to his bewilderment.

Tulloch just sat back and sipped his scotch. He paused and swallowed before offering some initial light.

"I'm not in a much stronger position than you, really. I have seen and read of big fraud cases in the past, but unlike you I haven't been involved personally in those sorts of investigations of any size. Only in case studies – on courses and things like that. What I have seen, though, is that they all involve people in positions of authority moving money or material into their own back pocket, while pretending to move it to where it belongs.

"Now, I'm not a copper like you; I'm just a bean counter – a numbers man. My simple approach is to try matching people and money, or the lack of it. What I need you to do is visit those people with an obvious question mark against them and try to stir things up in order to find out what rises to the surface. I'll try to get some more pointers and background from old Vanstraat and Madam K tomorrow."

Without those 'pointers', Tulloch knew that they were stumbling around in the dark. Even with the pointers, they would still largely in the dark but hopefully stumbling in the right direction.

17

Penniless pensions

Most of the employees, whether they were pension fund members or not, were worried sick about the state of the company and their future employment. On top of that, pension fund members were due to have their dreams of secure retirement dashed on the rocks of Grand Cayman.

A circular was issued to all, stating bluntly what many knew or feared: that the company had suffered losses from unspecified financial transactions and had filed for protection under Chapter 11 of US bankruptcy laws until its solvency could be established. The note added that severe cost-cutting and other remedial action had already been taken and there was reason to hope that much of the company's trading operations might continue. The Antwerp operation and offices in Zurich and Stuttgart had already been reduced in size and cost, as was about to happen in the head office in Vaduz.

Once the initial round-robin to all employees had been circulated and its contents had time to be digested, a separate circular to those who were members of the pension fund was composed. Each copy included a personal calculation of the stated values of each member's portion of the fund and warnings of the considerably lower pensions that members might expect to claim on retirement.

Apart from the shock and bitter disappointment at the prospect of large reductions in the values of their pension contributions, there was what has been described as a 'double whammy'. Due to lowering interest and annuity rates, the members were also informed that what was left of their contributions would not generate the rates of income that they had previously expected. The lower annuity rates could be blamed on higher life expectancy, but the lower values of their pension contributions could only be blamed on P.O. Holdings Inc. and its directors – particularly, they could assume the late and now un-lamented chairman, Patrick Klevic.

As the directors expected, several angry calls were received, demanding more meetings of members with the company board. Probably followed by a lynching party. Tulloch was content regarding his own safety at the hands of the discontented. After all, he reflected, he had probably saved what was left of their fund and saved the company – at least temporarily – from immediate and complete collapse.

"Where there's life," he had reminded the board, "there's hope."

His own hope was that the employees' representatives would accept the weak straw offered to the drowning men and women. He added that there was also a good chance of continued employment for many in the profitable trading offices. With luck, that would deter them from any thoughts of violence or sabotage.

He just hoped that this would be enough to soften the blow to the employees and their shattered hopes of financial security. It would be of some comfort, he thought, but very cold comfort to most – especially to those near to retirement age. They were the people who would suffer the most; the victims of Klevic and his reckless plundering. A meeting with representatives of the pension fund members was agreed and took place in Vaduz within the week.

As befits representation, those who had the most to gain or lose were high on the list. Of the fifty or so employees at the meeting, more than thirty of those were approaching retirement age and had long service with P.O. Holdings Inc. or companies previously acquired by them. They had contributed the maximum that they could afford into the fund and banked on their employer's contributions to increase the value to a level that would ensure financial security.

Tulloch listened and tried to assure them of his best efforts to minimise their losses. He was sure that he could justify this, but he knew that they could not simply accept his efforts as compensation for the damage to their future. The overall mood after he had spoken was one of numb depression. The older employees quickly realised that their employment had little or no future and that their savings had little value. One elder statesman from the Stuttgart office took Tulloch to one side.

"Are you sure that the company can continue trading?" he asked. Then, before Tulloch could think of a positive response, he added, "No. You cannot be sure, can you? No-one can. But is there no hope of a better return of values in our pension funds?"

This time, Tulloch – and Carlsen – tried to offer a tiny gleam of hope. But, only a one candle-power gleam, which was not reflected in the eyes of the old man.

The meeting crumbled to a sorry halt and the employee members left, like a detachment of zombies. Many appeared to have aged beyond retirement in the two hours of the meeting. Tulloch checked the personal details of the man from Stuttgart who had spoken with him. His dependants were listed in the HR records – a wife and three grown children, one of whom was handicapped and in a care home.

The old man had a life expectancy of eighteen more years and his pension expectancy was now less than half of the average income in Germany. Two days after the meeting, the HR department was informed that the man had been found dead in his garage. It was rumoured that a length of hosepipe was attached to the exhaust of his car and placed next to him in the driver's seat. True or not, it was just one less for the pension fund to finance.

Watching and listening to the dazed and frightened employees and Tulloch's sympathetic attempts to explain and comfort them, Lloyd felt as though he was just a spectator to a human catastrophe in another world. He had heard something about people living longer and annuities (whatever they were) getting smaller but that was something for insurance companies and old age pensioners to deal with. *How,* he asked himself, *could he or Tulloch do anything about it?*

Whilst Lloyd appreciated the candour of his colleague and his simple approach, he still did not understand the sheer scale of the problem. Nor did he understand precisely who or what had suffered the losses or, who might have gained. What he did understand, from his police training, was that two key points in crimes of any nature were motive and method. Perhaps he should start there.

Tulloch felt that he had to adopt a similar approach, remembering the wise words of Rudyard Kipling and his 'friends who served him well':

...six honest stalwart men.
Their names are Who and Why and How,
and What and Where and When.

He would start with Mr 'Who'.

After the employee representatives had departed to lick their wounds and consider what remained of their futures, Tulloch and Lloyd re-convened in the conference room. Tulloch tried to plan their next move.

"Obviously, the main victim is the Group Pension Scheme. I don't give a monkey's for the useless trustee in the Caymans, but the people who will really suffer are the employees expecting a decent pension. They'll be lucky to get the price of a beer unless we find a large dollop of cash for them. No point in asking them anything. There's too many of them and they don't have any inside information other than an annual statement of how much they thought they had coming.

"We do need to get all we can from the trustees and whoever works for them. I'll find out what I can of the technical side and the name or names of the trustees from

Goldsmit. He's the consultant actuary on the board. Then, I'd like you to fly over to the Caymans and grill him or them. As soon as I have some details from Goldsmit, I'll pass them to you with suggested questions. If you start with those, some more leads should come out of the woodwork.

"What we're looking for is: who authorised the loans; where did they go; how were they transferred and when. Then we want names, dates and amounts for whatever came back. I'll be looking out for the same sort of detail here and in the trading divisions' records."

Lloyd was more relaxed now. He knew how to get on a plane, especially if someone else was paying. Tulloch said he would get the seat booked by Madam K. Lufthansa wouldn't argue with her. In fact, he didn't think that even the Luftwaffe would dare to. They agreed to meet once more in the office on the next day, at eight a.m.

As anticipated, Madam K organised a seat on the earliest flight available, which was later that evening. The trip would involve changing flights at Atlanta, the massive hub airport in Georgia. Although a British citizen, Lloyd's residence in Hong Kong suggested that a US visa would be a sensible precaution and this was procured by Madam K within two hours.

During that time, Tulloch discussed technical and organisation details of the pension fund by phone with Goldsmit. Like his colleague Carlsen the investment banker, Goldsmit lived and worked in Zurich. The details were skeletal but sufficient for a short-list of people and questions to be given to Lloyd before he took it and his luggage to the airport. On a long overnight flight to Atlanta, he wondered who the unfortunate dispossessed employees were and what they had done to deserve this financial calamity.

His arrival at the apparent chaos of the Atlanta hub and the delaying and offensive immigration procedure brought no consolation. The connecting flight was all but disconnected by the hour wait to get past two particularly rude immigration officers. They questioned his visa, his passport and his right to enter or leave the state of Georgia. Thoughts of a large denomination banknote in the passport, as employed by Chan at Guan Dong, passed through his mind. But, as he said later, he would rather have eaten razor blades than give any money to the nasty morons.

With the help of a very sympathetic American attendant, he and his baggage were whisked along a mile of corridors to his connecting flight. By the time they landed at Owen Roberts International Airport, on Grand Cayman, he was exhausted but happy to be back on more friendly territory.

In Grand Cayman, the pension fund trustee had booked a room at the Turtle Nest Inn, near the old capital of Bodden Town. There, he had assured Lloyd of a quiet rest at a reasonable price. It was near his office, which was a little distance from the financial centre in the new capital, George Town. It was indeed comfortable and clean, with all that the visiting security officer needed for his short stay. The room included a telephone and a fax machine, which he used to announce his arrival to Tulloch in Vaduz and to Betty in Hong Kong.

P.O. Holdings Inc.'s pension fund trustee George Armstrong was originally from Bradford but lived and worked, as he had done for the last twenty years, in the Cayman Islands. He had made his little pile as the local manager of a hedge fund registered in Grand Cayman but mainly operated by bigger fish in small offices in Mayfair, London, and Fifth Avenue, New York.

Without great financial pressures or a spouse to apply them, he had found a nice easy retirement job and remained in his tropical paradise, surrounded by almost limitless supplies of food, drink and female tourists. The trustee of P.O. Holdings Inc.'s group pension fund looked after his own before worrying about the pensioners. 'Nowt for nowt, unless thee do it for thyself' was his maxim.

On the next morning, blazing hot despite the cool off-shore breeze from the ocean, Lloyd donned a light cotton hat and walked to where Armstrong had established his office. The building was in an area that could only be described as 'faded' at best. It had originally been described as 'affordable' by an estate agent, which appealed to Armstrong nearly as much as 'cheap'. A large second-hand table served as his desk, surrounded by several easy chairs and one sprawling office chair in which the relaxed trustee sprawled and relaxed. Lloyd was ushered into the office and offered his choice of easy chair in which he could follow suit.

Although Armstrong had been briefed by Tulloch of the importance of Lloyd's investigation, his attitude towards his visitor was as relaxed as the chairs would allow. The personal computer on his desk was there for show as far as he was concerned – or for displaying his favourite film or to play some music. As Lloyd entered the room, it was rendering a scratchy recording of an ancient tenor aria from a Verdi opera.

"Enrico Caruso," explained the portly incumbent. "You can't get better than that."

Could be Robinson bloody Crusoe, for all I care, muttered the tired investigator. *Let's hope that Man Friday's coming with the drinks soon.*

For Lloyd, time was now of the essence on this mission. Apart from the cost of staying in Grand Cayman now of concern to a company in administration, he needed to extract as much information as he could discover and report it with his initial conclusions to Tulloch as quickly as possible. He started by outlining the dramatic events of the past few days at P.O. Holdings Inc. to trustee Armstrong.

Armstrong had been made aware of the huge discrepancy in the records of loans to the trading divisions and had already prepared copies of computerised accounts and bank statements. The loans had not been forwarded directly to the trading offices of P.O. Holdings Inc. but to banks, which had then advanced the money to the traders. Lloyd didn't really understand why the cash had been moved around banks and offices in this complicated way but he guessed that it was designed to hide something. And he knew from long experience that people only hide things when they have something else to hide.

The fund's accounts certainly agreed with the entries in the bank statements, but Lloyd was puzzled by the variety of names and account numbers, listed as the receiving banks. He would have expected, he said, that the loans would have been transmitted to only one single bank account and returned from the same one. In fact, several entries did appear to have a similar reference but the others varied in description and number. In the absence of detailed knowledge of his own, he had to rely on Armstrong to explain the irregular pattern of transactions.

To some extent, any explanation was a case of the short-sighted leading the blind. However, Lloyd had the list of questions from Tulloch to guide him through the unfamiliar financial maze. The trustee had checked the fund's regulations, as contained in its trust deed. They had allowed for 'secured loans to registered financial bodies'. The loans had then been made on Klevic's written authority to nominated banks in different countries, including the bank with the regularly appearing reference.

Armstrong's understanding was that when the money had been made available by those banks to trading divisions of P.O. Holdings Inc. they would, with one exception, reverse the transaction with an agreed amount of interest within two to six months. The exception was the regularly listed account number, which appeared to be to a small private bank in Vaduz. Initially, the loans were large – but not unreasonably so. More recently, the loans had been of much larger amounts. All of those were yet to be re-paid.

Apart from the details of banks and account numbers, the resulting situation was not unexpected, even to one not familiar with bank accounts. What Lloyd had not been convinced of, however, was Armstrong's reason for restraint and not screaming for the overdue repayments or refusing further advances until they had been cleared.

Armstrong's sole excuse was that he had received assurances, not only from Klevic but also from the director of the principal bank involved in Vaduz. No mention was made of the large bonus that Klevic had promised to Armstrong or the thinly veiled threats of disclosure to the financial authorities in Grand Cayman and probable exile from his little bit of heaven. Even without the disclosures of promises and blackmail, the policeman's nose could smell the faint odour of corruption.

There was one other main task for Lloyd to complete. He switched subjects, from the plainly illicit movements of the fund's cash to the bereft and apparently helpless future pensioners who would possibly be pensionless and penniless in the very near future. Armstrong had copies of the actuaries' reports, showing names, ranks and serial numbers of the P.O. Holdings Inc.'s employees who had put their contributions and trust into the fund and its very untrustworthy trustee.

The lists and calculations of probable pension liabilities, payable from the fund if and when it was solvent, were afforded the most cursory glance and a few winces at the fate of some longer-serving employees. Then Lloyd carefully folded the documents and placed them in his briefcase alongside the bank statements and bookkeeping copies. He had expected to dine with the Bradford ex-pat, but after the whiffs of corruption and moral weakness admitted by his host, he made his excuses and booked an early flight back to Liechtenstein.

Fortunately for him, the earliest flight available was not until the following afternoon. That gave him enough time for a swim. This was topped with 'a large rum punch or three' and a barbeque dinner. His table overlooked the ocean and some of the scantily clad girls on the warm beach. All of these he would describe as 'very tasty' when he returned to his home. Wherever and whenever that was going to be.

Another fax was transmitted to Tulloch in Vaduz, outlining a minimum of detail but requesting transport and an appointment on his E.T.A. During the cool, air-conditioned night in the Turtle Nest Inn, and the alternate hot and cold rides to and from airports and aircraft, he pondered on the missing millions of dollars and, the drifting and dispossessed employees.

The one thing of tangible worth that he had taken with him on his exit from the police force was his own pension entitlement. Not enormous but, as his bank manager had said, 'beautifully formed'. Many of the P.O. Holdings Inc's employees had worked and saved for years more than his own brief career had lasted but they would receive a relative fraction of the generous and unfunded police pension. And they might well receive their marching orders in the very near future.

Back in Vaduz, the hotel-bar and Tulloch were awaiting his return and report with baited glasses and a hot meal. They didn't have to wait for long.

18

The other Pension Plan

Eating and talking simultaneously had never been Cocky's forte. The Hotel-Bar Brasserie Burg in Vaduz served a lip-smackingly savoury sauerkraut, with long red meaty sausages and spiced creamed potatoes. It was just what the travelling detective wanted after his long hours in an aircraft seat. Tulloch was keen to get hold of as much of Security Officer Lloyd's findings as possible but demurred to the Welshman's appetite and a bottle of Crozes Hermitage – his favourite 'Red Rhone', to slush down the red sausage and apple-filled sauerkraut.

When the munching and slurping and lip-smacking had died down slightly, Lloyd started to describe the Cayman Island office and records of the Group Pension Fund. He spared the dubious trustee from passing harsh judgement on his credibility, despite the natural suspicion of malfeasance and corruption. They had both accepted those dangers as probabilities before the investigation had begun. What Tulloch wanted most urgently now was the detailed record of bank transactions – dates, names and numbers. Messrs When, Who, and How much.

Printed copies of the pension fund's accounts and bank statements were handed to him without comment, other than a cursory and largely unnecessary explanation of which document was which. In addition, and after further munching and sipping, Lloyd offered his own opinions on the matters that stood out as less than normal.

First, he mentioned the repetition of the account reference relating to the bank, right there in Vaduz. Tulloch would be able to trace that bank almost immediately and expected to obtain chapter and verse through the bank's connection with Jacob Carlsen, the banker and non-exec director on the P.O. Holdings Inc. board.

Then, Cocky related Armstrong's excuses for avoiding responsibility. It all pointed back to Klevic and his iron grip on the company's affairs. But they both accepted that it was always easy to put all the blame on a dead man, even if it was justified.

"So, he voss only following orders, was he?" jested Tulloch grimly. "Surprised he didn't put the blame on Hitler." He then issued some orders of his own for Lloyd to follow.

"I'll have to spend some time sorting this lot out in the morning. Not much more we can do tonight. You look a bit pooped, Mister L. We'll have one more Scottish wine for the stairs and then you can get some kip. I'll just stay here for a few minutes and take another look at these numbers." He ordered the two glasses of scotch and a little spring water.

Mister L took the whisky, the advice, and his luggage up the hotel stairs and into his bedroom, where he flopped onto the soft duvet on his bed. When he woke up, three hours later, he realised that he was still fully dressed. He just managed to peel off his shoes and most of his clothes, replacing them with half of his pyjamas, before collapsing again – this time under the duvet. Below him, in the bar lounge, Tulloch was still pouring over the sheets of accounts and bank statements – rubbing his eyes and making brief notes for the morrow and for the banking non-exec.

Dawn brought both men down to the standard continental breakfast. Just a cold collage of ham, cheese and boiled eggs to support the croissants and coffee. Just enough to keep them going until they could get a real breakfast, they thought. It had to suffice. The office awaited, and Madam K was going to be asked to arrange some very prompt meetings – starting with the senior banker on the P.O. Holdings Inc. board.

Vaduz was home to many small banks. Jacob Carlsen had been an officer of some of them and knew many of the rest intimately. Arriving at the company's office at ten thirty a.m. and knowing the urgency involved, he quickly identified the home of the more repetitive referenced account. He wasted no time in putting in a 'most confidential' phone call, followed by confirmation of an appointment at two fifteen p.m. that very day. The bank was only a few hundred metres from P.O.'s offices so Tulloch and he could walk there after a snack in a mid-way café.

Andrew Tulloch prided himself in having what Napoleon described as the most important qualification of all for his generals. He was, he knew, lucky. Luck could fall either way. The trick in managing it, he suggested, was to limit the down-side risk whilst exploiting the up-side potential. That had kept him climbing up his career ladder, despite the over-caution of his last boss. That had kept him studying the documents and numbers until three thirty a.m. that morning and led him to guess the most likely correct path forward. Fortune, he believed, favours the prepared mind. Remembering his childhood role as a patrol leader in the Boy Scouts, he would Be Prepared.

Polite introductions were conducted by Carlsen as the three entered the bank and sat down in the tastefully furnished office of its director. With the details given by Tulloch, plus some of the opinions from Lloyd's report, Carlsen had been able to persuade the bank's director to waive much of the usual secrecy on which his bank had depended. The scandal boiling a few hundred metres away would damage him too if he resisted.

Within minutes, he had ordered a trace on the transactions passing through his very confidential banking operation. For the last two years, advances had been received from the pension fund's Cayman Island bank and paid over to P.O. Holdings Inc. During the months following those transfers, P.O. Holdings Inc. had returned the loans with agreed levels of interest. Then his bank had passed it back, less some of the interest and his charges, to what he assumed was the same fund in the Grand Cayman. The P.O. Retirement Benefits Fund. Until seven months ago.

"So… What happened seven months ago?" asked Carlsen. "Why didn't you return it to the pension fund then?"

"We did. Here, you can see our own statements. Very confidential, of course…"

"Of course, of course…"

"We returned the loans, as instructed and agreed, to the P and O Retirement Account. Here, you can see the entries in…"

"I know, I know. In your own statements." This from Carlsen. Silence from Tulloch. Something still didn't add up. Both of the bankers knew exactly what it was too. Tulloch was first to ask the obvious question: "What was the reference and account number of that account, and who or what bank is it in?"

The obvious question brought an equally obvious answer.

"Here's the details of the reference and account numbers. The account is not the same one used by the… uh… usual bank… used by the P.O. Retirement Benefits Fund. It is however" – slightly defensive, almost defiant, now – "the bank and account specified by your company. As authorised…"

"Yes, let me guess. As authorised by the late Mr Klevic. Who else authorised it? You know that the bank mandates always have at least two officials to authorise these things."

"Mr Vanstraat also authorised the instruction. You know all about this, don't you, Jacob? You're the senior non-exec director of P.O. Holdings Inc., aren't you?"

"Of course I know that Klevic and Vanstraat were authorities for major bank instructions. I don't see every cheque and draft that they sign, however. We… the non-execs – are directors of the supervisory board, not the executive management board."

"OK, gentlemen." Tulloch felt it was time to step in as referee before the big fight started. "We're not here to play the blame-game. Time – in fact life – is too short for that. What

we need to know right now is: who? where? and when?"
Kipling had entered again and had now come to the rescue.
"We have a great deal of work to do if we are ever going to
trace and possibly recover some of this money."

Carlsen jumped into action. Demanding to have full details
and contacts. He knew the procedures available to the local
banks and how to use them, in spite of Liechtenstein's famous
banking secrecy. First, the two bankers extracted confirmation
that all of the cash returned with the new authorisation had
gone to the same account.

The receiving bank was not one of the authorised banks of
the pension fund in Grand Caymen. In fact, it was not
registered in the Cayman Islands at all. But it was registered
in a location familiar to Tulloch's newfound ally – Lloyd. It
was registered in The People's Republic of China. The head
office was in Shanghai, with a branch in Guangzhou, amongst
other places. "Where on earth is that?" asked Tulloch.

Finding details of the account and the newly-discovered
pension fund – the 'P and O Retirement Account' – was close
to impossible. Chinese banks did not have much rapport with
Liechtenstein banks, and vice versa. Carlsen said he would
make what enquiries he could, at least to try to get an address
of the organisation or its agents. The Chinese bank must have
some sort of address and a name. Time was the problem, and
time was not on their side, as he knew too well.

Tulloch had another plan. Without risking any diversion
from Carlsen's plan of action, he would return to his security
officer friend – for by now he considered Cocky Lloyd to be
just that – and ask him what he knew about banks in The

People's Republic of China. Particularly about one in Shanghai, with a branch in Guangzhou. He also made tracks with the aid of another phone call, to visit his old precentor, Anton Vanstraat.

19

THE FOURTH MAN

Vanstraat lived in an old house not far from the castle. It was large without being cold, and imposing without being pretentious. Tulloch thought that as he approached the front porch but immediately dismissed that description from his mind. It sounded too much like one of those stupid wine experts' opinions of their latest bottle of cheap plonk. Descriptions of tasting everything except grapes. No. This house had real character – of bricks and mortar making a home fit for humans.

As he arrived at the door, the lights inside were still on and a maid welcomed him to the house, ushering him to a comfortable study and a warm leather chair by the fire. Declining a drink, he settled back to receive the retired elder statesman. The reception was less happy than he had hoped – not because of any disagreement but due to the clear decline in the former CFO's health. Tulloch pretended not to notice the deterioration showing in the drawn skin and simply asked how Vanstraat was feeling.

"It is not perfect," said the patient quietly, "but, it's better than being dead. And it helps to clear my mind a little. I think your Doctor Johnson reflected that when a man knows that death is near, it concentrates his mind. Is that right, Andrew?"

Tulloch smiled and nodded, without trying to correct the quotation. He could not disagree with the man's near death situation. He just hoped that it would not prevent him from giving some insight into P.O. Holdings Inc.'s near-death situation and the mysterious newfound pension fund.

Disappointment came almost immediately. The authorisation to the Vaduz bank had been made when Vanstaraat was receiving medical treatment in Switzerland. He had signed a few blank cheques and two bank instruction letters before he went to the clinic, for Klevic to use if required. When he returned, the cheques had not been used and copies of the other documents appeared to be in order. He had not scrutinised the details, knowing that Klevic would win any argument and that he was not fit enough to start one, let alone win it.

Tulloch turned the discussion to the subject of a second pension fund. He was met with an equally puzzled reaction.

"A second pension fund? Why would they, or why would he, want that? He didn't believe in the first one. That's why it was left to that useless Englishman – sorry, Andrew – Armstrong, just to keep the accounts and avoid tax. What was it called again?"

"P and O Retirement Account."

"Sounds like the famous shipping line. We have never had one of those. Umm… P&O, eh? Or, P and ORA. They, the shipping line, used to have a name like 'Pandora' for one of their ferry services. I don't think Klevic or anyone else wanted to start a ferry service either. Unless it was for his yacht and the smart launch he kept on that strange island near Greece. That was where he died, you know."

Tulloch nodded and murmured. Of course he knew, but he didn't want to say anything that might upset the sick man.

"Talking of the island, Mr Vanstraat, who lived there? Anyone else who might try to open an account for a pension fund? Perhaps one or some of the people around Klevic. I assume Madam Klevic was there with him, wasn't she?"

"I suppose so. If you remember, I had retired for some time before he died. But she certainly was there fairly frequently – with or without him. You would have to ask her about that. Be diplomatic – discreet anyway. She'll be very touchy about her relationship with Klevic – and any others." He laughed. "Now, what about some tea and one of the cook's nice cakes?"

It was a change from sauerkraut and red wine but nonetheless welcome on a wet afternoon in the mountainside town. Tulloch accepted gladly and waited in the hope of more scraps of revelation. The older man was very tired but comforted by the warmth of the tea, the cake and the fireside seat. As he swallowed the hot tea, his face tightened in a frown as he repeated the mystery name. Shaking his head, he resigned his thoughts to matters of cake and warmth. No further revelation was coming.

Cocky Lloyd was occupied with another phone conversation when Tulloch returned to the Hotel-Bar Brasserie Burg and knocked on the door of his room. Cupping one hand over the end of his cell-phone, he whispered, "My girlfriend, in Hong Kong."

That was another little stroke of the Tulloch luck. A contact still in China. Perhaps she could help to find something about the bank account and the mystery fund. The 'P and O R.A.' account.

Madam Klevic was less warm than the tea and cake in Vanstraat's house. She looked even more taught and edgy than she had been during the emergency board meeting a few days earlier. With a little effort, a semblance of a smile greeted Tulloch and she managed to look as if she was glad to see him. Her "Good evening, Andrew," was almost warm and quite the best he had received so far.

That's me. The widow's comfort, he reflected sadly. Still, in the same way that Vanstraat's illness had been awarded the 'better than being dead' award, so being a comfort was better than nothing. He hoped it would be good enough to survive his intended questioning and requests for more help. Waiting for the obligatory coffee, he tried to time his approach carefully.

"I think we're getting somewhere," he started brightly. "Lloyd has picked up a ton of detail from the company's pension fund in the Caymans and I've had some help and a lot of co-operation from Carlsen."

Madam K nodded over her coffee cup, waiting for the next move.

"I also had a good chat with old Vanstraat in his house. He's soldiering on bravely but I'm afraid he's not at all strong and couldn't tell me as much as I had hoped. He mentioned the, uh, island where you – Mr K – had the villa and yacht."

"Oh yes?" Madam K looked fairly disinterested. A flicker of tightened skin around her mouth gave the game away though. She was more interested than she wanted him to know. "What did he say about the... the yacht? I didn't know he was interested in sailing."

Sidestepping the attempted digression, Tulloch returned to the object of his interest.

"I'm trying to find out more about Mr K and the people close to him, and it occurred to me that some of them might have been staying with him – and you, of course – when he... when he was there."

"You mean when he was... when he died, don't you?" She snapped back.

Time to re-group, he thought, *without retreating*.

"Yes. And at the other times as well... before that."

He knew that Klevic had travelled extensively and would have been in many places at other times, but those closest to him may well have been with him on his Mediterranean island home. However and whenever he tried to open the subject, Madam K succeeded in closing it – softly but firmly. To help him to rotate to her attitude, she turned her attentions towards his social well-being.

"Why don't you have dinner with us... me, this evening? We can talk about the problem then – when my head and memory is clearer."

Tulloch could not think of a more blatant offer of attempted seduction. He couldn't think of a better offer for his evening either. After all, they had to co-operate as much as possible to try to rescue the company and pension fund from apocalypse so, why not? Why not indeed? Better not try anything funny, though, he warned himself. If she throws herself at you, make sure you finish your drink before catching her.

Dinner with the chic dark lady of Vaduz was not disappointing in epicurean terms. Veal escalope in white wine and fennel sauce vanished down his throat to the gurgle of cool Chablis. Other delicacies were light and of limited size, but beautifully prepared by Madam K's cook, while an elderly butler, who reminded Tulloch of Vanstraat, attended to their wine and digestif glasses. All through the meal and, over coffee and kirsch, the atmosphere was one of conviviality, if not actual friendship.

Eventually, Madam K returned to the subject of their earlier conversation. "The simplest way for you to understand who, if anybody, might have been involved with Mr Klevic in any unusual money transfers is probably to go to the island and get to know the people there. I could go there with you and explain anything else you wanted to know."

The last thing Tulloch wanted at this stage was to have Madam K looking over his shoulder when he was investigating Mr K's suspected fraud. He had another plan.

"That sounds very nice, Madam K. I have quite a lot to do before I can go there, as you know, but as soon as I – we – have completed those, then I would really appreciate your help and advice there." *Smarmy liar,* he thought. *But on the other hand, she could be very useful once I have the answers to other things. She should be quite attractive company too. Could be worse. Couldn't it?*

The smile that was returned as acknowledgement was waned rather than exhausted. All that she could add to it was the polite, "Please stop calling me Madam K, Andrew. My name is Rosa, as I am sure you know. I prefer that, or just Rose, if you don't mind."

Tulloch didn't mind at all. In reality, he didn't give a monkey's what she liked to be called, except that it might ease tensions a little. As much as he liked the mild flirtation in her conversation and the comfort of the handsome house and furnishings, he was more concerned with the next stage of his planned approach. He just hoped that Lloyd would be fully recovered from his lightning trip to the Caymans and back.

Downing the last sip of his kirsch, he rose to take his leave from his new confidante. In his eyes, she was an increasingly attractive, but still furtive, Rose. *This kirsch might even make me look attractive,* he thought, as he glanced again at the expensive house and fixtures. Perhaps he appeared envious. It possibly showed in his face.

Before he could bid his fond farewells, she read his mind.

"We didn't spend much time here. Moving around the world as we did, we hardly had time to make ourselves comfortable. If you would like to, you are welcome to stay here rather than in that hotel. It would save the company some expense too." She knew where to fire the most telling dart. "Think it over and let me know. Don't feel obliged but don't feel embarrassed either. There's plenty of room and you could come and go as you please."

Tulloch thought he should go quickly, before anything more personal developed. Also, the time remaining for a talk with Lloyd was shrinking fast.

"That's extremely kind of you, Madam… Rose. I think I'd like that very much, if you're sure it's not at all inconvenient."

She gave him another hard look. A telling look, to say that they both knew what was passing between them. He said goodnight and left for the Hotel-bar Brasserie Burg and what was left of the evening.

Cocky was still fairly 'shagged out', as he put it, wishing it was literally true. Betty was back in the Aberdeen apartment in Hong Kong and he missed the comfort of her bedtime company. However, he drummed up enough energy to listen to Tulloch when he returned and parked himself in his usual chair in the lounge.

"How d'you get on with the not-very-merry widow?" he said opening the conversation – and a bottle of cold Urquel pils, the original Czech beer from Pilzen.

"Oh, that was all right. Very nice house, as you would expect. She said they hardly ever stayed there. And… she offered me a bed. Not hers but a room there instead of here. Maybe she wants to get me under her power." They both smirked at the thought.

"Incidentally, her preferred name is Rose, so we had better use that when we're not in formal company."

Cocky shrugged. He was used to the standard female wiles and procedures, to impose an atmosphere of confidence.

Tulloch started again. "Now, my old banana, I have a couple more detective tasks for you. The first is to find out

163

what you can about banks in The People's Republic of China. Particularly one in Shanghai with a branch in Guangzhou. It'll mean some more fast travelling though. I'll give you the name of the bank when I get it from my briefcase. Sounds Chinese but might be some other Asian name."

Lloyd's response was heartening. "No need to worry about the travelling. I'm used to it. As for the bank, I can get my girlfriend to look it up. She's red hot – in the nicest possible way – at anything financial. And, of course, she ought to know her way around businesses in Shanghai. She comes from there. You let me 'ave the name and I'll phone her and get on the case, as they say. By tomorrow. Tonight even. Now. What was the second thing?"

Tulloch was not sure of what details of his European investigation he could ask of the security officer for Asia, but in the absence of the counterpart security officer for Europe, detailed instructions and protocol were superfluous. General background and questions to stir up the mud would do at this point.

"I want to find out more about the people Klevic dealt with in private. Starting with whoever he met at his villa on that Greek – I think it's Greek – that island of his. Again, I'll get more gen on the geography for you, but if you fly over there, or near there, you might be able to trace someone or some people who can put us on the track to the money transfers. Can you do that, d'you think?"

Another approach would be necessary to elicit the information from Madam Rose without inviting interference or diversion from her. He would appear to be looking at travel

164

arrangements and make the excuse that he needed to check the times involved, to fit in with his other scheduled jobs. Assuming that he would be travelling and staying with her, Madam K seemed relaxed enough to give him the name of the island with the villa and the larger island nearby with the essential airfield.

The information concerning the Klevic conclave on Lenios was passed to Lloyd, together with a very short list of targets. The name and what little detail they had of the Shanghai bank had been telephoned to Betty who was, as Lloyd had predicted, 'red hot' financially and, 'on the case'. While Betty would conduct her covert enquiries in Shanghai and Guangzhou, Lloyd would start his own in the Mediterranean islands. Tulloch felt like a puppet master pulling and weaving the strings. He realised that he must avoid getting his fingers enmeshed.

While he was waiting to hear from Lloyd, who had arranged to fly quietly to the main island near Lenios the following day, Tulloch relaxed and considered whether he should take up the offer of accommodation at the Klevic household. To relax further, though, a quiet night in his room with an old film on the hotel's satellite TV would be just what he needed now.

The TV programme guide offered him a choice of about a dozen, the best of which sounded very apropos: Carol Reed's production of Graham Greene's story set in post-war Vienna – *The Third Man*.

When he viewed the scene of Harry Lime's supposed grave being exhumed, only to find the corpse of the villain's accomplice, the little hairs on his neck seemed to reach out towards his collar. Perhaps it was the thought of Rosa Klevic and her invitation. But perhaps not.

As he watched Trevor Howard and Joseph Cotten pondering the disappearance of Orson Welles – the villainous Harry Lime – he was overcome with feelings of, as the baseball player Yogi Berra said, 'Déjà vu, all over again'. Certainly, the character and early career of Harry Lime bore a distinct similarity to that of the late Patrick Klevic, assuming that Klevic really was 'the late'.

Breakfast in the Hotel-bar Brasserie Burg was taken earlier than usual by the two UK nationals. Cocky was spirited and living up to his nickname – looking forward to his clandestine trip to Greece. The overnight phone chat to Betty had already borne fruit. Strange fruit, perhaps, but fruitful fruit at that. Betty knew, or could find out, most of the banking details that were common knowledge to those Shanghai businessmen involved in finance. Moreover, and to Lloyd's delight, she recognised the bank's name as one contacted regularly by her employer's smart-suited friend: Joseph 'The Face' Chan.

Feeling almost stunned by the suggested revelation from an old British film still playing on his imagination and mental hypotheses, Tulloch listened to the progress from China. His mind started to put together as many links in the confused jigsaw of commodities trading and pension fund money as his breakfast could accommodate. Concentrating on the characters of missing people and money whilst trying to eat cold ham and pour hot coffee was about as much multi-tasking as brain and stomach could manage.

With each sip of coffee, he determined that the fate of Klevic was, or might be, as yet unproven. The obvious questions now were: 'if not Klevic, who was in the grave?' and 'if not in the grave, where was Klevic?' Sensitive to the dangers of mind games overpowering facts, he retained the hypotheses and questions in the back of his mental filing cabinet. Only the most essential facts and questions would be entrusted to Cocky. None of those would be shared with Rosa Klevic.

20

ANOTHER PATHOLOGIST'S REPORT

To maintain what silence and secrecy they could, Lloyd drove a hired car to Zurich airport, where a connection to the main island via Athens had been booked for him by Tulloch. Someone no doubt would report it eventually to Rosa, but by the time she heard that, he would have obfuscated that part of his investigation with a smokescreen of other details. Meanwhile, Tulloch would try to get some of those details from Vanstraat and Carlsen. Carlsen might even have some more information about the Chinese bank and Joseph Chan.

From his overnight stop-over hotel in Athens, Lloyd had reserved a room at another, near the harbour on his main island destination. It was not exactly the Connaught or Claridges, but it was almost clean. There was a café with a noisy bar nearby, so it could remind him of some of the watering holes in Mumbles – apart from the language. On arrival at the local airfield, the part-time duty officer there gave him some friendly advice, including a warning to avoid a rather fat local fisherman who held court at the café bar as the official town gossip.

That was also just like being back in The Gower, he thought. With a plentiful supply of low-denomination folding money in his wallet and another wad in his briefcase, he accepted a lift with the duty officer to the town centre and a small hotel near the harbour. The friendly airfield official explained that he was also the town's main purveyor of ships' chandlery – serving fishermen and tourists with equipment for their launches and yachts. He could also arrange for a launch to take the British visitor to some of the smaller islands around the coast.

All of the information and advice proffered by the Greek airfield officer-cum-chandler was gratefully but quietly absorbed by the Welsh copper from China. As much as he could, he would maintain his interest until his new host and advisor turned the subject of conversation to that which Lloyd wanted to hear the most. By the time that they reached the town centre and small hotel, Lloyd had a mental sketch of the who's and what's on the island, if not the where's and when's. How and why were for him to determine later.

An evening meal of fried fish and an olive-strewn salad with feta cheese were also gratefully absorbed, in conjunction with a carafe of indifferent white wine and strong coffee. He had never understood the difference between Turkish coffee and Greek coffee. They appeared to be identical, but *when in Rome...* he thought, even if he was nowhere near Rome. He ordered some more Greek coffee and a slice of baklava.

With his second cup, the rising decibels of voices from the bar told him that the fat gossip, of whom he had been warned, was trying to win the 'Noisiest Nuisance in Town' award. Whatever he did, Lloyd felt that he should not approach the talking time bomb directly. That would soon result in the entire population of the European Union knowing every little detail of his visit and enquiry.

Only the smallest amount of information could be carefully and discreetly disclosed and only to the most discreet ears and mouth in the hotel or bar. The ships' chandler would be a perfect conduit for verbal bait to catch the town's gossip. With luck, he would have been quizzed by most of the gossips already about the visitor seen riding as passenger in his car. Sure enough, the better mousetrap had been set and the portly Pathos Paramides was soon beating a path to his door.

It was only a matter of time before Pathos started to answer questions that Lloyd had not even thought of asking. Indeed, so much was being poured out from the fat mouthpiece that Lloyd could not take it all in. Despite the language of the delivery being in very understandable English, Lloyd's verdict on most of it was inevitably, 'it's all Greek to me'.

There were, however, a few little diamonds among the ashes and paste jewels of the gossip's dramatic exposures. When Pathos unearthed the port of Lloyd's arrival as the airfield, he immediately donned his most impressive mask, pulling a long, dark expression and lowering his voice to a muffled shout.

"I could tell you a few things about the goings on and goings off at that place… that would make your hair sit on end," he started.

Lloyd tried to look nearly as bored as he was feeling – wishing that the fat nuisance would cut to the chase with some real information – if he had any.

Failing to get an astonished response, Pathos continued. "People – really important people – flying out and flying in. Some alive – some not alive."

How some dead people, even very important ones, could fly in or out, was of no immediate interest to Lloyd, but he responded with a faintly questioning look of puzzlement.

Pathos warmed to the task. "Oh yes. I could tell you about some very strange travellers. Only last month… four with a body on a stretcher and another one. Not a dead one, you understand, a doctor from the mainland, flying in and out within half an hour. Half an hour! What was *that* all about, then?"

Without an answer, which would have deflated the questioner if he had received one, the sage was ready to continue. "I'll tell you what. He flew in just to stamp a death warrant" – he couldn't think of 'certificate' – "and fly off again. The others could then take the body off somewhere and hide it, you can be sure."

Before adding more fuel to his little barbeque, he thought he should broach the subject of thirst and how to quench it.

"How do you like our raki? Ever tried it? Oh, thank you, yes. Thanks. Tastes best in a large glass with water, or a large glass without water." He laughed.

Two large glasses of raki and a flask of tepid water were placed on Lloyd's table. Pathos accepted an invitation to a chair in front of it before it was offered. There was no need to invite further information on the subject of air travel and travellers. The real source of that was sitting in his own apartment, a few metres along the street and above the ships' chandlery. Meanwhile, between slurps of raki and the occasional belch, Parthos droned on, about sailors and boats and islands – like Lenios.

"And the people sailing over there and back – if they came back this way, some of them wouldn't be welcome to stay here, I can tell you. Russian oily-gards with their nasty bodyguards, I think. Definitely some sort of Slav or other Eastern lot. Not your usual Albanian or..." His voice started to trail off. "Could be Kosovan, though..."

Trying to remain uninterested, Lloyd casually mentioned that he didn't really like sailing. Not even short trips by boat, although he might just manage to survive as far as the nearest island without being sick. He was genuinely surprised when Pathos started laughing at 'being sick'. An explanation was delivered with snorts and sniggers.

"If you weren't sick, you wouldn't fit in over there."

"Why not? What's wrong with the place?"

"Nothing wrong, if you have leprosy. It's an old leper colony!" He laughed.

The raki was sipped by Lloyd with a slight shudder. He would have to find out not only the who and where of the flying corpse but how and when and... was it the body of a dead leper? "Are there still lepers there?" he asked, now more concerned than before.

"No, don't worry. We don't have leprosy here. At least, not as far as I know, apart from the barman. He can't hold a bottle to pour the raki without spilling half of it." He laughed yet again.

Jokes like that might be termed 'inappropriate' in most circles of politically correct imbibers. Lloyd had been a real PC but was no more politically correct than ninety-nine percent of the other police constables. He ignored the joke but did take the unsubtle hint and ordered two more glasses of the pungent absinthe. He also ordered another coffee for himself. Time to make excuses, not that he needed them, and to slope off to bed.

Dawn saw another example of the indigo and grey blend of mist and sunlight that had bridged sea and sky and island shore on the morning of the burial party from Lenios. From his hotel window, Lloyd could see a dark splodge of cliff and some olive groves, about eight or ten kilometres from the harbour. He wondered if that was the island of his quest. A visit to thank the chandler for the lift from the airfield could be good start. Hopefully, the raki would have taken its toll on Pathos the sheep-shagger and he could and should be avoided.

His friendly chandler was busy. Another regular flight was due and a chartered Beechcraft twin baron had asked to land with a small party of tourists on the same morning. Two aircraft in one day was capacity traffic and capacity landing fees with commensurate extra pay for the part-time duty officer. Lloyd browsed around the town centre, studiously avoiding the harbour and café. He managed to walk to a slightly higher street from where he could get a better vantage point to see Lenios. Even in sunlight, it still looked dark and dismal. Not exactly forbidding, but not exactly inviting either.

As the visiting aircraft departed for wherever, the chandler completed his duties and entries in the airfield records, before driving the short road to the town centre and his shop near the harbour. By the time he arrived, Cocky was waiting.

"Morning, Mr Constantiou. I just wanted to thank you for the lift yesterday and I wondered if you would care to have a drink or some lunch with me – as my guest, of course. I'd also ask you to suggest somewhere more, uh, less noisy than the café here." Cocky waved towards the last refuge of Pathos, the town scoundrel.

"Yes. Thank you, but no need to pay for my lunch. First, my name's Cyrus, and second, there's a better café about two hundred metres from here. Less noisy, as you say." He grinned and looked at his hands as he thought of the din that would greet them if they ventured into the harbour café. *Dante's Inferno*, and *Abandon all hope, ye who enter here* ran through his mind.

A short walk was completed in near silence, apart from a brief mention of the dark island on the horizon. "Yes. It was once a leper colony. I sometimes wonder if it's something worse now. There was a nasty accident to the owner a few weeks ago. Fatal, it was – quite fatal."

Once in the quiet café, Constantiou directed Lloyd to a corner table, barely visible from the street and respectfully distanced from the bar. Olives and pitta bread were delivered with the menu. The bread was plentiful, in contrast to the selection of items on the menu, which had the gift of brevity if not variety. Cocky asked for a kofte kebab – warm and smelly but with an intriguing flavour of herbs and lamb. Cyrus only ate the bread with some houmous and olives. A carafe of red wine arrived with the food, without being ordered.

When the niceties had been completed and a few mouthfuls of bread and wine consumed, Lloyd gently opened the conversation again, with vague questions of Cyrus's duties at the airfield. On receipt of similarly vague answers, he returned to the subject of Lenios and the fatal accident. "How did that affect you and the chandlery?"

"It didn't affect my chandler's business. Just my duties at the airfield. They had to take the body away by air, to bury it somewhere or other near his family home, apparently. A rush job. I suppose, they wanted to bury it before the heat and flies got to it. Only a very small group took it away. Even smaller one came back the same day. I don't know what they do about mourning and grieving, but it looked as though they just wanted to dump it and get back. Those that did come back."

"Who was the lucky corpse, then? With friends like that, it sounds as though he was better off dead."

"Yes, it does, doesn't it? He – the stiff – was a big noise in business apparently. Not making much noise now." He chuckled softly, but Lloyd wondered if Cyrus would say that if he knew what financial chaos 'the stiff' had left behind him. Time to drop the subject until more wine was downed, he decided. Another kofte and more bread and houmous were ordered. With it, another unordered but welcome carafe of red wine appeared, which was splashed liberally into Cyrus's welcoming glass. Before swallowing any more of his own wine, Lloyd returned to business.

"So, someone went off with the body but didn't come back, did he? Do you think he – or she – went down with the coffin?" Now it was Lloyd's turn to chuckle. He tried not to make it sound forced. "I think the Indians used to cremate widows with their dead husband. Suttee, or sottee, I think they called it. After the bonfire, she was just Sooty!" *What a dreadful thing to say,* he thought. *Dreadful practice too. Call themselves civilised, do they?*

Cyrus either didn't care or didn't hear or try to understand the poor pun. He sipped more wine, put another olive in his mouth, and continued with his story whilst chewing on it.

"It did seem a bit strange, but you know what it's like when people are in a near-panic to get on a plane. After the poor chap had such a bad accident – his hand was torn to pieces and his face was completely smashed in, you know – the others probably felt awful and might not even have known what they were doing half the time. One of the group was a woman – I think it was his widow. But she came back. No coffin for her, then. The others were either the two who carried the stretcher and body on board or one of them and the one who paid the doctor. But only two men came back with her."

"Who stayed behind with the coffin, then?" Lloyd tried again, to appear almost uninterested but just mildly curious. "Was it the undertaker? Maybe he had to do something more at the cemetery. Probably had to show he was important, otherwise he might not get paid."

"No. I don't think he was anything to do with the undertaker. If there was one, he would probably have been at the other end of the flight. I don't know where that was, because the plane was going to land in Montenegro for fuel, and then go on somewhere else. It wasn't on the flight manifesto. The names of the group were, though. And, the

176

doctor who flew in to certify that the corpse was dead. That should have been bloody obvious but I suppose they have to do it before the body's taken away. He was a Doctor Aristotle Panalides. From the mainland. In and out like someone with a free pass at the brothel."

While Lloyd was trying to work out how a brothel could issue free passes and if there was one on the island, he stayed silent, waiting for Constantiou to get back to the main target of his investigation – the fourth member of the group accompanying the body of his erstwhile employer. Eventually, Cyrus Constantiou delivered, as Cocky knew he would.

"So, apart from the doctor in the other plane, and the widow, there were just the two stretcher bearers and the other man on the flight out. I've got their names in my records but still can't tell which man was which. They were all about the same height and build. So was the corpse for that matter, but we all know which one he was!" Another muffled chuckle.

"Yes, I think one was a local who worked as a guard on Lenios, but the other two I don't know, except that one had the same name as the stiff and his widow. That might be a common name, where they come from, of course."

"Oh yes. Where was that?" Lloyd was almost tingling with anticipation now. Hoping it still didn't show in his voice or on his face.

"Albania originally, I believe. Or somewhere where Albanians live now. Like Serbia or Macedonia or Kosovo. Of course, they tend to change their names when they go to live and work somewhere else. Like the Jews in your country, after they went there from Russia and Germany."

Cocky felt that he was in danger of overstaying his welcome in the chandler's company. He still needed to get a better insight into the characters at the time of Klevic's death but did not want Cyrus to feel that he was poking his nose in any further than he actually was poking it. Perhaps another tack was required.

"You mentioned a doctor – at the airfield? That's a bit unusual, isn't it?"

"A bit, perhaps, but you know that some sort of medical report – pathologist's or even coroner's if it come to that – has to be registered before burial after an accidental death. That Doctor Panalides – the one from the mainland – he must have been contacted by the family or staff from Lenios. He flew in here to certify death and register it for burial. All very quick. No messy delays for the flies get to the body. Otherwise, it would have to go to the mortuary on the mainland anyway."

"Fascinating," observed Cocky. "Have you still got a copy of his report? I don't think I've seen one – not in these circumstances, anyway."

"Of course. I have to keep a copy in the office at the airfield. You can have a look at it if you like. I don't suppose you read Greek, do you? Don't worry. I'll translate for you. Why don't you drive over with me tomorrow. Say, about ten thirty a.m."

Cyrus Constantiou felt that he had found a new companion – one worthy of his own intellect. Llewellyn Lloyd felt that he had found a little goldmine of information.

As the two men left the quiet café and walked back to the town centre, they failed to see a large man watching them from the doorway of a shop near the harbour. After the chandler departed to his chandlery and the ex-Hong Kong policeman to his hotel, the watching man walked to a small boat, which he boarded before setting sail – or rather motor – for the small dark island on the horizon.

Athos Carolides, who was, as Cyrus the chandler had surmised, 'local-ish', and one of the stretcher-bearers at the Klevic funeral, handled the small motorboat easily. He had been brought up on another island some ten kilometres from Lenios and knew the waters intimately. As a senior member of the Klevic family staff, he also knew where his loyalties lay.

Arriving at the jetty serving the villa on Lenios, he tied up the boat's mooring line and went directly to the telephone in the reception hall of the imposing stone building. Initially, he spoke to an operator in Greek. Soon after the connection was made, the conversation was conducted in Gheg-Albanian, with another party in a distant land. The subject of conversation was 'the visiting Englishman' and his encounter with Cyrus, the part-time airport official.

21

BEAN-COUNTER'S ACCOUNTS

Frustration was beginning to creep into the mantra of Andrew Tulloch's thoughts. His earlier nagging doubts concerning Patrick Klevic's death and the missing millions had not been dispelled by anything in the company accounts. His emotional appetite, suppressed by the financial emergency and cold weather in the lee of the mountains, was being whetted by the attempted friendship of Rosa Klevic. That was the nearest to sex and seduction that he had experienced since his arrival in Vaduz.

Relief from frustration came to him from three directions:

First, a phone call from Lloyd telling him of the information and pathologist's certificate at the island airfield in Greece. That could possibly fit in with his own hunch about a faked death and switched bodies. Lloyd had seen the description of the corpse and its damage together with the note of 'distinguishing features' in the form of the red star and crescent tattoo on one arm. His friend Cyrus had also described the other men in the group, including two who could possibly resemble Patrick Klevic.

Secondly, Tulloch had visited the offices of a few of the main trading operations. Under the protection of Chapter 11 in Delaware, trading had resumed using existing contracts for commodities and currencies. Although they were desperately in need of short-term cash, the contracts in place appeared to be yielding good profits overall, and a 'white knight' buyer for trading operations might be interested enough to ride to the rescue of the company – at least to consider some sort of deal to take over the trading business.

Finally – as he suspected – a more personal variety of relief arrived in the form of mild seduction by Rosa. Madam K had appeared impervious to her social vacuum following Klevic's death, but now, as the budding Rose, she appeared ready to warm her bed at the drop of a man's trousers. At their current rate of progress, Tulloch's trousers were odds-on favourites for the drop.

Although not top of his social priority list, accepting Rosa's offers of accommodation and company had generated quite a lot of fresh information, some of which might well yield another form of dividend. It had also generated a good deal of body heat.

Within a few days of Lloyd's departure for Greece and Tulloch's departure from the Hotel-bar Brasserie Burg, the relationship between Madam Klevic and Mister Tulloch had become a cosy, if not passionate, Rose and Andrew. Would the next step, he wondered, be to share secrets during pillow talk? Not something he would resist to the death, provided that the pillow was the only cool thing in bed.

With the reports from Greece, and a few drops of inside information from Rose, Tulloch began to build up a picture of the possible fraud and death surrounding Patrick Klevic. The unrecognisable state of the face and upper body at the airfield, apart for the bare arm with the red tattoo – the extreme haste accompanying the burial in the Balkans and the huge money transfers to a previously unknown fund in a previously unknown bank account – they were all features of a likely crime scene.

They also matched his conspiracy theories of a staged false disappearance. A vanishing act of Postmaster General Stonehouse quality after an embezzlement of Robert Maxwell proportions. It all fitted into the theory. But still, the same old question remained amongst his imagined dramas; if there was a 'third man' body substitute, who was the 'fourth man' in the grave?

His theory suggested that a substitute body would most likely have been that of one of those three men assumed to be in the burial party. The one who did not return to the island airfield. Of those three, two had been close to Klevic and not to Greece – one being his European security officer and the other his cousin, who had originally formed the business with Klevic.

Rose had explained, or tried to explain, the red tattoo on the body's arm. It was the badge of a support organisation for ethnic Muslims in Kosovo, worn by activists in certain sections involved in supply of weapons and money to resistance fighters. That could have been on the arm of either of those two of Klevic's close friends. Or it could just have been on the arm of a very dead Klevic himself.

Tulloch returned to Kipling's honest men, particularly 'Who' and 'Why'. His next port of call would be to old Vanstaart.

Arriving at the imposing front of Vanstraat's imposing house near the castle, Tulloch became both excited and nervous. How would he explain his theory to the former CFO without implying that he had been implicated in the fraud and murder? How would he extract the information that might involve international police – Interpol itself – without irreparably damaging his relationship with Vanstraat and the ailing man's health?

He need not have worried. On hearing the bell, the old man's butler gently and quietly opened the thick oak door, pausing for breath and quiet. "Good morning, sir. If I can assume that you have come to visit Mr Vanstraat, I'm afraid I have some sad news. Mr Vanstraat died early this morning – at approximately three a.m.

Tulloch was sad as well as feeling a sense of shock. He had imagined that the older man, who had appeared in fairly good spirits during their last conversation, was strong enough to survive a comfortable last few months. But now he was gone, and with him a source of support as well as information about past activities. The butler, walking slowly and softly, invited him in and conducted him to the warm sitting room. After a brief disappearance, the butler returned with a sealed letter, addressed to 'Mr A. Tulloch – personal'.

Taking a chair near the fire and accepting a cup of hot coffee, which the butler had thoughtfully heated further with a glass of Kirsch, Tulloch opened the letter. It was written in a slightly shaky hand but clear enough to read in the morning light. It was dated on the previous day and carried a brief message of encouragement.

Dear Andrew,

I know that you are very concerned about the unauthorised transfers of money and the large discrepancies. I am not sure that I will be able to help you for much more time but hope that this will assist you in tracing the missing money and restoring the company's finances soon enough to avoid a complete collapse.

You told me that the account to which the money from the company was transferred was in the name of – something like 'Pandora'. Although I don't know what that means, it was a name that Patrick Klevic sometimes used to call Madam Klevic.

Be very careful, Andrew. It is possible that she is involved in some sort of money laundering or embezzlement that has gone wrong due to the death of Klevic.

If you can trace the bank with that account and discover who is authorised to pay money from it, that is an obvious route. Carlsen might be able to help there.

You might also examine the trades contracted by Klevic at the time of those transfers and the parties involved in them. If you find any connection between the trading parties and Madam Klevic, then you should know what, if anything, has happened to the money.

Of course, if any of the money is still in that account, then you should be able to reverse the transactions and refund the

correct pension fund. Carlsen will arrange that, I am sure.
He has too much to lose to refuse you.

Good luck with your quest and I hope to see you soon.
Best wishes,
Anton.

No mention had been made to Vanstraat of the 'third man' theory but now, with the sad little note from a dying man, another brick was laid in Tulloch's conspiracy wall. This one represented by his present hostess and her possible connection with illicit trading operations. The words *Be very careful, Andrew...* reverberated in his mind as he thanked the patient butler, left the warm house and walked to his cold office.

Reports from the trading operations had been encouraging in terms of current short-term profits but he knew that 'short-term' was getting shorter by the hour. However, they had given him a better understanding of the legitimate trades and the features of their operations. Following the late Anton Vanstraat's advice, he started to examine the trading accounts of the latest period, during which the pension fund's cash had somehow twisted around and landed in a Chinese bank account under a new name. That afternoon, he took a train to one of the main trading offices of P.O. Holdings Inc., in Basel.

Over the next two days, the trading accounts of the Basel office were put under detailed scrutiny by the company's new chairman and CFO. With the help of a very willing chief clerk, over a thousand conventional and mainly profitable purchases, sales and options trades were examined. All of these appeared to be correctly recorded and were completely regular dealings with completely regular trading partners. Tulloch thanked the chief clerk for his help and returned to Vaduz. The next six days saw him in similar circumstances, repeating those exercises in Oslo and Antwerp.

In Oslo, apart from the exceptionally warm weather, everything seemed to be as normal and correct as it was in the Basel office. At first, the Antwerp office records displayed a boring similarity. But there were also some unusual trades in oil and metal supplies and future options, which did not appear quite so boring. The parties involved included an oil trader in the former Belgian Congo and a buyer of tantalum ore and other rare minerals based in China. Both parties acted through an agent whose office appeared to be in Guangzhou, China.

The market in tantalum, the rare and high value grey-black powder used in the circuits of electronic instruments, from mobile phones to computers and military systems, was extremely volatile. This was due to the erratic supply of coltan, its basic ore from the former Zaire, now known as the Democratic Republic of Congo. Much of the supply was smuggled by the warlords controlling the impoverished miners, over the perforated borders to Rwanda and Uganda, leaving only very small and intermittent supplies to be exported officially from the DRC.

The Chinese agent's location in Guangzhou was a geographical pointer but insufficient to relate the very complex deals with the Klevic clan. There was no obvious connection with either Patrick Klevic or Rose, but the dates of the trades coincided roughly with those of the money transfers from the pension fund.

The other strange feature was the repeated buying and selling of what appeared to be the same consignments of some commodities. Each trade was at a higher price than the previous one. In the insurance markets, such transactions between underwriters and brokers were notorious. They were usually methods for the broker to generate multiple and increasing commissions from the same policy in a spiral of re-written contracts, known as 'churning'.

These repeated sales and purchases were not standard open market deals, as the buyers seemed to be nominees for an organisation that appeared later as the sellers of the same commodities. It occurred to Tulloch that these trades were oscillating between two separate offices of the same group. The offices were in Stuttgart and Antwerp – and that group was P.O. Holdings Inc.

In an inter-office game of 'pass the parcel', profits were being recorded each time the parcels of commodities were passed. Eventually, the last office to buy the products was left holding a parcel of heavily over-priced goods or options. Unless the market price rose to meet the over-valuations the group was recording profits and paying commissions on its own purchases, which were left in the balance sheet of the last office at the end of the financial year 'at cost'. A very highly inflated cost.

It was apparent that the group had overstated its profits and was now sitting on a financial time bomb of over-valued goods and options, which would explode when auditors or regulators discovered the scam. Memories of the infamous Pergamon Press scandal involving book sales between subsidiary companies of the same group, flooded back to Tulloch. In the case of the churned commodity trades, the Chinese agent was due to receive several commissions from what could have been the same original transaction.

To add further injury to insult, the final payment to P.O. Holdings Inc. for the genuine high value coltan or tantalum trades with the Chinese customers had still not been received. It was supposed to have been paid a few months ago, but Tulloch knew that it was still outstanding. Payments from other contracts had been received by the trading offices and corresponded to payments back out, but those re-payments during the last few months had been transferred to the mysterious 'P and O R.A.' account and not to the group pension fund's bank.

Trading in oil futures was relatively plain sailing. They could be conducted on international commodities markets or directly with the producer. In the case of the Antwerp office's deals, the producer was a company operating in West Africa – and in a region quite close to the supplier of tantalum ore. There was no mention there of the Chinese buyer and the unpaid bill, and Tulloch could not place his finger on the relationship of oil and tantalum in the DRC. But as a fully qualified and card-carrying bean-counter, his experience told him that there would be one somewhere.

The beans were beginning to fit into the holes in the accounts. He made copious notes of the companies and contact names, which the Antwerp office manager freely supplied, fearing (correctly) that his job and reputation were in danger. After three hours of questioning, Tulloch had several contact names and locations but still no obvious connection with Klevic. The only common factor was, quite literally, the agent in Guangzhou.

Another searching task loomed. This one appeared to be designed specifically for Cocky Lloyd's girl, the financially red hot Betty T'Sang.

22

THE CHINESE CONNECTION

Returning from Antwerp, Tulloch immediately went to the company treasurer's department in Vaduz. The unpaid bill involved nearly a million dollars. This was substantial but almost modest by comparison with the total drained from the pension fund. It had been overdue for a short time, starting just before the death of Klevic. Legal proceedings were slow and difficult in China, and the normal bank guarantees through letters of credit or documentary acceptances had been delayed. The only guarantees initially had been those of the agent and the approval of Klevic.

Lloyd had returned from Greece that afternoon. Although tired from the broken journey, including a four-hour delay at Athens airport, he was elated at his success in obtaining the information on the island funeral party without having to sail to Lenios.

He was even more pleased when he heard from Betty, who had started to get more information about the bank in Guangzhou. He was about to become almost ecstatic when he and Tulloch met that evening; back where he was ensconced in the Hotel-Bar Brassiere Burg.

Only a limited amount of paper would fit onto the small round tables in the bar lounge. Tulloch kept most of his haul of documents safely stowed away in his briefcase. The main catch had been landed by Betty. It was the name of the agent and his firm in Guangzhou. He read the details on the message from her.

It read: *Chou Li Chan (Joseph)* and *President, Chan Industrial Corporation.*

To Tulloch, it represented a large piece in an even larger jigsaw puzzle. To Lloyd, it was the winning number on a lottery card. He thought back to his original Chinese connection and to Betty's wise words about her employers' 'less than straight' contact.

He pictured the many faces of the crooked Cantonese agent: Mr C. 'call me Joe' Chan. Back came the memories of the smarmy spender of Klevic's money in Hong Kong clubs and tailors' shops; the procurer of instant visas and passport lubrication, who appeared to have taken the application of palm oil to new greasy heights. Surely he was the missing link, or one of them, to the missing millions.

Cocky felt as though he had a huge weight lifted from his shoulders. A weight that he may well dump on Joseph Chan's smartly-dressed neck.

His elation was contagious. Tulloch immediately knew that they were on a fast track leading to the heart of the fraud and financial smokescreen. Champagne was too light to be called for a celebratory toast. Too loud to avoid a confidential discussion being overheard, anyway. No. It would have to be large glasses of Highland Park from Orkney – or larger glasses of Spaten beer from Munich. Or both.

The two financial detectives quietly toasted each other, before Lloyd retired to phone Betty T'Sang again. Tulloch prepared to slip into Rose Klevic's house without waking her. Before leaving the hotel, he had transferred any documents relating to Chan into Lloyd's care and then, locked his own briefcase very firmly. If Rose managed to open it before he woke, she would spend a lot of time trying to unravel some very complex details without finding any mention of Joseph Chan.

Rose was very clever, but Tulloch did not consider her to be so well versed in trading deals or their finances. She might spend a lot of time finding a lot of trivia. That should leave her none the wiser. He remembered the words of legendary barrister F. E. Smith, – later Lord Birkenhead – to a puzzled judge who complained of being 'none the wiser': 'None the wiser, m'lud, but doubtless better informed'.

Sleeping in Rosa Klevic's house without allowing her to be 'better informed', was always going to be less than completely secure. Sleeping in her bed under similar circumstances was even more risky, but Andrew Tulloch convinced himself that he would be better placed to monitor her movements if he was as close as humanly possible. He recalled the Italian advice: 'Keep your friends close but keep your enemies closer'.

At this stage, he would have to take a chance on his new bedmate being a friend or an enemy. He persuaded himself to take the risk. It didn't take a great deal of persuasion. Risk management was, after all, his stock in trade.

After the glasses of elixir and elation in the bar lounge, he was ready for as much close contact as his alcohol-softened genitals and Rose would allow. Elation overcame erection and he slept soundly but he was confident that it would be securely. If she tried to open his briefcase, he would be unaware of it, as he was almost comatose from the moment his head hit the pillow until she brought a morning coffee to his bedside at seven thirty a.m.

"Feel better now, Andrew?" The question was put gently and without admonishment. "You certainly had a good night's rest. Sadly, so did I." Still gently teasing, without complaining. "What's your schedule for today – in fact, for the rest of the week?" There was only one day remaining until the weekend but she wanted it to sound like an invitation to rest and recuperate.

"I have to check in at the office and go through some more, a lot more, accounts. Sorry, but that's a bean-counter's lot. Especially in these circumstances. After that… what did you have in mind?" He sensed that her mind might appear to have some very human activities in it at the moment, but in reality she was constantly seeking information relating to his inquiries about her past.

"Why don't we meet for a late lunch and see what we can usefully do over the weekend?" *Not too much lunchtime booze or I won't be anything resembling useful to anyone*, he thought.

Ablutions and dressing took longer than usual. He didn't get back to his desk until eight thirty a.m. and then fumbled in his pocket for the key to his briefcase. He found it, but not in the pocket of his jacket where he had left it. The key had been taken and almost certainly used to inspect the contents of the case. Some of the papers were not where he had left them, either. They contained details of the tantalum trades but no mention of the traders or the agent in China. Rose, or someone in her house, was interested in those deals and dealers and wanted to know more of what he had discovered. Maybe more than she already knew.

None of the usual staff at the Klevic residence were likely to know what the papers contained, or care. And there was no temporary or new recruit in the household. It had to be Rose herself. Rather than use the office phone, he dialled directly to Lloyd's own mobile.

"I'm fairly certain that Madam K has been sifting through my briefcase. Don't worry, I left anything that had Chan or his cohorts on it with the papers that I gave you. Did you manage to speak to your girlfriend back home?"

Cocky confirmed happily that he had indeed done so, adding that at least one percent of the call involved company business. He mentioned that Betty had been delighted to hear from him but sounded apprehensive at the request to get so much information about Chan's business. Like Klevic, some of Chan's associates had unfortunate reputations and dispositions. Not all of those who had dealt with him and with them were still in circulation, unless it was at the bottom of a whirlpool outside Hong Kong harbour.

T'Sang Xi Lao (Betty) was not one who feared death, but she was not applying for an early release from life either. Life was, she hoped, due to continue for many years. She also hoped that many of those would be happily spent with ex-

Inspector Lloyd. Although her contact with Chan had not been direct, her boss knew him quite well and might, albeit innocently, let some of her activities be known to him.

She would have loved to be able to confide in her boss but that invited suicide, so she asked Lloyd if he could obtain confidential help from one of his former contacts within the Hong Kong police force. One who could be absolutely relied upon for secrecy and without any association with the Tong gangs or other criminal societies.

That was quite a big ask but ask it she did and her Welsh lover understood only too well. His best bet was a fellow Brit who, had spent years with the Hong Kong police in the fraud squad. He knew most of the banking fraternity and the local regulatory authorities so might be able to get details that were not available to any outside those circles. He had spent much of his working life fighting organised crime and criminals without ever falling into their pockets. Lloyd would contact him.

James Watson, known alternatively as either 'Jim' or 'Elementary' to friends and colleagues, did indeed know who was who (or 'Hu was Hu', he regularly jested) in the South China banking fraternity. Nevertheless, when telephoned and asked by Lloyd to find out what he could about the mysterious account in the Guangzhou branch of a small Shanghai bank, he expressed puzzlement.

"To be honest, I've never heard of them," he said, adding hopefully, "They may be a new bank or a spin-off from a bigger group. Either way, they should be registered in Shanghai and that will give me a starting point. Getting details from the

Guangzhou branch will be more difficult but I'll see what I can find."

Lloyd was more than happy with that. He didn't want to compromise Betty or risk her safety. Nor did he want anyone to link the enquiry to him, either through her or her boss, or more likely, through their shared apartment address in Aberdeen. He thanked Elementary Watson profusely and made a vow not to call him that to his face. He hoped instead that he could think of him as 'Lucky Jim' after the enquiry's successful completion.

Watson started with a call to a contact in the financial regulators' security department who owed him a favour. In fact, they had both helped each other in the past and knew the benefits that could accrue from such favours. Although Shanghai was not within the Hong Kong regulator's area of control, he knew a man who's area was. The bank in question, he told Watson, was relatively new to Shanghai.

It had been a subsidiary of a bank based in Khazakstan and had received most of its capital and initial deposits from sources in the former Soviet Union. Sources, whose own source of funds might have been questioned in other countries where dealing in surplus Soviet army weapons was less commonplace. It had been permitted to operate in Shanghai and Guangzhou shortly before Hong Kong had reverted to the PRC.

Of the bank's customer base, most were small Chinese companies trading with others in the old Soviet Union and in satellite countries such as Poland and Bulgaria. There were others who might have traded in similar areas, plus a very small number of Chinese and non-Chinese individuals and funds. One of those was indeed the 'P and O Retirement Account'. Another was none other than Chou Li Chan (Joseph) and the Chan Industrial Corporation.

Even before he had passed this exposé on to his colleague, Cocky Lloyd suspected what he would be asked and he knew what he had to do even if not asked. He took the precaution of booking a flight from Zurich to Hong Kong and told Betty to keep well away from Chan or any of his contacts, including her own employer.

Betty took the orders with pleasure, announcing to her boss that she had some leave due and was taking a trip to see her parents in Shanghai for a week. There, she knew she would be protected. Lloyd also asked his old colleague Jim, now beginning to qualify as 'Lucky Jim' Watson, if he could visit him in a few days' time.

Having completed his line of attack and Betty's line of defence, he told Tulloch that he would be flying to Hong Kong the next day and asked him for a short-list of questions to add to his own list for catching Chan. Tulloch was again delighted, at the rapid results gleaned from Cocky's contacts: Inspector James Watson and 'Red Hot' Betty T'Sang.

He now knew, with more certainty, that Chan was the lynchpin to the articulated embezzlement and fraudulent dealing. With Klevic's death, or staged death and disappearance, Chan was the only contactable party, and that contact might also disappear as soon as it realised that it had been uncovered.

What still puzzled Tulloch was why, or if, Chan would still be involved when a huge sum of money was sitting in the Guangzhou bank account. Was he waiting for Klevic to surface from his staged disappearance and pay him from his ill-gotten gains? Or was he hoping for more, from further scams of his own? The market prices of oil and tantalum were still open to fluctuations, which might cover another 'churning' fraud if he or Klevic could get another corrupt trader to establish spiralling contracts.

If his hunch about Klevic's staged disappearance was right, there had to be some other reason for the fraudsters to delay extraction of the fortune waiting for them in Guangzhou. His doubts and questions were set out, before Lloyd set off on his flight to Hong Kong. Lloyd didn't understand the detail of the churned trading deals, but he knew that he had to catch the slippery little fish of Chan Industrial Corporation and not let him go, even if his little finger was bitten.

Arrival in Hong Kong's new airport on Chep Lap Kok never failed to impress Cocky, with its huge terminal building designed by Norman Foster's firm and admired throughout the world. He was equally impressed by the automatic electric trains connecting passengers with Hong Kong island, which took him straight to Central without having to involve a human driver or conductor. The old Kai Tak airport, with its approach below the level of the high-rise apartments and washing lines surrounding it, had been fun to land on but Chep Lap Kok was the business. Although it did sound like one of Betty's less well mannered Chinese relations.

From the rail terminal at Central, Cocky made straight for Aberdeen and his apartment. Even without Betty in it, the apartment felt warm and secure. Before he made any other arrangements, he telephoned to Betty's parents in Shanghai. To his relief, Betty was there and assured him that she would remain there until the end of her week's leave, when she would return to Hong Kong. By that time, she calculated that Cocky would have cornered Chan and his co-conspirators and her way would be clear to return to her work and the apartment.

Lloyd casually mentioned Tulloch's puzzlement at Chan's continued involvement and the huge mountain of misappropriated money sitting quietly in the Guangzhou bank account.

"What's he doing waiting for a dead man to come back when there's all that cash there?"

She thought for a moment, then gave him her guess at the probable reason.

"If Chan and his friends are dealing in very high value imports, then they will need a great deal of capital to finance the purchases. The banks won't give them credit on their own or on the back of their friendly relations with the local party officials. They will have to either pay up front (she said, 'up flunt') or get the bank to issue Letters of Credit. And, the bank will only do that if they have at least an equal value of money or property in their hands as collateral." (This time, she managed the 'l's and 'r's correctly.)

"Even if your old boss is not there any more, as long as the bank has a charge on the money and the people controlling the account are still alive, they can probably get documentary credits issued by the bank without touching the money in the account. The imports could be sold before the goods arrive or are even shipped, so that the sales value is payable to them as soon as the shipments arrive.

"They could even get the bank to open a letter of credit in the name of their customers, to allow them to buy without payment 'up flunt'. That way, Chan and his friends can finance millions of dollars of trade in whatever they're dealing in, and make massive profits for themselves.

"At some point, your boss could have taken his share of the profits and returned the money from the bank account to wherever it belongs. Before the year-end accounts are due and before any audit starts."

Lloyd was dumbstruck. Why on earth, he wondered, did giant international companies like P.O. Holdings Inc., bother to hire smart and expensive finance executives like Andrew Tulloch when they could have just hired Betty T'Sang?

"Betty, I'm still not sure that I understand all of it, but as long as you do, that's all that matters. I'll try to explain what I can to Mr Tulloch and we'll have a go at unravelling all this financial crap with Chan and those villains in Guangzhou.

"I've said it before and I'll say it again. You're a bruddy malval! Pity you can't cook."

The sound coming back to him over the phone line from Shanghai was a softly delighted cooing noise. And a demure but very sincere: "Do be careful, Cocky. Do be careful…"

The rest of her conversation dissolved in warm tears of genuine concern and devotion. Cocky hardly knew where to put his face, but as she was hundreds of miles away from him, he managed.

23

A DEAL WITH THE DEALERS

Faced with warnings of visiting violence, Cocky Lloyd was not exactly living up to his name. However, the mask of confidence was required. Not just to assure Betty but perhaps more so to assure himself.

"Never mind me, love, just you watch out for yourself. I don't know who Chan's friends are – if he's got any – but they won't be members of the Salvation Army. If I'm not here when you get back, leave a message at Inspector James Watson's office at the police station in Central. They'll get it to me, I'm sure." *As long as I'm back in one piece to take the message*, he muttered to himself.

Armed with the expert opinion and explanation from Betty, not to mention his unused Smith & Wesson automatic, Lloyd was beginning to feel a little more like James Bond. As long as he could think up those verbal quips to throw at the villains, he could probably save the world. With a bit of luck, he might save himself too.

A short nap and then a phone call to Jim Watson set up a meeting of the two policemen and arrangements to interrogate Joseph Chan. Watson had made copies of some official-looking documents, which he would 'accidentally' allow Chan to glimpse, in the hope of inviting terror to strike him into confession and exposure of the facts.

With a few phone calls to friendly contacts in the commercial harbour area and one to a Repulse Bay resident, Chan's whereabouts were traced. Fortunately, he was not visiting his own office in Guangzhou or the metal importing firm. An impromptu visit to his Hong Kong office brought no sign of him but Watson's official looking file of documents – what he called his 'weapon of mass distraction' – brought a frightened cry from one of the staff, who directed the two Brits to a nearby restaurant.

In there, hugging a bowl of wonton soup, sat a very nervous Joseph Chan. Somehow, he had heard of the investigations into the Antwerp trades in oil and coltan, and had not slept properly for some days. Seeing Lloyd and a European stranger coming towards him elicited a gurgled squeal through Chan's mouthful of hot soup.

He tried to rise from his chair but his napkin, tucked firmly into his shirt front, was caught beneath the soup bowl. Whilst the two investigators watched and tried not to laugh, Chan lurched back into his chair and wiped what he could from his shirt and the paper tablecloth. Lloyd put on his best James Bond presence and spoke first.

"Hello, Joseph. You seem to be in the soup today. But I think we might be able to help you – to save your bacon even." Lloyd pointed at a dish containing pieces of fried pork on an adjoining table and waited for a smile. He would have to wait forever to get one. Not wishing to allow the nervous Chan to recover by uttering useless epithets in order to gain time, Lloyd went straight for the jugular. Under Chan's rising blood pressure, that was getting larger by the second.

"This is Chief Inspector Watson and we are going to discuss certain transactions regarding illicit trading in the Peoples Republic of China – with you." He paused between the deliberately emphasised PRC and 'with you' for effect. It had the desired effect, for Chan knew only too well what the penalties for corrupt practices were in the PRC. Some of his contacts had ended their days in labour camps. Some had, simply and painfully, just ended their days.

Human rights policy in the PRC tended to err on the side of the ruling party. They had plenty of humans and insufficient rights to go round. They were rumoured still to charge the criminals' relatives for the cost of the bullets expended in the executions. No discrimination in capital punishment was made between murderers and fraudsters, particularly if they involved rival politicians or similar authorities. And Joseph Chan had dealt with several of those. The restaurant's hard floor reverberated to the rhythm of Chan's ninety-decibel pulse and the drumstick rattle of the soup spoon in his trembling hand.

Watson stepped in to steer the conversation and Chan towards an atmosphere more conducive to voluntary co-operation. For the moment, he would be the good cop, weaving a pattern of guiding suggestions towards explicit and detailed confessions of the complex trading crimes. By this time Chan was so weak he could have confessed to the assassination of Abraham Lincoln if it would remove him from the harsh justice of the PRC criminal courts.

Without another word, he allowed Watson and Lloyd to take a limp arm each and propel him through the restaurant doorway and into their waiting car. He slumped into the rear seat with Lloyd, while Watson took the wheel and drove the trio to Chan's office. Entering the office building, Watson waved one of his copy documents at the staff and plonked Chan, wet trousers first, onto a hard chair. As usual, Watson adopted a firmer tone, without losing a sense of reason.

"Now, Mr Chan" – too early to call him Joseph – "I am going to take notes while you answer questions from Inspector Lloyd, whom you already know as an official security officer of P.O. Holdings Inc. There's not a lot of time to get all the details we require to save the situation and possibly save your neck."

Chan felt the sweat on his collar running down the vulnerable neck to meet the wet patch in his trousers.

Lloyd took over, not needing to harden his tone artificially. He didn't have time to spare either. He would need to report back to Tulloch in order to make sense of some of the strange tale he was about to hear.

"Look, Joseph" – time to drop any formalities or the James Bond act and get to the hard heart of the financial matter – "we know that certain persons in P.O. have been conducting illegal forms of trading, with you acting as agent for the other parties. Particularly that one in Guangzhou and others in Shanghai and Africa.

We don't have time to mess about, so if you want to save your skin" – now getting very wet – "you must, repeat *must*, tell us everything about the trades – who the other parties are;

where the money and the commodities are; what happened to the late Mr Klevic; and how you are going to get the stolen money back to its rightful owners." *That should do for starters,* he thought.

Watson nodded in silent agreement.

"Let's start with the others. We know" – we'll say that anyway – "Klevic was involved. Right? Yes, right. Your gang in Guangzhou too. They won't be pleased with you now but that's their problem. We know that the money went to Guangzhou. Into the same bank that they use for trading transfers…"

At this point, Chan looked round desperately, a mixture of puzzlement and fear. "I don't know anything about that," he blurted, almost sobbing. "That's something only Klevic dealt with. If you look after me properly, we can get the people who control the bank account to tell us… you… who can access it." Wriggling mentally and physically, he could see a glimmer of hope before the executioner's gleaming pistol. Lloyd put that to one side. The bank and access to the account might have to wait until they visited Guangzhou, and that would take a little more time.

"Now, who are the other parties and what happened to the payment for the tantalum sales?" He didn't really know how that was supposed to work, but Tulloch had told him to find that out.

"Let's start with the people who have been dealing with the Antwerp office traders. Who are they? And who was directing the dealings from Antwerp?"

Chan gulped. He didn't realise that Lloyd and his police colleague knew so much about the nefarious dealings between Guangzhou and Antwerp. In reality, nor did Lloyd. Chan did know that he should move quickly if he was to put some space between his position as helpful advisor to the police and that of master criminal facing the pistol of certain dreadful justice.

"Klevic, of course. He was behind it at first. He had the assistant manager of the trading floor in Antwerp to make the deal and then buy back the same property at higher prices, before making the deals again at even higher prices."

"Yes, we know all that," Lloyd lied smoothly, "and you shared the false profits with Klevic."

"No, no! I only got a small commission on the deals. And I haven't received any from the last deal either. They owe me a lot of money." He tried to appear like an injured man.

"That's a laugh," said Watson, without a smile on his lips. "What makes you think you should get anything other than the labour camp – *if,* you don't get the chop?"

Chan's lips were neither smiling nor dry. He licked them nervously at the thought of the type of chop involved. It certainly wouldn't be a chop suey. He realised that all too well.

"I was entitled to commission on all completed deals. But," he added quickly, "I will waive that and add it to the money refunded, if we can complete them. And… of course, if you treat me as a collaborator… on your side."

Deadpan faces greeted the last outburst.

"Now then. I ask again. *Who* are the other parties? To the traded deals and the money salted away?" Lloyd was getting fidgety. Chan was pouring out his bellyful of mixed confessions, complaints and conditions, but once again time was of the essence. "Let's start again with the people at this end, those who were dealing with Antwerp and Klevic's assistant manager. Are they the same people who we met in your pal's place in Guangzhou?"

Chan nodded rapidly. He was getting the same sense of urgency. More than the prospect of a judicial bullet in the neck was driving him now.

"They are genuine importers and traders in the commodities, but they got, uh, ambitious and… there is a problem with the money now."

A sarcastic and hollow laugh was returned by Lloyd.

"Yes, We all realise that. And you are the biggest part of problem."

"No. Not just my involvement. I was only the agent. They… the traders in Guangzhou… they can't get the delivery of tantalum ore from Africa. And they can't pay up until they do. That part is actually legal, as you must know."

There's actually a legal part to this is there? Lloyd wondered.

Chan continued. "If we can get the minerals delivered, they would release the payment to P.O. Holdings Inc. and we could persuade them to re-pay the rest at the same time."

"It can't be that easy," thought Lloyd aloud. But not wishing to apply the principle relating to gift horses and mouths, he added, "You had better take us there and do the persuading very quickly, because I don't believe you. Also, we have to get the money from that other account in the bank there. How do you propose to do that?"

"They will do all the persuading necessary, when I explain the... the situation." Chan was exhausted. Partly due to the physical strain of activity since his soup hit the floor and the proverbial hit the fan, but mainly due to the mental anguish of lost commissions and possible lost life. He meekly consented to obtain fresh visas immediately from his source of freshly forged documents and to handle the authorities at Dong Guan port.

By four p.m., the visas were ready. By eight p.m., the three men were taxiing towards Guangzhou and the office of Chan's surprised associates in crime. For once, Chan had told the truth. A frenzied conversation reached a crescendo of shouting and screams. But the partners of Klevic's false trading were as aware of the penalties as Chan was. They were, if anything, more vulnerable than he was, being so close to the local justice of the PRC. Names of two others involved in Antwerp were disclosed as were details of the commodities subjected to the spiralling churn of multiple deals at ever-increasing prices.

Two more vital pieces of the puzzle were missing: the trading parties in Africa who had blocked the shipments of tantalum ore and what was required to unblock them. Without the shipments, the banking authorities would not permit payment to P.O. Holdings Inc. Even more vital, in terms of value to P.O. Holdings Inc. and its insolvent state, was the huge amount of cash lying in the account labelled P and O R.A. The Pandora fund which Klevic – and possibly Madam 'Pandora' Klevic – had embezzled from the P.O. Holdings Inc's pension fund, via P.O. Holdings Inc.'s treasury.

Lloyd still assumed that Klevic was dead. Tulloch had not confided his fears or 'the third man' theory to Lloyd. But he felt that there was a very real danger of Madam K or others, obtaining the money before Lloyd and Tulloch could get these scumbags in Guangzhou to return it to its rightful owner.

Under more powerful persuasion from Chan, the Guangzhou traders explained the situation regarding shipments of coltan – the tantalum ore – out of Africa. The problem there was horribly simple. They had already paid a deposit in order to get the metal shipments from the mines to the docks in Africa. There, the consignments had been prepared for shipping to China but the shipments had been blocked by the local exporting officials. The Muslim African dealer in oil futures was in league with an Arab official in the only port of the former Zaire, who controlled export permits for oil and other minerals including tantalum.

The crooked African dealer in oil had received a backhanded bribe – as commission – from Guangzhou, based on the oil trades, and the Arab official had found out. Naturally, the official wanted to have the same or more for himself and refused to release the export licences until he did. Whilst he was stopping the licences from being released, all shipments and payments were frozen.

He was not going to budge on this. He was a very large part of the corrupt local constabulary and expected to receive at least as much in bribes as anyone else. Preferably much more. Guangzhou had already opened letters of credit with their bank for the money for the Guangzhou contracts to be paid to P.O. Holdings Inc. when the goods were certified as shipped to China. Since they had contracted to buy the metal and had paid the deposits, the market price had soared. Now they were as desperate to get their hands on it as the Arab policeman was to get his hands on the bribe money. He had insisted on personal cash payment and the Chinese gang had insisted that they would not travel to anywhere as dangerous as the Democratic Republic of the Congo.

The Guangzhou bank would not pay P.O. Holdings Inc. for it until all the shipping documents, including the Bills of Lading and supporting documents to prove that the goods were as ordered and on their way to China, were presented by the buyers to the bank. Almost a catch-22 situation. Meanwhile, the coltan, needed to extract the tantalum, could not be shipped and P.O. Holdings Inc would not be paid.

The Guangzhou gang did have more encouraging news of the P and O R.A. account. They had helped Klevic to open it and knew that he could not withdraw – or had not withdrawn any of it. Moreover, two of the Guangzhou gang who had opened the account with Klevic were the only people authorised to deal with it. Provided that they received their shipments of coltan with the shipping documents, their customers would pay them and the letters of credit would automatically action payment from them to P.O. Holdings Inc.

They accepted that they would then have the money mountain in the P and O R.A account, returned to its rightful source on the basis that it was – officially – the result of a banking error. There were plenty of those around. And sometimes for even larger amounts. Inevitably, as they would blame the banks, so the banks would blame their computers.

Lloyd was over the moon at this news. He still could not believe unwinding the tangled scam could be that simple. Before building up the hopes of Tulloch and himself, he decided to stay there with the worthy Watson and the worthless Chan to ensure that the Guangzhou gang kept their word. If they did not, he and Watson might have to fight their way out, but as usual Watson had taken the precaution of informing other police contacts of his mission and where to strike if they were in danger. The Guangzhou gang had been made aware of that before they started to get into serious negotiations.

Too late to visit the bank personally, Lloyd and Watson insisted that the bank officials be contacted by phone and agreed to do as instructed by the gang and authorised by the bank mandates. The entire conference continued into the night, ending with Lloyd agreeing to help free the blocked shipments, and the desperate Guangzhou importers agreeing to fund his travels and a large cash bribe to the Arab official.

At nine thirty a.m. the following day, the combined forces of crooked importers and honest detectives made the banking equivalent of a dawn raid. By midday, the money was traced. Theoretically, it could be on its way around the world to P.O. Holdings Inc.'s bank within a few days of confirmation of the shipments and presentation of the documents. That was provided, of course, that they were released by the corrupt officials in the former Zaire, and provided that they were shipped with the valid shipping documents.

But they had not been released yet, and payment for the shipments – or the millions in the P and O R.A. account would not be either until the Guangzhou gang, the sole remaining authorised signatories of the P and O R.A. account, received proof of their precious metal shipments and the documents to release their payments.

After yet another phone call to Vaduz, Tulloch was naturally delighted at the news from Lloyd, subject to yet another old cliché in the bean-counter's head, concerning chickens and hatching. He decided to maintain complete silence to all, even from his most confidential contacts in P.O. Holdings Inc.'s bank and from his hostess's bedroom.

24

IN AND OUT OF AFRICA

If Lloyd had been living up to his nickname – Cocky – he would soon lose it. His ebullient conversation with Tulloch after his success in Hong Kong and Guangzhou only brought the inevitable instruction. This one more unappealing and more dangerous than the trips into the PRC and to the gang of Chinese fraudsters.

When the gang had confessed to their past crimes and present predicament in China, Lloyd realised that someone would have to confront someone else in Africa. There was no one else that he knew who could do it. The European security officer had still not surfaced. He had not claimed his monthly salary or contacted anyone at P.O. Holdings Inc. Even if he had been available for the task, he probably wouldn't want to touch it with a Kalashnikov. The only obvious candidate for the title of the 'someone' was the former D.I. – Lewellyn L. Lloyd.

Once again, travel arrangements were completed; Betty would be advised by the faithful Jim Watson and ex-Inspector Lloyd's job description amended to include 'will travel'. This time, though, he would also 'have gun'. He was aware of the dangers of travel in Africa, and this part of Africa was more dangerous than most. Since the former Belgian colony had become independent from its European colonisers, the entire area had been torn with multiple revolutions and so-called 'civil' wars. Law and order, like Bismark's diplomacy, was conducted through the barrel of a gun.

Flying in to the Kinshasa airport at N'Djili was relatively easy. He hoped that flying out would be equally easy. Travel to the mining area and to the Atlantic coastal port of Matadi was fraught with delays and problems. The Chinese gang had supplied him with a wad of US dollars, to placate the Arab's itchy palm, and as a representative of a Delaware corporation, Lloyd had taken the precaution of enlisting help from the US consulate in Kinshasa. As so often happened, that amount of help diluted with each of the three hundred and sixty-six kilometres between the capital and the port.

Flights to Matadi had been cancelled for a week due to accidents in the turbulent thunderstorms of the season. The road was more dangerous than swimming in the crocodile-infested river. Road accidents in Zaire were second only to gunshots as a form of population reduction. Lloyd took the ONATRA railway. Still less than safe but it was the lesser of several substantial evils.

Arriving in Matadi, and in one piece, he managed to obtain a taxi from the station to the only hotel recommended by consulate and paid for by the Guangzhou gang, who were now eagerly co-operative. It was basic but quite comfortable and not far from the railway station, which might be useful in case of an emergency exit. It was also within walking distance of the police station dealing with export licence matters.

The gang had contacted the Muslim African oil trader, who had tried to get an appointment for Lloyd, with the Arab official blocking the coltan shipments. For six frustrating days, Lloyd tried in vain to contact the Arab police and customs official. Finally, he managed to speak to someone in the police station who spoke English and promised to get an appointment. When Lloyd phoned again, he was told to piss off in the nicest possible French language way. Another call brought the same response, but like his friend Jim, Lloyd became lucky on the third attempt of the day. By then, most of his sweat-stained clothes had been in and out of the hotel laundry three times.

The appointment was scheduled for the late afternoon of the following day. Central African weather delivered thunderstorms and high humidity almost every day, so he was not surprised at the distant lightning and loud explosions as he rode in an old Citroen taxi to the police station. Alighting a few hundred metres before his actual destination, due to an unforeseen but commonplace lack of petrol in the taxi, he took the only option left to him and set out on shanks' pony.

Walking the remainder of the way along crumbling pavements, he came to a grim, stone colonial building, with an open front leading to a large dark courtyard. He strode in and stepped up the few stairs to an empty reception area. By now he was feeling hot, sticky and damp, in the warm rain. But at least the thunder had kept away – for now. Eventually, a sweating policeman appeared, and after some difficult conversation in schoolboy French, he was escorted to a bench outside a very solid mahogany door and told to wait until called.

Waiting was more uncomfortable than usual, due to the hard bench and increasingly humid atmosphere. Thunder, and the sound of more tropical rain, told him that the storm was closing in on the town. Occasionally, the lights would flicker and even go out completely for several seconds. With the increased noise, he didn't hear the barked order from inside the official's office.

Soon, an angry man in plain clothes opened the door and snarled at Lloyd in English to get a move on; waving his fist towards the desk and chairs near the open window. Lloyd took a chair beside the desk nearest to the window and relief from the stuffy air of the corridor.

The plain-clothes policeman was clearly confident of his authority and the strength of his bargaining position. He was also in command of a good grasp of English as well as French and the local African dialect. Evidence of his authority was made more obvious by the large Colt automatic lying ready and waiting on his desk next to a fly whisk, which he waved to reinforce his conversation. This was opened with demands to see the money that he had claimed from the Chinese purchasers. Failure to produce it, he said, would terminate everything. Lloyd took this to mean his own existence as well as the conversation.

Summoning up as much composure as he thought the situation required, Lloyd assured the belligerent Arab that he could satisfy the demand, patting his jacket pocket to indicate possession of the bribe consideration. In reality, the pocket contained his own Smith & Wesson. The pat was to reassure himself that it was still there, in case of emergency. He was less sure about the safety catch, which he had fiddled with but not checked. In fact, he had never actually fired the handgun in anger – or in calm.

"Before we get to any exchange of the US dollars" – *that should impress him,* he thought – "which I am authorised to do, I must have evidence of the merchandise being released for shipment. I presume that you do have the authority to release it? What documents do you have to get the goods out of bond and on to the ship?" *That,* he thought, *would show that he was no mug and put the onus on the Arab to perform his part of the transaction.*

Lloyd's show of composure was met with surprised scorn by the intolerant police officer. People didn't speak to him like that. Not unless they wanted to be thrown in jail or in the river. And certainly not in his own office. Snorting with suppressed rage, he took a deep breath to recover and opened a desk drawer. Lloyd expected to see another gun in his hand but the Arab grasped a single sheet of paper with printed words in French and English, and an official looking stamp next to a blank line for signature.

"All I have to do is, sign here" – he pointed at the blank line – "and your goods will be released as soon as this form is presented to the shipping agent at the docks. And all I have to do, " he added in a lower tone, "is to shout out an order and your head will be blown away by my men downstairs."

Throughout the long pause, a silent, unblinking stand-off ensued between the two men. Lloyd kept thinking of Tulloch's anecdotal sales training instruction. He would not be first to speak and lose the game. On the other hand, the greedy Arab wanted the bribery money to continue flowing. Shooting the messenger would stop the flow permanently. After a few more long and pregnant seconds, the Arab ended the short game.

"I'll sign it right now and you will give me the money right now too. Right?"

"And," added Lloyd, "you will give me the form and safe conduct to the shipping agent, *and* back again to Kinshasa – right?"

Without further bluffing and threatening, the form was stamped and signed, and handed to Lloyd for inspection. He took the form and had a quick look at it, pretending that he knew what he was looking for. Then, his hand, with the form, moved towards his inside pocket. As he tried to push the form into the pocket, his jacket opened sufficiently for the Arab to see the butt of his automatic, which bulged suspiciously towards the police official's desk and chair.

At the sight of the unused Smith & Wesson, any form of mutual confidence or respect disappeared from the office, as did the electricity for the light in the ceiling. The Arab emitted a scream of abuse as he grabbed for his own gun on the unlit desk. A short flash of lightning outside the open window gave just enough illumination for Lloyd to see that his would-be collaborator was now his would-be assassin. The Arab was of similar build to Lloyd and managed to take hold of his gun at the same time as Lloyd tried to take hold of the Arab's arm.

Wrenching his arm free, but with Lloyd's other hand striking the Arab testicles, another scream of abuse was accompanied by a volley from the Colt, which went straight up and into the electric light fitting in the whitewashed plaster ceiling. All hope of internal light disappeared and the heavy fitting descended onto the head of the furious Arab. Badly stunned, he still managed to hold his gun, if not his temper.

A vast shower of white plaster crumbled down and covered both men. Another attempt by Lloyd to disarm the angry bearer of malice and Colt handgun was partially resisted. Several more bullets were fired wildly into walls and ceiling. The air in the office was by now thick with white dust and plaster, much of which stuck to the two assailants' sweating heads, hands and clothes.

More screams from the police official brought the sounds of heavy footsteps and shouts from the duty police below. Two of the duty staff, resplendent in dark olive uniform and loaded AK47s, stumbled up the stairs in the dark to their boss's unlit office. Lloyd related later that what followed fell into the category of being 'serious if it hadn't been funny'. At the time, it was deadly serious, albeit bizarre.

Crashing into the closed door, one of the duty policemen tried to shoot his way in. Splinters of wood and bullets sprayed into the room, causing Lloyd to wrest his hands free from the big Arab and dive for the floor at the side of the desk. When the initial burst of gunfire stopped, the second policeman turned the unlocked door handle and pushed what was left of it open. In the darkness, both policemen could hear the shouts, including the order screamed in their local dialect to "Shoot the white bastard! Shoot him now! Kill him! Kill him!"

The window frame and office space nearest to it was suddenly lit by a huge flash of lightning, accompanied instantaneously by deafening thunderclaps. In the brief instant of light, the gun-toting duty police saw a large figure, quite white with plaster as well as with rage, waving a large handgun. Trained to act rapidly, the first one loosed an entire magazine of thirty-nine bullets from his AK47 into the armed and rabid white apparition before him. The weight of bullets drove the whitewashed body right through the open window frame – out into the night and down onto the cobbled courtyard below.

With two trigger-happy half-wits in dangerously close proximity, Lloyd froze in the lee of the whitewashed official's desk. Both of the AK47-wielding men retreated as quickly as they could in the darkness. Down the stairs and into the wet courtyard they raced to examine their prize on the ground. Lloyd followed quietly, out of sight as best he could, keeping a safe distance between himself and the policemen before him.

At the foot of the stairs, he noticed a police cape and peaked hat hanging on the duty officer's rack by the door. Slipping the hat over his white plastered hair, he snatched the cape and slipped out of the door. The cape was then draped over his shoulders. Anyone looking in the dark street would have seen a wet policeman wearing a cape and peaked hat over a strangely mottled white and grey suit walking quickly towards the railway station.

Running and stumbling into the courtyard, the two excited sharpshooters took a flashlight and switched it on, pointing the beam at a crumpled mess of flesh, bone and bullets on the ground. By now, the tropical rain was falling heavily, washing some of the white plaster from the bloodied corpse. A heavy boot prodded the remains of an arm and turned the torso over, revealing a half-washed distorted face. A gasp of horror from one of the policemen followed a second of shocked silence.

"You stupid arsehole! You've shot the boss!"

Excitement of the wrong sort then turned pride into panic. They both realised the very real peril that they faced. Time to go off-duty, very quickly and probably permanently. Time to vanish from the police station. Ignoring the mess behind them and the absence of a cape and peaked hat, they ran to a car in the yard. Snatching at the keys in the ignition, they drove immediately from the dark, wet town, racing towards what they hoped would be the sanctuary of their own village, several miles up-country. The village elders there would confirm that they had never left it for days.

The next batch of duty officers would find the mess and would explain that the sudden demise of their superior was due to ill-health. After all, Matadi was a very unhealthy town, in a very unhealthy country.

25

BRIBERY AND CORRECTION

At the railway station in Matadi, Lloyd walked straight onto the platform, beside which were two stationary trains. No-one tried to stop or question the policeman in the cape and peaked hat as he boarded the nearest train carriage and sat on the hard wooden seat. Recovering some of his composure, he sat for fifteen minutes, trying to work out which train was bound for where.

After he removed the hat and cape, the sound of a diesel engine suggested an imminent departure. The locomotive engine appeared to be pointing along the line to Kinshasa. The other train, he guessed, would be bound for the terminal at the docks only two stations further west.

During his elongated wait for an appointment with the Arab police official – now 'no longer available' – Lloyd had contacted the shipping agent, whose office was in the dockland area and who had been as helpful as he could be. They had discussed the frozen export licence and the agent was as keen as anyone to get the shipments of tantalum ore, stacked in containers at the docks, out of Africa and on the water to China and receive payment of his shipping costs.

Before the train could move from Matadi station towards Kinshasa, Lloyd suddenly opened the far door of the compartment and the near door of the train on the adjacent line. He crossed from the eastbound train to his new westbound transport, leaving the police cape and hat behind, to go on to Kinshasa without him. Some twenty minutes later, the docklands-bound train also moved away, but in the opposite direction, containing one weary and relieved white passenger.

At the terminus, Lloyd resorted to the use of the most effective form of passport or ticket in Africa and many other continents. The bundle of US dollars that had been reserved for bribery and corruption was applied to its intended use. Ten dollars into the ticket collector's hand was gratefully received. Another ten bought a taxi ride to the shipping agent's office and the driver's guarantee of silence. If the agent was not exactly expecting to see him, he was certainly hoping and relieved to do so.

In the agent's office, a comfortable chair and a cold drink were provided to the exhausted messenger with the export licence form. While Lloyd recovered from his near-death experience, the agent eagerly checked the signed licence form and made the necessary arrangements to file it, with copies of the Bills of Lading, invoices and packing notes. Once those documents were completed in quintuplicate, he issued the orders for immediate shipment of the containers of coltan and handed one set – the top set for the bank – of the copy documents to Lloyd.

The agent would receive a comfortable and legitimate fee for his overdue work but, as usual, some form of commission was also standard practice. Five of the hundred dollar bills were freely offered and freely accepted. Lloyd felt that the assistance and co-operation from the agent was well worth the commission. More was to follow. Rather than risk another train journey and possible manhunt in Matadi, the agent suggested an alternative form of transport. A few kilometres from the docks there was a small airport and a light aircraft.

The shipping agent explained that high-value shipments could sometimes be 'shipped' by air-freight. This would normally fly out from Kinshasa, but if the 'shipment' was small and not too heavy, it could be flown from the nearby airport to link with the main air-freight from Kinshasa. The same aircraft could – at a price – be employed to fly human cargoes. More thanks were expressed with more dollars from the bribery envelope, which was now resembling the 'good guys' welfare fund'.

During the time taken for flight arrangements and a bumpy drive to the airport, Lloyd's clothes and luggage were collected from his hotel by an employee of the agency. They were then driven to meet Lloyd at the tiny air-freight terminal. A grateful European exchanged more dollars for his belongings and yet more for the flight to Kinshasa. All in all, he thought, the bribery and corruption business provided good value for the needy traveller.

Despite the poor flying conditions, in humid and thundery weather, Lloyd enjoyed the two-hour flight across thick tropical forest and brown rivers between coast and capital. By the time he alighted from the small sky-van and walked across the tarmac to present the return portion of his intercontinental flight ticket, he was relatively sprightly, if not actually refreshed.

This time the welfare fund was applied to legitimate commercial business, exchanging twenty more dollars for a cold beer and a sandwich. Waiting for five hours in the passenger terminal at Kinshasa airport was less stressful than five minutes in a dark Matadi police station.

Some days later, a local newspaper carried a 'breaking news' report of the arrest at a railway station between Kinshasa and Matadi of a well-known thief. The arrested man was charged with impersonating a policeman by wearing a stolen police cape and peaked hat. Another report told of the sudden death due to ill-health of a high-ranking police official in Matadi and the acute shortage of trained police officers there.

The short walk across wet tarmac to an aircraft of most welcome appearance included a brief glimpse of glaring blue sky between the threatening clouds. Lloyd never really enjoyed flying in thundery conditions, but an established airline with a scheduled jet aircraft controlled by an Antipodean pilot and Cantonese cabin crew was reassuring and as good as it could get at that stage.

Just before entering the cabin, he saw a pair of large birds, apparently engaged in an aerial courtship dance. He recalled watching something similar on a wildlife programme broadcast with David Attenborough – two albatross in graceful flight appearing to have an invisible thread between their bodies, synchronising every movement more precisely

than the best ballet dancers. A vision of Betty with himself –
or might it be another couple in physical and mental harmony?

Could there be a deeper understanding than he had been
told between Tulloch and Rose Klevic? Could Rose be
controlling both of them in order to take the benefits of their
most difficult and dangerous efforts? Could she be plotting
with a very alive Klevic, or even one of his former 'dangerous
associates'?

He realised that conjecture was as useless as the penniless
pension fund at this stage. Concentrate on the immediate
objective: into the cabin, comfort and safe conduct.

Cathay Pacific Airlines food and drink was good – slightly
better than typical airline fodder. It was an awful lot better
than the Matadi hotel restaurant's fare though, and Lloyd
accepted everything on offer during the long flight to Hong
Kong. As he settled back in his business class, fully reclining
seat, at thirty-three thousand feet above Africa, he ordered a
large after-dinner Courvoisier cognac. Digesting the warm
brandy, he thought back to the potentially deadly encounter in
the coastal town's police station and the sudden rash of staff
shortages there.

Better an empty house than a bad tenant rang through his
tired mind. Lloyd dozed off before his half-full glass was
discreetly removed from the tray before him. By the time that
the Cathay flight circled Chek Lap Kok airport, Cocky was
almost fit for human contact again. The series of catnaps,
alternately dozing and waking, often wondering where he was,
sometimes confused his exhausted mind. At one stage, half-
asleep, he saw only swirling clouds and flashes of sky, thinking

he was a lone aerial navigator, before realising that he was flying in the company of others – and in a large jet aircraft.

He had not died and gone to heaven, he told himself, it just felt that way. A bottle of cold Spa water was delivered with an approving smile and consumed gratefully. The water soon re-hydrated body and soul, bringing both back, if not to earth, at least to the reclining business class seat. As his head cleared, he reflected the extraordinary event of the past week.

Had he been dreaming? Or had he narrowly escaped a gory end down a god-forsaken plughole of the old Belgian Empire? King Leopold had a lot to answer for. And now, Joseph Chan and his Guanzhou gang would have a similar task. Talking of Chan, would he continue to co-operate under the threat of being reported to the PRC authorities? Or would he resort to his natural imitation of the scorpion riding on the back of a swimming frog – instinctively killing his carrier only to drown them both?

Lloyd's main concerns were now two-fold: completion of the deal with Guanzhou and safety of Betty. Although he had insisted that she should go to her family in Shanghai while the potentially dangerous liaisons with Chan and his friends were in progress, he knew that she would probably return to Hong Kong as soon as she thought fit. That might not be coincidental to what he would consider as the 'all clear' signal.

Throughout the transfer from aircraft to the automated rail link into Central, and again from Central to Aberdeen and home, he wondered where, and if, she was safely tucked away. In the apartment there was no letter, or fax, or telephone message on their TAM. No sign. No sound. He phoned her parents' home in Shanghai.

Worrying news – Betty had indeed left their house a week ago, saying that she was returning to Hong Kong. A message to her employer's office brought even worse news. She had returned for one day only, but then she had phoned in to say that she had been detained somewhere. Nothing more.

Cocky tried to live up to his name. Betty was... is... resourceful and smart. She would have realised that any danger would be directed at places where she was well known, such as her parents' home or her employer's office. She would have quietly slipped away to where she would be anonymous and safe. He then phoned Jim Watson and told him of his fears – that Betty had been abducted by Chan or one of his henchmen.

Watson was sympathetic but realistic. His long experience in Hong Kong police work had made him almost philosophical about crimes against the person. Life in China had been as cheap or cheaper than Chinese manufactured goods for centuries. This had been an accepted situation since the first dynasty of emperors used human life as a commodity. If Chan had arranged some form of kidnap, however, killing the hostage would reduce the bargaining power to zero. Although Watson was trying to look on the bright side, Lloyd failed to see any sunshine.

Despite his fears and continuous nagging worries, the object of his visit to the Congo had to be completed. The documents carried from the helpful shipping agents, and the information gathered by him and by Watson should prove to be much more powerful in China than the life of one Chinese girl. That was the hard but pragmatic truth of the situation. He decided to contact Guanzhou directly – supplying the gang with what they needed, provided that they procured Betty's safety and returned the embezzled cash to P.O. Holdings Inc. and its insolvent pension fund.

Initial contact was aborted when the receptionist handling the call advised him that 'his friend Mr Chan' was there and would Mr Lloyd like to speak to him first? The second phone call brought a more discreet conversation with the head of the Guanzhou company and authorised signatory to the P and O R.A. account. Arrangements were made for a meeting of the bargaining parties in a neutral corner of their sparring ring. The negotiating table chosen by Lloyd, with Watson's advice, was to be the head office of the bank in Shanghai. Referee and seconds would be provided by the bank, who would be primed to transfer the P and O R.A. funds immediately on the authority of the Guanzhou gang.

The demand for a meeting at the bank's head office suited both parties; it suited Lloyd, on behalf of P.O. Holdings Inc., because the bank held the missing money. It suited the gang, because the bank had issued the Letters of Credit to P.O. Holdings Inc. Neither they nor their customers could obtain possession of the coltan or receive payment for it until they had the shipping documents carried by Lloyd. He remembered what Betty had told him – that the gang had probably already sold the precious metal forward, but now they couldn't get paid for it either without possession of the shipments and documents to prove ownership

To add some weight to his side, Lloyd had asked Jim Watson to accompany him. Jim could stay silent and just look as though he was acting as an official representative, and he could take Lloyd to one side and advise him if he noticed anything suspicious.

Suspicions abounded during the meeting but all parties were eager to succeed. The importers and the bank were both worried about the documentary credits being overdue and likely to expire. They had already been extended for a month. Further extension was unlikely to be offered. The Guanzhou gang were desperately worried that they would not be able to take delivery of the coltan, which they had contracted to sell for tantalum extraction. Lloyd was just worried about Betty. Nothing more had been heard from her since he phoned her employer.

Once the documents had been examined and checked thoroughly by bank officials, the atmosphere eased. Cathay Pacific's 747 had returned Lloyd much faster than the sea freighter would carry the containers of coltan from Matadi but only a few days would separate their arrival. Even if the ship struck a rock and sank, the cargoes were insured. Payment to P.O. Holdings Inc. could proceed and the goods would belong to the gang. They in turn could deliver to their customers and receive payment and a massive profit.

The second vital part of the operation could be more difficult. Getting the two members of the gang to authorise transfer of the entire balance in the P and O R.A. account required rather more than a gentle reminder. Before the bank officials could take the documents from him, Lloyd used

Watson as a supposed official from Hong Kong police to insist that the authority for transfer was recognised by the bank and immediately acted upon.

There was surprisingly little opposition to the demand for the return of the embezzled money in the P and O R.A. account. The Chinese importers insisted that the huge sums had been 'arranged' by Klevic, to be available to them in order to be used as collateral for the high value imports, which they or their customers could not finance themselves. They forgot to mention that they had been trading in this way without agreement from the local authorities in either Guangzhou or Shanghai. Once Watson agreed not to remember this lapse, provided that the money was returned immediately, the gang's co-operation was assured.

Klevic, the importers conceded, was to have received a direct share of the profits from their trading in the metals and, had assured them that the cash in the P and O R.A. account would be repaid 'in due course', to the banks who had originally advanced the money from P.O. Holdings Inc. They claimed innocence and ignorance of the true source of the money or any other use to which it might be applied by Klevic, whether for more precious metals or for more arms shipments from Russia or its old satellites.

Realising that nothing could be gained by refusing to co-operate in full, and that much could be lost if the shipping documents were withdrawn, the gang leaders and the bankers then acceded without a struggle. Transfer of the proceeds of the illicit P and O R.A. account back to P.O. Holdings Inc.

was set in motion, albeit with the usual 'old Spanish custom' of several days' delay during which both sending and receiving banks could make use of the money.

Tulloch had previously instructed the P.O. Holdings Inc. treasurers department to contact the Shanghai bank in order to establish legitimate relations and, advise Shanghai of a new account to which the money was due. All this detail was of little or no interest to Lloyd, who just wanted his part of the operation to be completed so that he could search for his personal emotional rock, the financially red hot Betty T'Sang.

By late afternoon, the formalities and banking arrangements had been completed and several phone calls to and from Tulloch confirmed that the money transfers were in progress. As far as Lloyd was concerned, he had performed a near miracle of modern commerce in extraordinary circumstances. He and Watson declined an invitation to dine with the Shanghai bankers but did have some China tea and a scotch at the airport, before flying back to Hong Kong. Once there, the two men discussed the problem of Betty's disappearance without any obvious solution.

The immediate financial disaster, huge as it had been, was in process of correction to some extent. There was still the very serious problem of embezzlement and false trading, with overstated profits in P.O. Holdings Inc. and the scandal of Klevic's involvement with very dubious, if sometimes officially legitimate, traders.

And there was still the problem of Joseph Chan and his commission on phoney transactions, as sanctioned by the late chairman. They would continue to be problems for Tulloch, for Carlsen and the other directors. They could be a problem for Madam Rosa Klevic too, but she would have to find her own solution. The most serious problem was that of Betty's disappearance.

26

Death and transfiguration

Tulloch's nagging doubts of the true circumstances of Klevic's apparent but probably staged death had not been shared with anyone. Not even his usual confidante and current hero of Africa and China. Not with the senior banker, Carlsen, or his late financial mentor, Vanstaart. And certainly not with his hostess, Madam – 'call me Rose' Klevic. He had tried to be as careful as possible when dining with her and even more so when sleeping in – or near – her bed.

Before Lloyd had worked wonders with Patrick Klevic's shady associates in Guanzhou and their corrupt contacts in Africa, a curious story was relayed to Tulloch from somewhere in the Balkans. Someone purporting to be an old comrade of Klevic, in his gun running days, had left a message to the effect that he thought that he had seen his old friend in Kosovo. The reason for the message was that he wanted to make contact with him to discuss old times and perhaps re-open business arrangements.

Remembering the warnings from Vanstaart and the reputations of Klevic's associates and 'old comrades', Tulloch had been glad that he had not received the message personally. No name had been left by the caller – only a poste-restante address and a phone number in Pristina. To avoid direct contact, he asked a receptionist to phone the number and say that she had the message but could not hear the name of the messenger. Without a name, she was to say, she would not know to whom the message was sent. Without a name and further details, she could not pass the message to anyone.

On the third attempt, the receptionist obtained a name and the barest of details. The messenger gave his name as Mr Bela Fark or something she could not quite understand. The name meant nothing to Tulloch and he wondered how to obtain some background without igniting more suspicion. A call to the house of Vanstraat and the old butler proved nothing and he thought he might have to resort to confiding in Rose. First, he would casually mention the name to Carlsen, in case that brought any sign of recognition.

"Bela Fark? That's a funny name. Where did you hear that?"

Tulloch pretended, or wondered, if he had not heard it properly.

"That's just a name that I have heard mentioned. I can't remember exactly where. Why is a funny name?"

"FARK was an acronym – the name given to a splinter group of terrorists, or freedom fighters if you prefer it, in Kosovo. They broke away from the KLA – the Kosovo Liberation Army. They sounded like a proper bunch of gangsters, I can tell you. Even Klevic was touchy about contact with them."

Vanstaart's account of Klevic's activities and double-dealing in Kosovo flooded back to Tulloch. No wonder Klevic was touchy. He – Tulloch – would not touch them either. Not if he could help it. However, someone – the mysterious Mr Fark or whoever he was – claimed that he had seen a supposedly dead man. It could be the lead to his conspiracy theory coming to life. Fark and Kosovo were quickly abandoned as a subject for conversation with Carlsen, but Tulloch was determined to discover much more.

Before he could glean more about 'Mr Fark' and his search for a dead man, another unusual report arrived. One of the bank officials in Shanghai had received a telephone request for details of the Guanzhou bank account in the name of P and O R.A. As the request had not come from an authorised signatory, nothing had been revealed. Not even the fact that the account was now officially closed. The Chinese caller had said that he had been doing so on behalf of 'a client' whose name, he claimed, was Klevic.

To receive one claim of sighting Klevic was disturbing – two claims, as Lady Bracknell might have said, were perhaps not careless but too close to Tulloch's theory to be dismissed as coincidence. Was Klevic not only still alive but travelling the world, seeking access to his ill-gotten gains? Tulloch's mind raced with theories and possibilities verging on fantasy.

One possibility was that it was just Chan trying his luck with the Shanghai bank to tap into the money he thought might still be there. Another, darker possibility, was that 'Mr Fark' had heard of the financial scandal at P.O. Holdings Inc. and suspected that Klevic was on the run and open to blackmail. But if Klevic was really alive and running, who was the unfortunate late owner of the body from Lenios?

He really needed to hear more from Lloyd about his brief investigation on the Greek island. But Cocky was still in Hong Kong and had his own problems. First, Chan had spoken to him, insisting on a personal meeting in a crowded restaurant where he could be seen. There, Chan had discussed his situation and the threat of criminal prosecution and awful punishment. To alleviate his worst fears, he said, would require a cast-iron guarantee of non-disclosure regarding his involvement with Klevic and Guanzhou.

That guarantee could only be cast in iron if Lloyd swore an affidavit clearing Chan of all and any charges. Cocky was outraged but suspected that Chan would add some sort of threat or incentive to get such an affidavit. Perhaps the bribery fund was not yet closed. Alternatively, what would Chan threaten? Cocky's fears were not groundless. Chan suddenly talked of family and loved ones and the dangers they faced in 'these circumstances'.

What circumstances? thought Lloyd. And, what dangers? He faced up to Chan.

"I don't know what you're talking about, but I have to tell you that I don't have any family in Hong Kong and I'm happy to take care of myself, in case you are threatening me."

Chan's face tightened. His attempted show of pleasant demeanour, completely gone. "No, not you, of course. But, your loved ones always need protecting, don't they?"

Lloyd's attitude also hardened. *So, that's it,* he thought. *Either I ensure this miserable shit's protection from justice or he'll ensure Betty's bad health or worse. It's blackmail, of course but what if he really has abducted Betty? Or has he heard that she hasn't*

238

surfaced and is trying to pretend that he has got her to scare me? If so, he has succeeded. I'm scared all right.

Lloyd rose from the table without answering. He wanted to make Chan think that he was considering compliance without immediate confirmation. He had to gain some time to get help. To find Betty and protect her. His old police presence took over, although he didn't know how to apply it. He told Chan that he would have to think about it. Chan looked daggers at him, wishing he had a few to stick in Lloyd's back. If he wanted to harm Lloyd, he didn't have to wait long.

Within a few hours, Watson had phoned Lloyd with the news he dreaded. The body of a young Chinese woman had been extracted from the harbour near to the rocks off Lantau Island. Positive identification was very difficult due to the injuries and the effects of the Hong Kong harbour on a lifeless body. Watson couldn't say if the body looked anything like that of Betty but it was a possibility. Nothing more. Not to Watson perhaps, but much more to a now very un-cocky Lloyd.

Immediate plans for dreadful retribution flashed through Lloyd's mind. He wanted to get Chan by the throat and choke him slowly in a pool of piranha fish. Rather than going to all that trouble, he wanted Watson to phone him again to say that he had made a mistake. Most of all, he wanted Betty back. He couldn't believe that Chan could have abducted her in Shanghai. She would have gone to another place of hiding rather than stay there or risk returning to Hong Kong. She was somewhere safe, he knew it. He hoped it.

Hope springs eternal, someone had told him. But with time and no further news, hope started to unwind. Slowly at first, then faster and more surely. Watson's further bulletins only confirmed what he had already said. Identification turned from possible to probable. The next report would be almost certain.

Lloyd decided to do the only thing he could think of. He would report Chan's corruption formally to the police and file charges for prosecution. Then, he would pack up the apartment in Aberdeen and sell it, before returning to the United Kingdom. He was beaten senseless.

Despite the critical shortage and resulting high values of property in Hong Kong, selling a short-term lease on an apartment would take longer than Lloyd expected. In the meantime, he duly reported to Tulloch with the awful report of Betty's suspected death and his decision to quit Hong Kong and P.O. Holdings Inc. and go home to Wales.

Tulloch's reaction was understandably sympathetic. Betty had been an essential agent in their inquiries as well as being Lloyd's closest companion, and he knew how much Cocky would miss her. The latest strange reports, claiming contacts with – or sightings of – Klevic, however, generated an urgent need for renewed alliance with Betty's forlorn and distraught lover.

In the continued absence of Dmitri Petric, now adopting quite sinister possibilities, Lloyd would be appointed as the single official security officer, reporting still to Tulloch but with a higher salary and authority. The combination of the last two points, Tulloch hoped would renew Lloyd's interest in

P.O. Holdings Inc. and perhaps take his mind off his missing rock. After a few hours deliberation, Lloyd agreed. After all, what else was there to do? His plans and destination focused back on Vaduz and the Hotel-bar Brasserie Burg, although his mind remained on Betty.

Trying to resume the chase, after tracing the missing pension fund cash and receiving settlement of the last contract in tantalum, seemed like an anti-climax to Lloyd. He had done all that could be expected of him and more. However, a few days in the cosy but dull Hotel-bar Brassiere Burg reminded him that he had to occupy the rest of his life with something worthwhile. What would be worthwhile without Betty? The thought left him in a shell of remorse and self-pity. The cold reality of his bean-counting colleague brought about a crack in the shell and took his thoughts back to continuing existence.

Meeting at their old spot in the lounge bar, Tulloch outlined his remaining and developing concerns with some ideas of the part that Lloyd could play in finding solutions. It was all rather vague at this stage, he said, but perhaps the two of them could work out a plan, starting with the objectives. The company was still in a very restricted financial state, despite the anticipated receipts of money from China.

Trading profits had been overstated by the churning of contracts, making the company liable to re-state its financial statements and probably break up the trading operations for sale at a distressed price. Once what was left of the missing money had been recovered, he would have to break up the pension fund too. Probably assigning the individual employees' reduced values to one or more insurance companies, as a series of small personal pension pots.

All of this dull information left Lloyd cold. What possible interest could he have in pensions and financial statements? What, for that matter, would anyone apart from the Financial Services Agency, be interested in it? Then Tulloch revealed his conspiracy theories and the mysterious reports and sightings of Klevic. Neither man could fit the pieces of his latest jigsaw puzzle together, but perhaps some lateral thinking could establish some sort of correlation.

Tulloch thought that the key elements seemed to be Klevic, his apparent death and the embezzled money. Lloyd was more interested in the circumstances and which individuals might be involved in the death. He had visited the scene of the corpse's departure and heard quite a few scraps of information concerning the individuals. If they compared notes and facts concerning those, perhaps the link to those key elements would appear.

As a starter, Lloyd said, he had discovered that either Dmitri Petric or Ostal Klevic had not returned to Lenios after the funeral in the Balkans. Petric, the devoted minder and former company security officer had for some time been rarely seen before that event and not at all since. The funeral had been conducted with exceptional haste, even by Balkan Muslim standards.

Then Tulloch reminded Lloyd of his 'third man' theory and of the apparent sighting in the Balkans of someone resembling Klevic by a man wanting to contact him. He also told him of the gun-running and double-crossing events during the

Kosovo civil war, as described by the late Anton Vanstraat. To Tulloch's slight surprise, Lloyd did not reject the idea completely. He even admitted that something similar had crossed his mind as the events in Lenios and the island airfield had been unravelled to him.

Despite the reported devotion of Petric to Klevic, they both knew that Klevic would not have issued a guarantee of faithful reciprocity. And they both were aware of the physical similarity between the two ethnic Albanians. That suggested that the faithful Petric, or another person close to Klevic and his nefarious activities in the Balkans, had possibly paid the ultimate price of loyalty.

If there had been a conspiracy involving Petric's murder and substitution, then others in the Klevic clan – Rosa and cousin Ostal – must have conspired equally. What then, were their parts in the deceit and murder? More puzzling, what was their motive? Klevic would naturally want to pocket the embezzled cash and disappear without a trace. Would Rose and Ostal simply wait until he paid their share to them? How could they trust him to do it after such a heinous crime?

More questions. Few answers. And again, the limited answers only generated more questions. In the absence of the departed Vanstraat, Tulloch might obtain some pointers from Carlsen and his co-directors, but he concluded, sadly, that in the event of a Klevic family conspiracy, he would have to say goodbye to any passionate relationship with Rose. He would have to get to the truth one way or the other. Her warm bed might well turn into a death bed if he was not extremely careful.

Yet another question appeared before him. One that made him wonder why he hadn't asked it before. What personal investment or involvement, if any, did Klevic and the various relatives and associates have, in the real pension fund? It would be normal for the CEO of a big corporation and his wife to have big shares in the company's pension scheme, if only to demonstrate confidence in it. Robbing the fund would be tantamount to self-abuse, unless they thought their own investments would provide some form of alibi.

In Klevic's case, a staged death and disappearance, combined with such a robbery, would appear to be more like suicide. Perhaps, he thought, it really was suicide, to take 'the coward's way out' and avoid humiliation. As Lloyd had been to Grand Cayman and the pension fund trustee's office, Tulloch decided that he should ask him to contact Armstrong again, while Tulloch quizzed the nervous company secretary in Vaduz to get lists of fund members and their investments. "You never know," he said cheerfully to Lloyd, "if we get two lists of what should be the same employees: one from the trustee and one from the secretary, they might even agree."

Thoughts of flying pigs flew past the windows of their minds.

27

FAMILY TRACES

Within hours, pausing only to allow for the time difference between Vaduz and Grand Cayman, George Armstrong had been woken from his post-prandial slumbers by a slightly refreshed and re-invigorated Lloyd. Without telling him of the success in tracing much of the missing millions, Lloyd simply ordered him to extract a full list of contributors to the pension scheme and the value of their contributions.

At the same time, Andrew Tulloch, adopting a more gentle approach to his nervous flatulent colleague, obtained a similar list from the P.O. Holdings Inc. company secretary. To the surprise of both Tulloch and Lloyd, the two lists of employees names actually matched. What did not match were the total value of contributions and the value of the fund's cash and investments. Even allowing for the best scenario and full recovery of the missing cash, the total value would still be almost thirty percent below the amount contributed by the employees and miles below that required to finance the cost of reasonable retirement pensions for them.

Once more, the hand of Patrick Klevic was writ heavily on the value and state of the investment portfolio. A minority of the value was in authorised trustee investments such as government bonds and shares, or in 'blue chip' companies quoted on leading stock exchanges. The majority, however, was stated as investments in unauthorised managed funds, none of which was recognised by Tulloch. Meetings with Carlsen the banker, and Goldsmit, the consultant actuary on the board of P.O. Holdings Inc., shed no further light onto the investments' provenance or market values.

Asking the pension fund's trustee or the company secretary for details was as enlightening as a wet match in a damp cellar. George Armstrong pleaded a pathetically believable ignorance of anything resulting from Klevic's orders. Similarly, the increasingly paranoid company secretary, rightly predicting his imminent dismissal or another cardiac arrest, pleaded something more akin to insanity. His nervous disposition was on the verge of a complete breakdown, particularly as he also assumed by now that his dreams of a retirement pension would be more imagined than real. For him, responsibility had diminished completely.

There was one more common thread running through the list of high-risk investments – most of the companies or funds had commercial operations in Asia, Africa or Eastern Europe. The metal importing connection with Guangzhou was just one of the beneficiaries of the pension fund portfolio. Organisations based in Asia or Eastern Europe would probably be involved in arms trading or the carpet-bagging exports of former Soviet Union state assets. Once more, Klevic appeared to have been using the fund to feather his own nest, gambling with his employees' savings.

By now, Tulloch realised that he could no longer postpone interrogation of his bedmate. She must have known something of Klevic's investment scams, and there must be other people involved in them, the names of whom would probably be known to her. More than likely, they would include the men who had been reported as making enquiries of Klevic in Greece and the Balkans.

As he was almost ready to have something to eat, he phoned Rose to invite her to have dinner with him at a quiet restaurant not far from her house. The response was encouraging. Either she was feeling romantic or she desperately wanted to find out what he had found out. It wasn't just hunger or thirst for food and drink.

Berggasthaus Matu is situated on the side of the mountains near Vaduz – a typical Alpine-style wooden building, with a typical Alpine-style menu and atmosphere. Before even thinking of grilling Rose, Andrew's thoughts were aimed at grilling lamb or chicken and sipping cool Johannisberger Riesling or Provencal wine. The half-lit evening views over the valley were romantic enough, but not enough to distract either of the two diners from the prime objectives on the table or from each other.

Throughout the first and main courses, no mention was made of business, money or Patrick Klevic. Rose appeared relaxed and happy. Andrew could not relax completely, but in part, his inner tension was caused by a growing affection for her. If not a completely merry widow, she was certainly not morose. She was also not at all unattractive. In fact, he found her downright sexy. More than once the thought crossed

Andrew's mind as to whether Klevic would have staged his death and disappeared forever if he had not arranged to reunite with her soon afterwards.

Against that train of thought, the other side of such a situation occurred to him. Would Rose want to reunite with someone of Klevic's nature? Would she, for that matter, have wanted to continue their lives together? Perhaps it was a case of being a Black Widow before becoming a merry one. A man such as Klevic must have had many very dangerous enemies and probably even more dangerous friends. Vanstaart had warned him about them. Vanstaart had not mentioned Rose as either of them but she might have been both.

All those thoughts were put to one side in the comfort of the Berggasthaus Matu restaurant. The possibilities might be almost endless but the immediate task, apart from a pleasant dinner, was to discover as much personal detail as possible about Klevic, his family and, his associates.

Rose was not particularly interested in drinking wine or anything more intoxicating. After one small glass of the Johannisberger, she accompanied the rest of her meal with plain water. Tulloch sipped water with his wine too and had to admit later that it was of particularly clear and sweet tasting quality. Good enough to accompany a good Scotch but that would have to wait. He also wanted to maintain a particularly clear head.

Ignoring coffee, he invited Rose to chose a dessert. She declined but instead invited Tulloch to take her back to her house where, he guessed, she might invite him to take their relationship to bed. Driving back down the mountain road to

Vaduz, she relaxed further, leaning towards him and almost causing some distraction from the controls of the large Mercedes S-Class. Drinking the clear water had been worth the effort, to avoid either embarrassment, an accident or a ticket from the traffic politz in Vaduz.

Sooner than Tulloch might have wanted under different circumstances, they arrived at the house, entering the hall and further negotiations. Conversation to date had been limited to a few casual comments and compliments, with non-specific questions regarding Rose's family occasionally slipping in. From her reaction and generalised answers, he gathered that she had originated in the Balkans and had arrived in Liechtenstein with Klevic some ten or twelve years previously.

Guessing her age was difficult. Tulloch thought that she might be a few years older than he was, but it could well have been a few more than just a few. Whatever the number of years was, she had the gift and habit of presentation, making the years seem less and the attraction more. To add to her striking appearance, the quality of her conversation and obvious intellect always seemed to strike a chord with the company she kept. *Quite the most dangerous female companion of his close acquaintance,* he thought.

"Are we going to bed or are you going to sleep?" she challenged.

Tulloch rose to the challenge, giving her a warm half-smile and gentle squeeze. "Come on then. We can start with the bed and, see what sleep we get later." *Be careful now,* he thought, *pillow talk after a hard night in bed could go either way and give away much more than you get.* He delayed his entry to her room and her bed, striving to fly a simple intrusive kite into the limited conversation. Trying not to appear too inquisitive but trying to encourage more disclosure of her background and more details of the Klevic clan history.

Two hours later, when they had both enjoyed a half-hour's snooze at what he expected to be half-time in their game of passion and pleasure, Tulloch revisited the scene of Rose and Klevic's past.

"Whereabouts in the Balkans did Patrick originate, then? I don't know anything about that region. Was he from the same town – the same country – as you? And, about some of the others from his clan" – he felt safe using 'clan' as a generic noun – "are they all – what would you call them – 'Balkanites'? *No* he thought, *that sounds like some sort of polymer material.*

"We are – were – all from Kosovo, if that's what you mean. Patrick – incidentally, that's not his real name, you know. He was called 'Prek' in Kosovan, after Prek Cali, a famous Albanian freedom fighter. You can guess why he didn't want to use that name in his business. Patrick and his cousin Ostal, and Dmitri Petric – they all came from that area of Kosovo too, where the Albanians live. I think Patrick got the idea of his new name from Petric, the… uh… the security guy. His old friend…"

In the dark, Tulloch could almost see Rose looking away as she referred to Petric as 'his old friend'.

"Security guy? Some security guy. I don't think I've ever seen him. He seems to have got lost. Or maybe he was stolen!"

The sardonic laugh was met with a shrug of the eyes and mouth. No comment. No other response from Rose.

"What about cousin Ostal? Was he ever actively involved in the company? After all, he was the 'O' part of the 'P.O.' wasn't he?"

A bored sigh breathed back over the sheets. "Yes, he was. And yes, he was. But not now and, not now. There. Does that answer your questions? I don't know why you're so interested in them, anyway. Not now."

Not now that we are in bed together? Or, not now that Klevic is dead or done a bunk and not now because I don't want to go there with more of your prying? Tulloch wondered and pondered.

"Sorry. I was just interested in the history – your history – that's all. Just trying to get a picture of you and your life. You are quite remarkable, you know. Carrying on in the business and the company after what has happened. Not many women – not many men either – would have done what you have and borne themselves so well in these circumstances. But, you know, you can't stand up forever as if nothing has happened. You have to relax and let your feelings flow out at some stage."

A warm hand at the end of a warm arm reached out and onto his body.

"Isn't that what I'm doing now?"

There was no answer to that. She carried on 'doing it now' and, he stopped asking questions about Klevic and Kosovo. *Fair exchange,* he thought. *Got him,* she thought.

Breakfast brought hot coffee, toast and "English marmalade" – made in Scotland – and with it, a little time before returning to the office and daily chores. Time to think about the previous evening and night-time quiz. At the offices of P.O. Holdings Inc., they went their separate ways and into their separate office facilities. When he was sure that he was not to be overheard, Tulloch phoned Lloyd to arrange a discreet morning meeting.

With nothing much more than that which they already knew, they covered the same ground as before: recovery of whatever was left in the P and O R.A. account in the Guangzhou branch of the Shanghai bank, tracing the questionable investments of the pension fund and establishing the true identity of the corpse in the Balkans cemetery.

Of the current tasks, Tulloch expected the first to continue without any more than continued pressure on Carlsen and his banking friends to complete the transfers of cash from Shanghai to Vaduz and then from Vaduz to Grand Cayman. Only one doubt nagged at his mind – the second 'Klevic' contact to the bank in Shanghai. If it came from Chan, it would probably amount to nothing, but if it really originated from Klevic, anything was possible.

The secondary investment investigations were very much in Tulloch's hands. He had the contacts and authority to trace whatever value was still there, given time. Carlsen and Goldsmit would also use their contacts to extract what remained in them.

But without modern DNA fingerprinting, a buried corpse in a second-world country was unlikely to reveal any secrets. Some lateral thinking was required, and Cocky Lloyd delivered the sideways thoughts.

"Rather than trying to get an ID check on the body, which will be in an awful state by now," he proffered, "surely we have to find the likely or possible Klevic substitutes – those who he might be impersonating now. If he is still alive, then whoever he's pretending to be is probably dead and in the coffin. If, you know what I mean," he added lamely.

Tulloch understood very well and said so. "I know exactly what you mean. Exactly. Of course, Klevic could just be hiding out somewhere under his own or some other name, but he would have to have acted as one of the others in the first place to get away from the island – the proverbial scene of the crime. Cocky, my old banana, you're a veritable Hercule Poirot. Brilliant!

"Now, there's just one more small point. Who, is going to find 'Mr X?' Who has the skills…" – Cocky didn't need a degree in telepathy to know what was coming – "to track down the other men in the burial party?" continued Tulloch pointedly, " to check their proper ID? Let me see…"

Cocky wished that he had kept his big Welsh mouth firmly shut. In the absence of whisky or beer at ten thirty a.m. in the offices of P.O. Holdings Inc., he took a gulp of very hot coffee, scalding his throat and making him wish it again.

"When and where? That's all I ask. When do you want me to go, and where to?"

"Better get as much background as possible here," Tulloch advised. "Start with personnel records – sorry – "Human Resources" they call it now. When I started working, we called it the wages department. Whatever they call it, they should have some personal records for your former European equivalent: Dmitri Petric. I know he came from Kosovo so he's probably ethnic Albanian and a Muslim. I don't expect him to be, or have been, excessively religious, but you never know."

"No. I don't. But I don't expect him to be a Welsh Baptist either. Tell you what, Andrew, I'll get what I can from those HR people if you can get what you can on the other chap – Klevic's cousin Austin or whatever he's called. We can meet again this evening to compare notes – if you're not otherwise engaged, that is."

"Ostal. His name's Ostal. Don't ask me what that means. He isn't or wasn't an employee or a director so I don't know where I can get any information on him, apart from the usual suspects, that is."

"You mean Madam K? That shouldn't be such a challenge for you, should it?" Cocky asked that without smirking or sounding sarcastic. He was just following his policeman's intuition to ask more and more questions.

"I mean, all of the directors who have been around for a while – they might know something from the old days, when he was in partnership with Klevic. Of course, I'll try squeezing Madam K – for information – again. But she's a bit touchy about the past and almost certainly suspicious of my motives by now. She must be involved somehow, but again, I don't know how, and getting information from her – it's not as easy as you might think."

"OK. I believe you. I'll see you this evening. Same place?"

"Yes. Same place. I don't want any others starting whispers about our social habits."

Lloyd raised an eyebrow but said nothing.

28

BACK TO THE BALKANS

The Human Resources department of P.O. Holdings Inc. was more helpful than either man had anticipated. Dmitri Petric had entered the company's employment from its incorporation. His role was largely undefined. Klevic had simply brought him along as his bodyguard, butler or batman. He had worked and probably fought with Klevic, possibly as a sergeant to Klevic's officer rank in an unofficial army.

None of their combined military activities was in the company's records, but what was there, including references from Klevic and others, pointed to a military arrangement based on past performance. Tulloch knew that their past performance included sourcing and supplying arms to insurgents in the Balkans' civil wars. He wondered if the faithful Petric knew the details of Klevic's past double-crossing of his ethnic Albanians in Kosovo and the massacre in Djackovica.

Despite having quite a lot of information about Petric's past, neither Tulloch nor the HR department had any of his present whereabouts or activity. If Petric had indeed flown with the funeral party to Kosovo and stayed there, they had no sign of him – unless he was the man mistaken for Klevic by the mysterious 'Mr Bela Fark'. Or, if he was 'Bela Fark' himself.

Another flight and another search for Lloyd to undertake. This time starting in Adem Jashari airport – in Pristina, the capital city of Kosovo. To Lloyd's surprise, there were a few flights available, including some from Zurich and Geneva. Bearing in mind the warnings from Tulloch of Klevic's former dealings in Kosovo, he decided to include as much protection as the airline would allow, including his unused Smith & Wesson automatic in a suitcase with his clothes. He also carried the phone and PO box numbers left by 'Bela Fark'.

On arrival in Pristina, Lloyd settled in a small hotel and tried to phone the number given by Mr Fark. An answering machine invited callers, in Albanian – which he didn't understand – and in halted English, which he could only just decipher – to leave a message. This he did, including the hotel's telephone number. He then bought a street map of Pristina and a road map of the whole of Kosovo. On the map, he noticed that the scene of the massacre in Djackovica, which according to Vanstraat, Klevic had deserted, was situated near the southwest border, miles away from Pristina in the northeast.

Another place-name caught his eye. Not far from Djackovica was the scene of yet another atrocity. It was the town of Bela Cerkva where many unarmed villagers including women and children were killed by Serbian forces in the Drini valley. It became clear to Lloyd that the similarity between Mr Fark's first name and that of the scene of the massacre might be more than coincidental.

As he was studying the map, the ringing phone in his room announced a return call from Bela Fark. A deep voice introduced the caller in hesitant English, duplicated in German. Mr Fark then explained that he was unsure of the nationality of a visitor from Liechtenstein and would be happy to converse in English, unless the visitor preferred to speak in Albanian. This was politely declined. Lloyd suggested that they might employ Welsh if the caller preferred it but otherwise English – "One of the languages we speak in Wales" – would do nicely.

'Mr Fark' continued in his halting English. He was trying to contact the person he had seen in a town near the south-eastern border of Kosovo. The news of Klevic's death had come as a shock to him and received two days after he had seen the 'doppelganger'. He used the German term and was stopped from translating when Lloyd told him of its common usage in English-speaking countries. A meeting was suggested for the two men to exchange information and explanations of their reasons for trying to track the Klevic look-alike.

At this stage, Lloyd felt it wise to allow 'Bela Fark' to disclose the time and place of the sighting – and his own true identity – in his own time when they met. Later that evening, in the hotel restaurant, the two seekers of Klevic sat down to eat dinner and discuss their tasks. 'Mr Fark' admitted that he was using an alias and his real name was Arian Bogdani – "God given," he added, with a modest smile.

Although Lloyd could guess the origins of his alias, he put that to one side, hoping that the God given one would give a lot more information than that. Bogdani started to ask questions of his own first. Why was Lloyd trying to find someone whom he, Bogdani, may or may not have recognised, if he knew that Klevic was dead?

That was answered easily and very neatly. 'Bela Fark', or Bogdani as he was now known, had left the message with P.O. Holdings Inc. and he, Lloyd, was obliged to check it out in his capacity as security officer, in case someone was impersonating the former CEO of the company. Bogdani was now in the witness box – obliged to elaborate on his story to date.

His alias, he admitted, was drawn from the paramilitary unit to which he and Klevic had belonged – the FARK. Added to that, he had thought that the name of 'Bela' might trigger memories of the wartime massacre in the minds of any surviving comrades of Klevic. Lloyd continued to feign ignorance of any knowledge of these matters. That was also easy.

Bogdani then mentioned that Klevic had a team of insurgents, including himself, and one of them who was very close to Klevic might easily be mistaken for his senior officer. His name had been Petric and he had continued to work for Klevic after the civil war in Kosovo. "Perhaps," he added, "I might have seen Klevic, or it might even have been Petric or someone else." This was not new to Lloyd and he wanted to have much more detail of the sighting and any further developments. He adopted a different tack.

"Did Klevic have any other family or friends who might be mistaken for him?" he asked. He was thinking of Klevic's cousin Ostal, but there might have been others.

"Plenty of other men were involved. His contacts in Chetchnya and others supplying arms to us; they were mainly desperados – gangsters – we wouldn't want to get involved with any of them. They would shoot their own children for money. Family? He had uncles and cousins but no immediate family of his own. One cousin had helped him to start their business but he fell out with him for some reason. Maybe it was money – or he didn't like the way Klevic handled the arms supply."

Lloyd stayed silent again, letting Bogdani talk on.

"There were plenty of stories going round after some of the people here – particularly those down south near Djackovica – were killed and we couldn't get the arms to fight those Serb bastards. Some said that Klevic had double-crossed them. Some of us believed them, some refused to. Petric wouldn't hear of it. Perhaps the cousin would. As for me, I wasn't certain either way, but it was possible. That's the main reason I need to find out if Klevic or Petric are still alive and get to the truth once and for all."

Lloyd was uncertain of Bogdani's real reason but prepared to test it. First, he would open fire with a straight question. "You didn't kill Klevic in Greece, then? If he did double-cross you and your friends, that would be an obvious motive for killing him."

Bogdani hesitated. Looking daggers at no one in particular. "No. Of course I didn't kill him. I might have wanted to. So would lots of people but why would I be looking for him – or Petric – if I had already done so? That's crazy!"

So, Bogdani had joined the growing army of would-be assassins looking for Klevic. If the former CEO of P.O. Holdings Inc. was already dead, then the army would be short of a target. But if, as Tulloch and Lloyd suspected, he was alive and hiding with the stolen ID of the man in the coffin, then they would be in competition – not only with the two investigating execs from the company, but eventually with Interpol.

Bogdani felt that he had exhausted his supply of explanations and any useful information from Lloyd was limited to the fact that they were both on a similar expedition. "I must go now. I have a long drive in front of me – to Djackovica. If you like, I'll phone you when I get there, if I have any information about Petric or the other one." Lloyd wasn't sure who he meant by 'the other one', simply thanking the Kosovan and wished him a safe journey.

During his few days in the capital city of Kosovo, Lloyd made enquiries to try to find out if Klevic or Petric had been staying in Pristina. Police records were sparse, as neither person had been officially been a resident there for years, if at all. Further calls to similar sources in the southeastern towns were equally fruitless and Lloyd was beginning to think that he would have to scour the rugged country – possibly for nothing. He conveyed these feelings to Tulloch, suggesting that he should return at the end of the week.

A week, he reflected, could be a long time in Kosovo.

29

DISCOVERY

By the end of the third day, still feeling frustrated at the lack of progress, the hotel phone rang and he heard the voice of Bogdani. He sounded far away, which was indeed where he was. Somewhere between Djackovica and Prizren, he had found an older man who naturally recalled the killings in the area very well and had also been asked about any survivors of the FARK unit in that area. There were several other ex-FARK members around, but Bogdani was more interested in the man who had enquired about them.

The enquiry had come from a man who answered the description of either Klevic or Petric. The old man couldn't be very precise and both of the targets were of similar build. However, Bogdani intended to follow the tip and would phone again with any news. That was exactly what he did the next day, barely suppressing his excitement at tracing the enquirer and planning to challenge him that evening. Such a challenge might be innocuous or it might lead to physical danger. Not a problem for an ex-member of FARK but in extremis might leave Lloyd without his contact in Kosovo.

Once more, there were unanswered questions hanging over the situation. If the enquirer was Klevic, was he simply seeking sanctuary with old comrades? Not, Lloyd decided, if he had double-crossed them. If, on the other hand, it was Petric, then what was he trying to find? Bogdani soon supplied the answer to both questions. A brief call to Pristina and the hotel informed Lloyd that he had found and met with the loyal ex-sergeant and minder of Klevic – Mr Dmitri Petric.

Somewhat to the disappointment of both of the searchers, Petric was not looking for Klevic but for information regarding the suspected double-cross by his boss. And, to his bitter disappointment, Petric had found what he was looking for. Evidence, albeit anecdotal, of the failed arms delivery that had left FARK and the villagers of Bela Cerkva exposed, vulnerable and for many of them, eventually murdered.

Petric had been travelling in Kosovo and Albania for months, asking questions and hoping to get proof to clear his ex-boss but receiving more damning evidence as he went along. For Bogdani, it was reassuring to some extent. The mystery man was not Klevic, although he might well be alive elsewhere. And both Petric and he had determined once and for all that the failure to defend their compatriots had not been due to their own negligence.

For Lloyd, and later for Tulloch, it closed one door, leaving another wide open.

30

RECOVERY

Although neither Tulloch nor Lloyd had any further lead to trace a fugitive impostor in Klevic, the financial traces were beginning to bear fruit. Most of the cash in Guangzhou had been transferred to a new account, which Andrew had opened pending resolution of the pension fund's assets and obligations. The final settlement of the sale of tantalum shipments had also been made – this time to the company's trading account.

As no 'white knight' was likely to ride to the rescue of the trading company, Tulloch had drastically slashed any questionable overheads, including the entire Antwerp office, and announced that the financial crash diet would allow the company to continue *sine die*. The news had been taken by the business world as 'disastrous but not serious'. It would buy time for the company to re-group and try to bridge the gap in its pension fund.

The remaining dark area of the pension fund – the black hole and potential destroyer of the company was the real value of high-risk investments made by Klevic. A few of those had been successful but most seemed to be effectively worthless. Cocky was pleased to know that his dangerous work in China and Africa had been so successful, but unlike Andrew he was indifferent to the point of boredom, to the financial details of the pension fund.

Like so many employees, pensions to most of the P.O. Holdings Inc.'s staff were only important at the end of their careers. If the employees of P.O. Holdings Inc. were aware of the proximity of their own career-endings, they might – and probably would – take a more intensive interest. Cocky was happy to return to the hunt for a possible impostor and embezzler, leaving Andrew to deal with the boring stuff in the pension fund and the accounts of the company. Both tasks were to collide again soon.

Having traced the elusive Dmitri Petric, Cocky had established his reason for wandering so far from his former employment and his search for the facts behind Klevic's unsavoury past gun-running. If all that was correct – and it had been accepted by Bogdani – then the only other lead available to Tulloch and Lloyd was the report of someone acting for 'Mr Klevic' in Shanghai, trying to enquire about money in the Guangzhou bank account.

As that cash had now been transferred successfully to the new account opened by Tulloch, even 'Mr Klevic' himself would not be able to extract it. Nor would he be able to obtain any access to the Guangzhou bank account, as it was now closed. Nevertheless, the original report was all that Tulloch or Lloyd could go on. A return to Hong Kong and further investigation might lead to the true identity of the man presenting himself – possibly correctly – as Klevic.

This time, the request for Cocky to go back to China was agreed without protest. He had several contacts there who could help in the search, including Jim 'Elementary' Watson. He also had another reason for returning to Hong Kong – to try to establish if Betty had indeed been killed, and if so, by whom. Within a couple of days, he was on his way back to his former stamping ground – maybe, just maybe he hoped to be going back to find Betty.

Jim Watson was only too glad to help as much as he could, with the limited resources now available to him after the return of Hong Kong's sovereignty to the People's Republic of China. He was very sad at the reported death of the young woman assumed to be Betty T'Sang. Her identity had still not been confirmed although it was described as 'ninety percent certain'. Watson had heard that before. Experience told him that 'ninety percent certain' was often one hundred percent incorrect. Probable, perhaps, but by no means certain.

Investigations in Shanghai would be more difficult, even though relations with the police and officials there were actually easier after the return of Hong Kong to the PRC. Watson could get help from one or two of his Chinese colleagues but that would be limited to a very small range of official records. After that, the old shoe-leather and verbal enquiries would have to do. Neither easy for a round-eye in a huge city of several million Chinese.

When Lloyd met his old friend again, there was a harder look in the senior policeman's eye. Sympathy for Betty's surviving partner had been replaced by determination to hound down the perpetrator. Watson made it clear from the start that he regarded the investigation of her death as his top priority. Looking for the needle of Klevic, or his impersonator, in the haystack of Shanghai, would take second place.

He also suggested that Lloyd should take second place in the ranking of investigators.

"This is a current police matter, Cocky," he said, "and we don't want to disturb it with emotion – not even yours."

Lloyd understood that approach. He had been obliged to apply it all too often in similar cases during his contract period in the former colony.

"Besides which," Watson added, "you can be looking for whatever's available in the way of information about that caller to the bank in Shanghai, while I'm looking for the bastard who murdered" – he stopped before mentioning Betty's name – "the girl in the harbour."

Thoughts of Betty's lifeless body floating in the turgid waters and debris in the harbour swamped over Cocky's mind, already numb from a long flight without sleep. He nodded in agreement and thanked his friend for all the un-rewarded help he was offering and the unexpressed but genuine sympathy he felt. A good night's sleep, if he could sleep, and on to Shanghai in the morning would help to get his mind back in working order.

It occurred to Lloyd that he might be able to combine his initial objectives – sleep and journey – by taking the inter-city train to Shanghai. Total journey time would be twenty hours, but leaving Hung Hom station in Kowloon at three fifteen p.m., a de luxe sleeper berth would allow him to be reasonably refreshed in Shanghai central station by around eleven a.m. the next day. He smiled at the idea of Tulloch's approval when he told him of the cost of the train being less than a night in the Excelsior plus an airline ticket.

'De luxe' sleeping berths in the Chinese train were less than de luxe as far as Cocky's western frame and tastes were concerned, but they served a purpose. He was too tired to worry about absolute comfort and privacy on the journey and the usual noise from the rails helped to induce sleep, despite any misgivings.

As he had calculated, he was awake – and somewhat refreshed, and walking along the arrivals platform at Shanghai central station – by shortly after eleven a.m. By noon, he was in the office of a manager in the former bankers of P and O R.A., or Pandora as it had become known to him and to Tulloch.

By two p.m., Cocky wondered whether he had wasted his time and the company's money on the journey. All the bank could tell him was the same story as before plus the area code from which the Chinese caller had telephoned. It was from a phone somewhere in the harbour area of Hong Kong. Lloyd was too numb to make jokes about the meagre information ringing a bell.

He was not quite so numb an hour later as he reflected on who might have been calling from there. The first names that entered his mind were those of Betty T'Sang's employer and Joseph Chan. Initial contact with Chan had been through the shipping agency where Betty had worked, and Chan was the first suspect of involvement in Betty's disappearance and probable death. A vague coincidence perhaps, but the policeman's training had taught him not to put too much store on coincidence.

Before leaving Shanghai, Cocky telephoned to Betty's parents. Like Betty, her father spoke English very well and could tell Lloyd the little he knew whilst sharing their extreme worry and potential grief with him. Betty had stayed in Shanghai at least until she had left her parents' house. After that, her father thought that she might have gone to a friend in the city.

The only contact from her after that was a call from Hong Kong, some two weeks later, to say that she was all right. He couldn't tell Lloyd the area code from which she had called, but he had the impression that it might – only might – have been from somewhere near the location of her employer's office. Another vague coincidence but too close to the last one to be ignored. In any case, Lloyd intended to visit the employer's office as soon as he returned. And to find Chan – if Watson had not already done so.

He just had time to catch the return train to Kowloon, sleeping as best he could and trying to think of possible combinations of theoretical conspiracies between Klevic, Chan and Betty's employer. He dismissed the Guangzhou gang of tantalum importers as being too concerned with their legitimate business and too scared of corruption charges to get involved in either Klevic's or Betty's disappearance. Dismissal was somewhat premature, however.

Lloyd's assumptions of the Guangzhou importers' concerns were completely accurate. The combined fears of business interruption and corruption charges had turned them into unwitting allies. Before Lloyd could reconvene with Jim Watson, the leading executive in Guangzhou had reported their own experience of the Klevic connection.

Again, it had been a Chinese caller claiming to be acting on behalf of Klevic, but this time it had been a female voice on the telephone. They had called Chan in Hong Kong to ask him if there was any reason to co-operate with the caller. Chan had told them to call her back with the information requested. They had not done so but had given the phone number to Watson, who was waiting with the news to meet Lloyd on his return.

As suspected, the return call was answered by a female voice and traced by the Hong Kong police to the offices of Betty's employer. But the voice was not Betty's. On arrival at the employer's office, with two uniformed police in attendance, Watson and Lloyd quickly established the caller as a young clerk called Winnie Leung, who worked in the department dealing with Chan. She was genuinely frightened – nearly to, and of – death.

After an hour's quite robust interrogation by the uniformed policemen, Winnie tearfully confessed of her unofficial employment by Joseph Chan. Quite simply, Chan had paid her to telephone the importers in Guangzhou in an apparent attempt to extract some of the P and O R.A. deposit before it could be restored to its rightful owners. Suddenly, she blurted out her innocence in Betty's situation – whatever that was.

Under threats of a fate worse than that usually described as worse than death, she offered to help as much as she could. She said that she could contact Chan, who had given her a phone number to call and ask him how to get in touch with her friend Betty. At this, Watson jumped on her. "How do you know that he can tell you that? You don't even know if Betty is still... in Hong Kong, do you?" He stopped before saying 'still alive'.

Winnie's face was whiter than Watson's at the angry innuendo. "I'm sure she is here somewhere!" she almost screamed back at Jim. "I spoke to her – I'm sure it was her – yesterday. When I telephoned Mr Chan at his house – this number." She pointed to the piece of paper with the contact number for Chan. Rather than phoning the number, Watson gave orders for it to be traced.

It was not Chan's house or anyone else's residence. It was the number of a private line in a private, but well known to the Hong Kong police, house of certain but very ill-repute. It was a brothel. Not far from the new airport on Lantau Island. Not far from the shoreline that had recently returned the lifeless body of a young Chinese woman.

Without wasting further time at Betty's employer's office, the police patrol – with Lloyd in tow – set sail for Lantau and the house of ill-repute. The brothel – or private entertainment club as it preferred to be known – occupied a bland building that might have been taken for offices or a small warehouse, which it resembled in human terms.

Its small, smartly furnished reception area, might have been the front for another freight forwarder or air cargo handler. Immediately behind the plush front was a short corridor with a cloakroom and toilets, leading to another smartly furnished lounge with comfortable couches and armchairs and a small bar.

So far, Lloyd thought, it all looks innocuous. Give it a snooker table and it could be the local Conservative Club in Mumbles. Behind the lounge, however, another corridor – longer than the first – led to numerous small cells, each furnished with a double bed and lots of mirrors. Visiting businessmen might not know the reason for the preponderance of mirrors but each of the visiting policemen knew that they were twenty percent reflective and eighty percent transparent. Behind each wall-mounted mirror was another room for voyeurs to take part, as photographers or paying spectators to the naked all-out wrestling in the rooms.

Not exactly the domain of The Young Conservatives, thought Cocky. He wondered what sort of security would be in place, in a place like this. The tiny close-circuit TV cameras mounted above each cell door answered his question. They also answered Watson's next question: "Where do you keep the recordings," he shouted at the middle-aged madam, who had admitted the group without objection. She and they were fairly well acquainted and she always took the line of least resistance.

A substantial console with several sockets for compact disks was revealed. Each disk contained a video record of the activities in each of the cells over the past four weeks. The house management used the recordings to monitor the employees in case of customer complaints, theft or restrictive practices by the employees. To save time checking each disk, Watson's sergeant simply handed a photo of Betty T'Sang to the woman and demanded to know which disk contained her image.

Once more, the madam took the line of least resistance. She handed a disk to Watson, which she said was not from a cell-monitor but of the activities around the rear entrance to the house. Within a half-hour of screening, the police group and the madam were viewing an almost comatose female figure being manhandled into the employees' quarters. The man handling her was a stranger to the group but the man giving the orders to him was very familiar.

Chao Li Chan (Joseph) the president of Chan Industrial Corporation, was clearly identifiable, even without his calling card. Lloyd could not understand the orders given in a loud Cantonese dialect, but the police sergeant and his uniformed constable could make it out. It appeared that Chan was ordering the manhandler to take Betty into the employees' room and return with another girl. A few minutes later, on the CCTV recording, the man re-appeared with what was either the corpse or the unconscious body of a young woman. Not Betty but possibly the girl whose death had been reported three weeks earlier.

The co-operative madam of the entertainment club was either confused or deliberately confusing in making her replies to the police interrogation. As far as she was aware, the 'new girl' had been brought in from a drug gang on the mainland to replace the girl who was 'very ill'. That brought a grim smile to the faces of the British interrogators but an even grimmer stony frown from the sergeant. He barked something at Madam, which made her tremble and wobble at the knees.

"He just told her that she would be executed within the month after a quick trial for murder," whispered Watson. Justice was quick and final. Life, in the Chinese courts, was as expendable for murderers as it had been for the murdered.

A short burst of weeping and wailing by the madam, was followed by a longer series of 'explanations'. She swore that the dead girl had succumbed to a drug overdose, and one of the Tong gang, which controlled prostitution in that area, had ordered the disposal of the corpse in the sea, after damaging the body features to make it look like a boating accident. The harbours were constantly overcrowded with fishing and ferry traffic. Another body would not usually attract too much conjecture or even, a detailed post-mortem. The source of the replacement was more of a mystery to her than to the police.

All she could tell them was that the same Tong member who had ordered the disposal had obtained the replacement from a businessman who needed to hold a girl in captivity for a while. He would accompany the captive and the man- or woman-handler, to the bordello club but demanded complete anonymity. The replacement girl had been given some 'harmless' drugs to keep her quiet, so she would be unable to earn her keep in the time-dishonoured way of her co-workers. For an assurance of lesser charges, madam would do her best to find and release her to police custody.

Her best was as good as they could hope in the circumstances. A few kilometres away in a shabby residential area, the two uniformed police took great pleasure in breaking down an unlocked front door, reminding Cocky of his harrowing experience in the Congo. Once more, resistance was negligible.

The occupants were all young females who, quite literally, had been worked off their feet for most of the past twenty-four hours. All except one. In the corner of a small bedroom lay the semi-conscious and pale thin figure of T'Sang Xi Lao (Betty.) – barely recognisable to Lloyd and barely alive.

With the aid of a posse of police, a large police van and an ambulance, the girls and madam were whisked away to police custody. For madam, there would also be a trial for kidnapping. The ambulance took Betty and Lloyd to hospital, where she was placed into an intensive care ward to be treated for heroin poisoning and malnutrition. Lloyd's attentions were then focused on Betty's abductors and the ubiquitous Joseph Chan.

Having been relieved of his hostage, Chan could not negotiate his ransom of security from justice. He had not been able to contact Lloyd in Liechtenstein or Kosovo, mainly because he didn't know Lloyd's location. Watson had warned Lloyd that news of the raid on the bordello and its dormitory for sex workers would travel faster than the police van or ambulance. Chan would be moving even faster after he heard about it. Unfortunately for Joseph Chan, his contacts in the Tong gang could move faster still. Faster than he could imagine or evade.

Lloyd had always prided himself on not being a vindictive man. He was prepared to wait until he could corner Chan before garrotting him with his own silk necktie. Cornering the slippery colleague of Klevic and the Guangzhou gang would take Lloyd considerably longer than it would take the Tongs to detect and dispense their own version of justice.

The sentence for bringing the police down on one of their lucrative sources of wealth was elimination. Only the time taken to extract as much of Chan's personal belongings and the details of his hidden cash would delay the bullet and watery grave allotted by Tongs to the expendable.

In the event, Chan's accumulation of personal assets was to delay his demise. Like his associate Klevic, Chan had stashed away considerable sums in a number of different banks. It took several days and a great deal of pain for the Tongs to obtain access to the accounts and most of their contents. Ultimately, Chan's pain was their gain. His trump card, of a long-term option on Swiss francs at a favourable rate adopted from Klevic's modus operandi – was to save what was left of his life.

By the time that the options had been exercised and a large lump of Swiss francs passed to the Tongs, a badly injured and beaten Chan was able to disappear, at least temporarily, of his own accord.

31

Pandora's people

Under English Law, trustee investments are usually limited to certain classes of government bonds, shares quoted in recognised stock exchanges, cash and properties. However, the pension fund of P.O. Holdings Inc. was not governed by English Law. This had presented the trustees with wider-ranging investment opportunities, and Tulloch with a wider range of headaches.

P.O. Holdings Inc. was registered in the state of Delaware, USA, and operated in Liechtenstein. The pension fund was operated in and under the governance of Grand Cayman Island. Between the operating company and the pension fund, many potential hidden snakes existed to trap and swallow the unwary fund members hoping to climb the ladders to a secure and wealthy retirement.

Due largely to Lloyd's invaluable help, Tulloch had somehow managed to recover large parts of the cash previously swallowed by the former CEO. But there was still a vast gap between the actual value of investments and the amount required to finance pensions for the fund members.

Before returning the recovered cash to the pension fund bank account, it was time to take stock of the expectations of employees and his own expectation of their retirement income. He had obtained lists of employees who were members of the fund as well as their contributions to it. The list included several long-serving employees, such as Rose Klevic, but not the former chairman and CEO, who had tried to create his own, much larger but illegal, retirement fund.

Nothing could be done about the commissions and fees that Klevic and his associates had coined from making the original investments. All of the companies had been legal entities and attracted commissions commensurate with their high risk-high return category. Until and unless Klevic could be identified as alive – and brought to justice – none of those unauthorised earnings could be claimed directly.

However, under these circumstances, Tulloch and the other directors knew that if the commissions and lost values could be established, it might be possible to claim them from a dead Klevic's estate. That, and the value of his estate, was much easier to speculate than to prove.

The only likely avenue to evidence of the existence and value of the estate of 'Mr P. Klevic, (deceased)' was sitting in an office of P.O. Holdings Inc., a few yards from the boardroom. Namely, Assistant Company Secretary, Madam Rosa Klevic. Before Tulloch and his fellow directors could confront Rose, they agreed that further communication with the employees was essential.

Despite Lloyd's previous trip to Grand Cayman, Tulloch felt that he should go there personally to try again to recover some of the lost values of the high risk investments made by George Armstrong on instructions from Klevic. Travelling there from Vaduz was no easier than Lloyd had experienced, but with Lloyd's advice he was able to book into the same comfortable Turtle Nest Inn as his security officer had visited.

A hot and perspiring Armstrong was there to greet him – apprehensive and edgy at the thought of the fund in his trust being in such a perilous state. As a devout practising Yorkshireman, he could not be accused of profligacy concerning his own money. Other people's money was another matter. As long as he could see a piece of paper with the authorisation of someone with senior rank, he would fulfil his daily tasks as ordered and no more. In the absence of due diligence, George Armstrong relied on subservience and ample cover for his ample backside.

All that Armstrong could report to Tulloch by way of explanation were the detailed lists of investments and bank accounts, into which the fund's capital had been poured as quickly as Armstrong's rum punch sundowners. Tracing the companies involved would not be easy. Recovering any material value might be closer to impossible. Time required to re-value the fund and deal with the members was clearly against any lengthy process.

Tulloch guessed that his own time and skills would not be enough to complete such a task, especially as there was no guarantee of substantial recovery or agreement of the fund members. One thing was certain – George Armstrong and his office in Grand Cayman were surplus to requirements. Like the illicit traders and the Antwerp office of P.O. Holdings Inc., they would have to be labelled 'not wanted on voyage', and jettisoned promptly.

Rather than creating a drama in such a pleasant spot, Armstrong was invited to dinner. There, he was advised in confidence of the probability of criminal negligence charges, and he was directed to gather all of the available details and pension fund records. These were to be transported by him to somewhere offering more security for the records and for his own freedom from jail. Dinner, drinks and advice were all digested without objection or resistance as George Armstrong prepared to retire for the second time of asking to his former home in Bradford, England, via Vaduz, Liechtenstein.

Most of the pension fund records were archived in computer media such as CD-ROM or hard disks. Hard copies on paper of the summary lists of assets and members contributions were already in Tulloch's possession. By the following afternoon, Armstrong had marshalled the data and booked an airline ticket to Vaduz, travelling with Tulloch and the computer's records. By the evening of the next day, both men and their information were in Liechtenstein.

Frantic calls were made by Tulloch – first to Carlsen, the banker, and Goldsmit, the consultant actuary. Carlsen suggested placing the task of recovering value for the high-risk investments with certain agencies who were in reality, high-powered debt collectors. They would act for a small set fee plus a large commission based on a percentage of the value recovered.

Once a recovery report could be made and an estimate of the values to be gained, the entire portfolio might be assigned to another agency, acting as an insurance underwriter, who would buy the portfolio for a discounted amount of the expected recovery. By the time that the first agency had taken its fee and commission from whatever was expected – and the second had deducted its discount from the purchase price of the remaining portfolio – there would not be so much left for the pension fund.

The words of the dying Vanstraat came back to Tulloch's mind. It would be 'better than being dead'. It would also be better than being uncertain of any value at all for an uncertain period of time. Even these drastic measures would take some time to yield any dividends. In the meantime, he realised, the investments must be considered worthless and the employee-members of the fund would have to be informed. They must also be considered as potential litigants against the company and the pension fund trustees.

As possible co-defendants in a massive scandal and fraud case, Carlson and Goldsmit were prepared to pull out every stop in their wide organ of business contacts to demonstrate their activity in alleviating the fund members' hardship. Between the bankers and the insurance loss adjustors, the portfolio of dubious value investments was treated as a giant insurance claim and placed with several collection agencies.

Their first estimates of recovery varied between one hundred percent or more of the original investment and nil. Sadly, but not unexpectedly, the 'nul points' investments were in the majority. However, Tulloch was relieved that there were some possible recoveries available. The second part of the task was to find a willing underwriter to purchase the estimated recoveries for a reasonable price. A buyer for the 'bad bank' of dubious investments. Here, Goldsmit proved his worth, asking for quotes from insurers and investment banks who were willing to tender for them.

Like so many financial instruments, the various parts of the investment portfolio had different estimated values placed upon them by different agencies. Goldsmit was able to obtain several quotes for each section and place them with the companies or syndicates offering the best prices. Within three weeks, the previous potentially worthless part of the portfolio, with investments originally costing over two hundred million dollars, was effectively sold off to realise eighty-two million dollars for the pension fund, after potential fees, commissions and profits to agencies and underwriters.

His sharp brain quickly calculated that despite this loss in value, a majority of the 'black hole' in the pension fund was now either filled or due to be returned soon, thanks to the efforts of his new colleagues and himself. It was a fantastic recovery – from the brink of financial meltdown. The next question in Tulloch's mind was how to deal with the refreshed pension fund in order to provide the best of a bad lot to Pandora's unhappy people? Once more, Goldsmit would provide a solution.

With the trading position of the company in such a doubtful state, the existing pension scheme would be wound up and scrapped. Each member would have the opportunity to re-invest his or her portion, amounting to approximately eighty percent of the previously reported value in a personal fund operated by an independent insurance company.

Goldsmit's connections covered all the major insurance and re-insurance markets and companies. He would make sure that the personal funds would remain in each individual employee's ownership, directly managed by a company specialising in personal pensions.

The individuals could then decide, when they retired, how much of their portion they wished to take as a lump sum or an immediate annuity. In the meantime, they could leave the balance invested by the insurance company for their personal use in future. In time, they might be able to make up for the loss in their apparent fund share. If they had time, that is. For at least one former employee, time had already run out. For others, time was still running.

32

BENEFITS OF DEATH

Before the fund could be broken up and distributed to individual employees, the larger problem of the company's trading position continued to occupy Tulloch and the directors. The final loan from the pension fund, which was tied up in trading deals, had to be realised and repaid. Of more importance, the entire future of the company depended on its acceptance as a trading party with suppliers and customers alike.

Tulloch was painfully aware that he had to convince the US authorities and the business world that P.O. Holdings Inc. was now solvent and profitable. The recovery of pension fund assets would remove a massive overhanging liability from the company, but the scandal related to its joint founder and the lack of reporting transparency raised questions over any future dealings.

Madam Rosa Klevic, in her role as communications and PR officer, had issued comforting noises in press announcements, trying desperately to reassure financial markets of the company's viability. The scars left in the minds of commodity traders and financial authorities were far too deep for her comforting noises to take effect as hoped. They all accepted that there might be two roads to recovery. These included continuing in a reduced form, probably under a new and completely different trading name, or a merger with another company.

No-one in the board room, including Rose, believed that the markets would accept P.O. Holdings Inc. in any form other than under new ownership. Directors and shareholders would have to hawk the business of the company around a market of opportunist buyers. They would either sell the entire company at a massive discount to its previous share value or spin off the trading business of the company as a separate entity.

Under the circumstances, everyone agreed that the trading business was still a large and quantifiable asset, whereas the registered company, with goodness knows what other scandals and liabilities hiding under the Klevic stones, was an even larger but unquantifiable liability. After the sale of its trading business, P.O. Holdings Inc. would have to suffer the fate of its founder. Chapter 11 administration would become Chapter 7 bankruptcy proceedings and liquidation – the final chapter of its biography.

There were several possible buyers who would love to add the trading business to their own operations, provided that the revenue was large and the cost was small. To reduce the on-going costs of operations, the employee payroll would have to be put through yet another crash diet, involving redundancies by the bucketful. Senior traders would be offered terms that would include a period of consultancy, giving them income for a short while until the new owners could manage without them or their costs.

The entire head office would have to accept closure and dismissal within whatever period determined by the new owners. That could be anything from a week to a year, but a skilful buyer would make it nearer to the week. Until a buyer had approached and started negotiations, the office would be slimmed down severely to administer to the slimmed down operations. That would improve efficiency in the event of no buyer approaching anyway and possibly improve the attraction and price available.

Non-executive directors were expected to fall on their swords in the event of such a major setback to the company. Only Carlsen and Goldsmit were asked to remain on board. Carlsen was sounding out investment banks to act for the company in the sale of the business, with or without the company. Goldsmit, who was still acting in the assignments of the high-risk investments, was also expected to continue, pro temp. Tulloch had insisted that Rose and Lloyd should stay on, as so much of the mystery surrounding Klevic's death or disappearance remained unsolved.

The reported death of the older trader from the Stuttgart office still haunted Tulloch. The old man's office had been linked to false trading with the Antwerp office, but there was no hard evidence to suggest that he been involved in that personally. How many others, he wondered, were so traumatised that they were on the brink of suicide? He dismissed the question from his mind, as it could not be answered. His conscience, as the saviour of well over half of the damaged pension fund and the company, was as clear as it could be under these extraordinary circumstances.

Another employee's death was then reported to the HR department, who advised a worried Tulloch of it. A member of the trading team in the Antwerp office, working directly for– but not personally associated with – the manager of the illicit trading department had been killed in what was assumed to be a street accident.

Belgian police had been informed and were investigating the death. Witnesses had spoken of two men of 'foreign' appearance being seen near the scene of the accident. But what 'foreign' meant to witnesses in north Antwerp's suburb of Brasschaat was anyone's guess. That place was a haven for Dutch tax exiles, who could drive back to work in Rotterdam each day but claim Belgian residence and avoid Dutch income taxes. A 'foreigner' there might well be Belgian.

The HR department had also discovered a small consoling clause in the rules of the pension scheme. A group life assurance policy had been taken out earlier, offering a year's basic salary to employees' dependants, in the event of death in service. With that on top of the reduced pension pot, the family of an employee might qualify for over one hundred and fifty thousand dollars, if his death was accepted as being 'in service'. That would help to care for the widow or surviving partner, as well as any other dependants.

Normally, a planned suicide such as appeared to be the case in Stuttgart would disqualify the employee from such a posthumous benefit. But in cases of accidental death, the insurer might treat it as bona fide death in service. Tulloch instructed Rose to file a claim on behalf of the employees' dependants. She did as instructed, but he sensed that she might be wondering how much better off she could be had Klevic been a member of the pension scheme instead of being its plunderer.

Disappointment came back in the form of two reports:

First, a note from the police in Antwerp confirming that the cause of the man's death was being treated as suspicious. The apparently-respected trader had been seen shortly before his body was discovered on a busy highway with two men. The men, described previously as 'foreign', were now believed to be a Serbian and a former Soviet Union citizen. It sounded like a by-product of another of Klevic's high-risk investments in very high-risk commodities.

The risk also appeared to have hit new heights for the old Stuttgart trader. Police there had discovered that, although his body had indeed been discovered in a monoxide-filled car, the car doors had been locked – from the outside. Someone with either a warped sense of humour or a failed grasp of logic had left the car's spare keys in the locked door.

Secondly, the insurance company had investigated the Antwerp trader's claim and concluded that the man's circumstances were not as previously thought. Unlike the old man in Stuttgart, the Antwerp trader had divorced his wife years ago and his dependants did not include a handicapped son – or any son at all. His principal dependants in Antwerp were a mistress, a brewery, some expensive car dealers and several bookmakers. Death could have been delivered by any or all of them but his two gun-running companions were the short-odds favourites.

The two deaths might have been coincidental, but neither Tulloch nor Lloyd believed in such coincidences. It was now up to the police in both countries to investigate and liaise with Interpol. Lloyd considered contacting the former member of FARK – Arian Bogdani – in Kosovo but his whereabouts were unknown to him and he suspected that Bogdani was already aware of the deaths and of the circumstances.

As he advised Rose to cancel the insurance claims, Tulloch reflected on the level of corruption that often lies just below the surface of respectability. The deadly business of arms dealing appeared with disturbing regularity whenever the late Patrick Klevic had been involved. Whatever the morals of the old man's situation, there was no point in trying to pass judgement. Tulloch had a business to sell and a pension fund to save.

Days passed before Carlsen received a positive approach from one of his investment banks' corporate clients. Then, like London busses, two more approached at once. Three cautious indications of interest were better than one, making the basis for a market in the sale of the business. As expected, none of the three expressed any interest in the Delaware-registered company, provided that all intellectual rights and trading operations could be assigned without it. That was completely understandable. It represented a value of the fear of the unknown.

Carlsen and Tulloch were relieved at the interest shown in the business. With three parties already in the frame, others were likely to throw their hats into the ring, afraid to miss a bargain. The value of the business, securely inside a ring fence and protected against the wages of past company sins, was rising. They decided to act quickly, setting a short-term timetable to oblige interested parties to demonstrate firm and honourable intentions, with penalties for unwarranted delays by either side.

All three of the interested parties agreed and two of them, plus one later enquirer, offered to deposit financial guarantees at once, provided that any further offers would be rejected.

Massive volumes of due diligence enquiry forms were received in Vaduz, most of which were distributed to various departments by Rose, in order to complete and return the responses. Only two weeks were permitted for the replies and Rose enforced her own timetable on the company departments to complete the forms in time. In the event, they were finished in draft after five days, leaving more time for double-checking the information.

In theory, provided that the pension fund could be re-financed, the company did not appear to carry any other substantial undisclosed liabilities. In practice, however, no one could be certain that the employees would not instigate class-action litigation against the company and its directors. The directors certainly were aware and very apprehensive of this threat. So were all of the interested potential buyers. A clean sheet for the continuing business carried the value of certainty. To them, the remainder of the company was worth more dead than alive.

With all reasonable due diligence complete, the serious negotiations started. Almost like an adolescent's game of 'chicken' with cars racing towards a cliff edge, the negotiators knew that delay would reduce the value of ongoing business, by the hour. Trade continued, but with the uncertainties of their future hanging over them, the intuitive edge that makes the hardened market trader sensitive is dulled. Trading opportunities were slipping past them and profit margins weakening.

After two more weeks, one of the parties decided to pull out, leaving the remaining two to put their proverbial money where their mouths were. Sealed tenders were required to be lodged with the advising investment banks. It was now a straight two-horse race, with each party trying to out-guess and out-bid the other without over-bidding. The values would depend largely on how the successful bidders could merge the business with their own, adding trade and margins without adding overheads.

To no one's great surprise, the bids were fairly close. But inevitably, one bidder was in a stronger position to dovetail the company's business operations into its own. The geographic spread of trading offices and their specialist sectors of commodities markets threatened little or no significant duplication to them. What little there was would in any case be diluted within a short time, as staff retirements reduced numbers without compulsory redundancies. They could afford to pay a premium for the business and it would be repaid to them in two years – if everything went to their plan.

The trading executives' relief at the assurance of continued employment was reflected in the relief felt by Carlsen and Tulloch at having such a smooth transition of the business and a sizeable financial contribution towards the dissolution and liquidation of the company. That would cover the residual legal and professional costs, although little or nothing would return to shareholders.

The value to the directors would be to reduce the risk and cost of litigation. For other shareholders, it would only be freedom from the burden of worry about their former investment and its market value. But, unless their financial future was entirely dependent on that, then their situation was not much worse than that of the pension fund member.

In the company's death, there was indeed life for some, if not all.

33

With such tight timetables and pressure to recover the missing millions for the pension fund and then sell the business of the company, Tulloch's focus had been taken from his almost obsessive view that Klevic was still alive. If he was, and lurking undercover, then he would continue to pose a threat to what remained of the company and possibly to the former business.

If the business that they had just sold was polluted by a re-emergence of Klevic and the attendant scandals, then Tulloch and the remaining officers of the company would be in the firing line of litigation by the buyer. On the other hand, Klevic had no doubt amassed some fortune somewhere, which might be targeted for additional compensation for the shareholders and pension fund members.

To effect any recovery from Klevic, someone would have to claim against his estate, assuming he was really dead. Tulloch had long since ceased to assume anything and the obsession of faked death and impersonation returned to haunt him. To test his theory, he knew of only one way to direct his next move. That way led to his hostess, Madam Rosa Klevic.

She had not tried to do anything to hinder – and lots to help – his tireless efforts to rescue the shattered organisation and its employees. But she was living in their valuable Klevic residence and probably enjoyed possession of numerous facts, and perhaps assets, relating to the former CEO and herself.

No-one that he could think of would be in a better position than he was to pursue his conspiracy theories and enquiries concerning the Klevic family and its wealth. He returned to his hostess and bed-mate for some serious heart-to-heart discussions. Business before pleasure would have to be the priority but he still hoped that they could encompass both.

If the bidding parties to the sale of the former P.O. Holdings' business had wished to maintain non-disclosure with an air of confidence usually reserved for the poker table, they could have taken lessons from Rosa Klevic.

All efforts by Tulloch to elicit information regarding the Klevic personal wealth and the affairs surrounding his estate were parried politely with social graces and persuasion to divert the conversation, which was more than friendly. At some stage, Tulloch felt that he would have to tie her down and force her to talk. At other times, he wanted to tie her down but not with conversation in mind.

Whenever a suggestion of recovery from Klevic's available assets was raised, Rose – as she was at all times outside office hours – assumed a very attractive and appealingly seductive demeanour.

The constant oscillation of mind and eye, from and to business and social objectives, brought Tulloch almost to a state of nervous exhaustion. Almost, but not quite. Eventually, he would call 'time out' in his mind and accept whatever compliment or distraction that Rose would offer. His attempts to play cat and mouse were ending only with another game, in which he realised that he was too often the mouse being trapped by pussy.

Giving up, on either game, was not on his agenda. He determined to keep right on to the end of the road, even if that road ended in bed. Eventually, she would let her guard slip a little. Then, little by little, he would piece together a picture of Klevic and his surroundings of wealth and friends – or possibly co-conspirators. To aid progress in compiling the fragmented puzzle, he suggested a return match at the romantic Berggasthaus Matu on the mountainside.

Previous visits to the restaurant in the scenic spot had been in summer sunshine. As the two colleagues and bed-mates drove up the mountain road, the autumnal rain started to fall on the leaves and moss clogging the surface. At one point, the rear wheels slipped and spun under excessive power from the Mercedes V8 engine. Tulloch parked the car on a fairly flat space, with a rock behind the tyres to prevent slippage.

In an effort to get Rose's complete confidence, he started to ask about her childhood memories, hoping that it would lead to revelations of her family and its wealth. With Klevic's long track record in arms dealing and embezzlement, there had to be a latter-day pirate's hoard somewhere that should be returned to either the company or the pensioners. Rose, on the other hand, would try her damnedest to hide it for herself – whatever that entailed.

After a non-committal drink of dry Riesling with a little dish of smoked eel and olives, Tulloch added his own entrée, with an innocuous remark. "This eel is very popular in the

Netherlands, but I wasn't aware that they liked it here. Did you eat this sort of thing in... wherever you grew up?"

The response was deafening in its absence of information. "No. We did have some fish but mainly freshwater fish or something in a tin."

"In a tin? That doesn't sound very appetising. Didn't you get salt water fish – fresh fish, that is, but from the sea?" He thought that this would at least narrow down the geographic location, which he hoped would be either Kosovo or somewhere related to Klevic's origins. He was wasting his time. Rose wasn't interested in fish.

"I suppose we did. Can't really remember. Anyway, what are we eating next?"

"How about wiener schnitzel? I fancy that after this paling – that's what they call it in Holland – and we can stick with this dry white. If you like that combination."

"Yes. That's fine with me. In fact, I would be happy with a small portion of grilled lamb. Like shish kebab. Then you could have the red wine that you're trying to work your way to ordering."

Fantastic – how did she work that out? Crozes Hermitage, here I come!

"Just what I was thinking. Glad I thought of that." They both laughed and, Tulloch thought, thank goodness she's on my wavelength and seems happy to carry on. It suddenly occurred to him that if she was an ethnic Albanian like Klevic, she was probably also a Muslim and wouldn't normally eat eel. Perhaps she was too deferral to risk offending him or letting him think he'd offended her. Too late now.

The lamb and red Rhone wine was duly ordered and the apparently relaxed couple sat by the picture window, doing what relaxed couples do – staring out and thinking of something to say to each other until food and wine arrived to bail them out. He risked another dig into the past. More directly now. Can't wait all night to find something out.

"Are these mountains similar to those in your old homeland in the Balkans? You are from there, aren't you?" He stopped short of pinning it down to Albania or Kosovo.

"Of course they are. One mountain is very like another, isn't it? And if you're asking if I was brought up in Albania, the answer is yes. So... satisfied?" Without waiting for an answer, she continued; as if she wanted to clear the conversation for more important things, like dinner. "I was born near Shkodra but moved over the border into Kosovo when I was a teenager. That's where I met the Klevic family. That was where I married and that was where my son was born."

Tulloch felt as if he had landed a large fish when he was only trying to scoop for tadpoles. "I didn't know that. I mean, I didn't know where you lived before and I didn't know that you had a son." He paused, knowing the history of Kosovo and afraid to ask if the son was still alive. His silence was saved from embarrassment by the arrival of the lamb and red wine. "That looks good. Thank you. Just a half-glass, please."

Dinner after that was a quieter affair but not unpleasantly so. Rose seemed more relaxed, having bared a part of her metaphorical breast to Tulloch. Her actual breast was slightly bare too, which helped to warm the atmosphere. Whether by accident or design – probably design – her more laid-back appearance dissolved any frost between the diners. Desert was waived and coffee served with little chunks of Turkish delight and cointreau.

Rose was the first to speak. Not losing anything – but taking the lead, in what she recognised as an exchange of confidences. "My family in Albania was poor, as everyone was. We had an advantage over most though. We had distant relatives in Yugoslavia – Serbia. In the region which is now Kosovo.

"After the terror of Enver Hoxha ended in 1992, my father managed to get some help in Prizren, near the Sar mountains. You asked about mountains? They are very beautiful – rather like this."

Rose waved a hand towards the skyline to the west of the restaurant. "Except, when it's –how would you say – peeing down with rain as it is now." The rain was not actually peeing down but heavy drizzle, combined with low cloud, set a sombre background to an otherwise delightful scene. "My family all died in 1999. There was a lot of very bad fighting during the war there. You know all about that, don't you?"

The last 'don't you' was not a question but a reminder to Tulloch of her knowledge of his enquiries.

On the way back to Vaduz, Rose was even more relaxed, as if she had scored all the points she had intended to win. The drive down the hillside was slow and careful. It had to be, given the state of the roads and the driver. By the time they reached the house, Tulloch was ready for a good sleep, while Rose appeared ready for close contact and murmured conversation.

The conversation took first place in the queue, starting with her own light interrogation.

"What about you, Andrew? You never told me anything about your home or your family. Were they always in England?" The questions were delivered as if she cared more about the reaction of her bed-fellow than the details of the answers.

Tulloch's muttering was as non-committal as he thought he could get away with. "Mainly in England. My family comes from the highlands of Scotland or they did originally. I still have some relatives there but don't see them very often. I have lived and worked in England for most of the last twenty years or so. Until I came to Vaduz, obviously."

"Whereabouts in England is the highland of Scotland, then?"

Tulloch groaned inwardly but he was resigned to this sort of geographic and national ignorance. Still, he knew how to score a return hit – tit-for-tat.

"Roughly similar to where Kosovo is in Serbia." That should generate a squeal of protest. But no. Only a silent wince, followed by a sharper form of squeal, as he pinched her bare bottom under the bed sheets. A different form of tit-for-tat was to follow. He provided the tat.

For a while, they both abandoned question time and settled for a draw.

34

Maracaibo

Dawn arrived after Tulloch woke alone in bed. A cup of hot coffee arrived shortly after that and question time resumed. "What time are you going to the office this morning? I thought we could take another drive up the mountain road. The weather's so much nicer now. We could maybe have an early lunch somewhere near the restaurant – not at the same one, but I know a nice café not far from there."

Taken aback at the early invitation to another mutual grilling contest, Tulloch could only nod agreement and slurp his coffee. He wanted to get much more information and this was too good a chance to refuse. "OK Yes, that sounds great. Could you let the office know while I get washed and dressed, please?" Then, an afterthought. "I had intended to meet Lloyd this morning to discuss his latest investigation into the pension fund, so could you pass a message to him to let him know where I'll be and what time we should be back? Two p.m. should be about right, shouldn't it?"

Ignoring further breakfast, the Mercedes was duly extracted from its stable and driven back up the mountain road. The weather was definitely warmer and the air clear, but the roads had been soaked overnight and debris formed a skin of sludge on the surface. More than once, the rear wheels turned faster than their fellows to fore and Tulloch had to ease his foot from the accelerator whilst countering the drift across the sharp corners.

After twenty-five minutes, they reached a clear patch of gravel outside a small café with flower boxes hanging from the alpine eaves. Too early for lunch but a coffee and some cake would be nice, he thought. That will bridge the gap inside and give me an excuse to dodge any awkward questions while my mouth's full. A smart tactic and only a little more devious than just being perfectly polite.

At that time, the café was almost devoid of other custom. Their table by the window was quiet and clean. The bog-standard red and white check cloth set the scene for a gentle morning's quizzing with coffee.

Before opening mouth, for food at least, time to engage brain, Tulloch thought, *and think of what she wants from me, as well as my own targets.*

"Now then. We didn't come all the way up here just for more coffee, did we? You're dying to ask me something – or tell me something. We don't need to have any secrets from each other by now, do we? Don't be afraid…" He very nearly said, "I won't bite you," but as his mouth was closing in on a large moist slice of ginger cake, he let it concentrate on its chosen task – his first solid food of the day. Now, he had the excuse he had planned. She would have to speak first or wait until he had munched through the whole slice.

"No. We don't need to keep secrets now, Andrew. Neither of us. I need to know what you expect from me, from now on.

Now on, being now that you seem to have recovered as much, or much more, than you could have expected of the money from the pension fund. And now that you have almost liquidated the company."

The term 'liquidated' was a surprise to Tulloch. He hadn't expected to hear such a relatively technical accounting expression from her, until he remembered its more sinister application in the days of Hoxha's tyrannical dictatorship. Had Klevic liquidated a stooge in order to avoid the repercussions of his company suffering the same fate? He applied the ginger cake defence, giving him precious moments of thinking time. Swallowing the last crumb, he licked his lips for time and effect.

"Hard to say at this stage, Rose. There's still a lot of work to do before we can complete the sale of the business, let alone liquidate the company. I hope that you can continue with me and help me as much as possible." He tried not to sound too much like a politician claiming clarity whilst obfuscating blatantly. "What I mean by help is to act as my assistant in administration of company matters and to get the information that I'll need to answer the cries of 'off-side!' and 'foul!' from angry employees and shareholders; you know what I mean, don't you?"

"I can imagine, but listen – this is not a football match and I am not a referee. I need some security for myself. And I don't see any of that coming from what we can see now. If you think that I'm rich because I live in a big house, you're quite mistaken. That house was leased by Klevic from some of his old associates. I don't own it and they will want it back without question or argument."

Tulloch inwardly chilled at the thought of an argument with the 'associates'. Rose added to the chill. "That goes for the other house – the villa on Lenios. None of it belongs to me. All I have is some cash – not much – and my own bit of what's left of the pension fund. I don't even know how much that is now. So, I will need some help and, I hope you will give it."

In a way, Tulloch was relieved. Partly at her apparent frankness and partly due to the probable removal of Rose as a target for ambulance-chasing lawyers, seeking a small slice of the justice cake for class-action litigants, plus a large slice for themselves. If she had told all of the truth, at least about her own fortunes or lack of them, then his work might not be compromised by their personal relationship. He felt obliged to be equally frank with her. 'No secrets between them' seemed possible after all.

"I have to admit that I have been worried about your position, vis-à-vis Klevic and litigation, or even revenge by some of those who lost the most. But obviously I have to do all I can to recover the losses and mitigate – to ease the effect of the losses. So, in a way, I'm glad that you're not sitting on some of the money that Klevic seems to have stolen. But, I'll be a lot more glad, and so will you, if we can be sure that we have done all we can to get it back."

"But you have got it back. Haven't you? Apart from some losses from the pension fund's investments. What else could you do?"

This was followed by silence and hard thinking. What else indeed?

"If I could, I would like to be absolutely certain that, uh, no one else has walked off with the money that was lost in all that false trading and dubious investments. If that came to light later, we would all be under attack."

"No one else? Who do you mean by that?"

"Perhaps, one, or some of his associates." That would be a good cover for his 'third man' theory. It might even be true, knowing what Vanstraat had said about them. "What can you tell me about them? You must have met some of them and heard what they were doing."

"That was almost all before Klevic started those latest things – what you call false trading and investments. They are mainly from the old guard in Kosovo and Albania. They helped with weapons supply from the USSR. Later on, they were involved with some personal investments by Klevic in their private businesses. That probably led to him ordering the pension fund to invest more there. I really can't be sure.

"Any false trading in the company was probably nothing to do with them. I suspect that Klevic organised it to siphon commissions out of the company and to create false profits to cover – disguise the pension problems. But I can assure you, I had absolutely nothing to do with any of that either. Look, Andrew" – Tulloch was on his guard when she repeatedly addressed him by his Christian name – "we could spend a year looking for trouble but it wouldn't get us anywhere. We have to make the most that we can of this mess – for ourselves."

'Ourselves', sounded more like a euphemism for 'me', but Tulloch accepted it as an appeal for unity. He also had to admit that he would need at some stage to add financial substance to his limited reputation, even though it had been enhanced already by the recoveries for the pension fund and the sale of the business. In that respect, 'Ourselves' sounded not all bad. A club that he might not refuse to join.

"Well, Rose" – he would respond in kind, with the un-necessary first name – "let's see what we can do about clearing up the mess, as you rightly call it, and then see what we can do for ourselves. I'm including our innocent colleagues in 'ourselves' as well. Lloyd, Goldsmit and Carlsen amongst others." Then, he received the latest thunderbolt.

"Yes, of course. As much as we can. But I have to include one other. My son."

"Your son? What's it got to do with him? Is he involved in all this too?"

"No. His only involvement is that he is my son and I want to make sure he's protected. No pressure on him from lawyers. No threats from employees or from any 'associates'. Theirs or Klevic's."

"Well. Since you've brought him into the conversation, you'll have to tell me some more about him. Is he at school here? Or… where is he?"

"He's not at school. He graduated from university in Berlin last year. He's now a qualified engineer and working for a big American oil company in Venezuela. I've no reason to believe that he's under any threat at the moment, but I – we – must make sure he doesn't come under any. Some of those people – associates – have very long arms and hard skins."

"Yes. So I have heard. So, what exactly do you expect I can do for him?"

"Just… try to make sure that he's not harmed by the bad business or the scandal. That's all. Of course, I would try to help him financially if I could. But, if he's going to earn what I hope he will, then he will more likely be helping me." A light laugh relieved Rose's lips as she ended her appeal. Tulloch was relieved that there was no further problem than that, but he wasn't laughing. He could do without an extra problem.

It was nearly time for lunch, so they ordered a sandwich each with their second cup of coffee. By this time, they were fairly well saturated and the toilets were receiving more than their fair share of inspections. A large baguette with thin slices of ham and some lettuce and tomato helped to absorb the coffee, but they both made the mistake of accompanying it with a glass of very clear cold mountain spring water. Then, back to the car and a careful full-bladdered drive down the mountainside road to Vaduz and P.O. Holdings Inc. offices.

Lloyd was in his own office waiting for Tulloch when he arrived.

"Cup of coffee, Andrew? What's wrong?"

"I'm breaking my neck for a pee, that's what's wrong. Be with you in a couple of shakes…" He almost ran to the nearest toilet, ignoring the extra comforts of the directors' rest room yards further along the corridors of power. 'Pee and oh!' kept running through his mind until he was in a position to unzip his flies and let loose. A wave of relief washed over him and descended through his urinary tracts. A more relaxed Tulloch re-appeared in Lloyd's office. "That's better. Now, where were we?"

"Well. I was about to take some coffee in, and you were about to let some out. That's where we were. Now, if we can get back to business, perhaps you can let me into your next batch of secrets. First – how was your tête-à-tête over lunch with madam?"

Lloyd was still unsure of the extent of the relationship between Tulloch and Rose. The pressures of the last few weeks had been enormous and the results of their efforts to investigate and recover so much had removed almost all of the restraint he might have shown.

As far as Tulloch was concerned, the relationship was a pragmatic solution to several problems. Of those, accommodation and comfort were a bonus but not the primary objective. That was to find out what really had happened to Klevic and the assets, which he, and possibly Rose, had plundered. His obsession with 'the third man' theory was taking priority over his daily task of saving the business and its employees.

"Did you know that she has a son? Well, I don't suppose it would be very important under normal circumstances, but to her it seems to be the number one consideration. I have agreed to try to keep him out of any knock-on scandal or threats as long as she comes clean with me over Klevic's wealth and what we could do to claw it, or any of it, back.

"I can't make up my mind whether she's involved or not – she swears blind that she has had nothing to do with it and has received nothing from his little scams. I just don't know. What I'm going to ask you to do is check with HR and the pension fund records to see just what she has been getting and what her share – her official share – is worth now. If it's not enough to live off, then we shall have to find out how she is surviving with the high-life and where it's coming from.

There's one other thing. She told me that their son is now an engineer with a big oil company in Venezuela. See what you can find out about that, will you? If Klevic is still alive, then he – and she – could be aiming to slip over there and start again. That would be a good place to get lost in and might be far enough away to keep some of those hard men from Kosovo and Chechnya at arm's length.

Oh. And one more thing, Cocky. Just in case we find him there, check out if there are any extradition agreements with Venezuela. I don't suppose they have any with Liechtenstein or anywhere else for that matter. Chavez wouldn't surrender Bin Laden if he could help it. But you never know."

Lloyd didn't share Tulloch's obsession with the thought of Klevic walking about under a dead man's identity, but he wanted to keep an open mind on the subject until all reasonable checks had been completed. "I like the way you say 'in case WE find him'. You're getting as suspicious as a policemen now. Still, can't be too careful, can we? I'll see what I can find."

"Thanks, Cocky. I really appreciate it – as usual. I know I'm still very suspicious. The more we find out about Klevic's past, the more I can see him walking free now. This latest gen about Rose's son, particularly as he's involved in the oil business, just makes me feel closer than ever to finding Klevic and what he's up to.

I'll just finish checking progress on the business sale with Carlsen, and then I'll have another go at Rose – Madam K – to find out what I can about her family affairs.

"If you're not otherwise engaged" – *Damn!* he thought. *I shouldn't have said that!* – "and fancy a drink this evening, why don't we meet at the usual place. Say – seven thirty? Or a bit earlier and have some dinner there?"

Lloyd didn't flinch when Tulloch let 'otherwise engaged' slip out, to hit his emotions and worries over Betty but he did feel it. They left his office together but immediately separated – he to the HR department, Tulloch to his own office and a meeting with Carlsen.

Carlsen's report to Tulloch was mainly positive, but still with problems to sort out before the buyers of the business would sign. The main demand was for the directors to give joint and several indemnities guaranteeing that the buyers would not be involved in any litigation against the business as a result of any problem before they had bought it. This was not unusual but – with the calamitous actions conducted by Klevic still not completely absolved – it presented a potential problem, especially if Klevic was still alive but unobtainable.

Tulloch suggested that one way round it might be for the company to give the indemnity, with the fall back of action against Klevic if he were to be discovered. He knew that the buyers would still demand personal indemnities from the directors, and frankly, he thought, so would he in their place. Carlsen was asked to get the non-exec director, who was an international lawyer, 'on the case'. He would be first in line if any action was brought, so he should find the best solution for them. One more step down the ultimate corporate road to freedom – liquidation.

Seven thirty p.m. saw the two Brits re-convening in the Hotel bar-Brasserie Brug restaurant over a very British meal of steak and kidney pudding with chips and peas. They tried to order pints of English bitter to make it feel like home cooking. As it was, they settled for draught Lowenbrau. Lloyd remarked, "I wouldn't mind it if it didn't come from the beer keller in Munich where Hitler started the Nazi party. If he hadn't been teetotal, he could have murdered a few pints instead of millions of people."

It was good enough to enjoy and made them both feel less tired when they settled in the easy chairs in the bar lounge once again. "Back to business, Cocky. What have you found out? Anything about Rose's wealth or otherwise, or her son in Caracas or wherever?"

"Not much so far. She's built up a pension pot, which is now down to quarter of a million dollars, US. That won't get her much of an income. Not nearly enough to stay here, even if she could carry on in the big house for free. I also don't know who owns it, but I think you said it might be one or other of Klevic's Albanian or Russian pals.

"It seems that the son is quite above board. He works for Exxon – in Maracaibo – not Caracas. That's the big oil-field area on that huge lake on the northern coast. Nothing else on him, but I've got someone trying to find an address or phone number in case you want to contact him. And we can forget extradition. It's a non-starter. That may not sound like much to go on, but it confirms most of Rose's story, at least."

Tulloch was pensive. The steak and kidney pie was sitting in his stomach and he didn't want it to think of standing up. He declined coffee and settled for another Lowenbrau.

"You're right. If Hitler had concentrated on beer instead of armaments, the world would have been a better place," he mused. "Same probably applies to Klevic."

35

ROSEBUD

Rose was indeed about to have her story confirmed. It would also be expanded with more interesting detail – interesting to Tulloch insofar as it referred to a certain bank account, of which he had not been aware beforehand. After thanking Lloyd for the results of his instant investigation into Rose's son and his location, Tulloch pondered on the possible involvement of Klevic Junior in his parents' financial situation.

The next morning, after dealing with correspondence and phone messages, a telephone call was channelled to his office from Carlsen. He had just heard from his non-exec lawyer colleague that the amended indemnities had been accepted and the buyer insisted on completion of the contract within the next forty-eight hours. As this was precisely what the vendor company wanted, the way was now clear for the business to be sold and the selling company to be liquidated 'in due course', i.e. by negotiation between Tulloch and an acceptable firm of insolvency practitioners.

Insolvency practitioners varied from the enormous international firms of accountants, such as Ernst & Young or Price Waterhouse Coopers, to smaller specialist firms such as Cork Gully – affectionately known in accounting circles as

'Undertakers to the Trade'. As P.O. Holdings Inc. was incorporated in Delaware, USA, it was considered practical to invite an international firm, acceptable to US authorities, without question.

The legal eagle on the board could now suggest and approach one such flock of financial funeral directors, in order to effect a smooth liquidation under chapter 7 of the U.S. bankruptcy laws, with the paid assistance of Tulloch and Carlsen – and himself, provided that the fee was large enough.

Tulloch left his office in the hands of the skeleton staff still administering to P.O. Holdings Inc. head office and walked back to the Klevic residence. He was beginning to feel as though the problems of the past months were finally dissolving. The thoughts of Klevic, or a look-alike, roaming free with unknown amounts of loot still plagued his mind, but he would try to establish the truth of that as the liquidation progressed.

At the house, Rose was waiting for him. Once more, she suggested a lunch but this time something more substantial than multiple coffees and a sandwich. The same little café would serve a more serious late lunch. It could be ordered by phone before they drove up there. She was hoping to receive better news of her pension pot value and offered to buy the lunch as a celebration.

The pension pot news was not exactly of a gold mine waiting to be extracted and spent but it was a big improvement on her earlier expectations – before the combined efforts of Tulloch, Lloyd and Carlsen had retrieved most of the embezzled millions and Goldsmit had liquidated the bad investments. She smiled wistfully at the valuation, amounting to over a quarter of a million US dollars, in the knowledge that it was much less than it had been valued before Klevic's problems had been exposed but much, much more than the 'estimated to realise' value shortly afterwards.

Once more, the Mercedes was trundled out from its warm berth and navigated up the mountain roads towards Liechtenstein's version of a Swiss Cottage café. On one bend, a herd of pasture-targeted cows clanged their bells as they wandered across the paths and road, dropping large wet deposits onto the road as they announced their curfew. The tyres on the car squelched into the mire and out through it onto equally wet leaf-mould and moss. The air, dank with the morning's drizzle, took a healthy countryside aroma.

'Serious lunch' was not quite as serious as it sounded. The light food and wine, consisting mainly of lobster and Chablis with salads and fruits, followed by a little local goats' cheese with a glass of Madeira, might have been described as 'gay' if that adjective had not acquired homosexual overtones. The atmosphere between Rose and her lodger was almost dreamy. When all excuses for remaining had been exhausted, Rose took out a cheque book from her brown Mulberry leather purse. "This is definitely on me." No arguments asked, and none given.

As the cheque, for a not inexpensive meal, was being written, Tulloch peered over her shoulder. It was drawn on a very confidential private bank, not well known outside of Liechtenstein or Switzerland, and the name of the account printed on it was 'R & P Klevic'. Nothing was said until the waiter thanked them demurely and escorted them to the car. Once inside it, Tulloch could not restrain his anxiety. "What bank account was that?" he asked quietly. "I thought you were, what we call, 'borassic' or 'skint'. You don't seem to be as poor as you feared."

If they had been in a dream before, the dreamers suddenly awoke with a start. "What do you mean? Why on earth should I not have a bank account? I don't understand you."

"It's just that you said earlier that you didn't have a bean. Klevic had not included you in his money-grabbing schemes, and you were very anxious about the value of your pension policy. Now, you have an account with one of the most exclusive private banks in the world, who wouldn't open one unless you had a fortune to deposit into it. And it appears to be in the name of you and Klevic. Shouldn't that account have been closed when he died?"

Rose's expression changed again. One of anger mixed with fear. "It's nothing to do with him. *And* nothing to do with you, either. Just because you sleep in my bed, doesn't mean that you can pry into my private affairs. Now, if you don't mind, kindly drive me home." Tulloch could feel the daggers in her voice and looks but had to remind her of a few home truths. He took the wheel without pausing to secure their safety belts or adjust their seats.

"It certainly *is* something to do with me, Rose," His voice was as low and temperate as he could make it. "You know very well that I have been scouring every avenue to establish whether Klevic has, or had, secret stores of money that he had taken from the company or the pension fund. Which, incidentally, you also know that I have been instrumental in recovering for you amongst others. That's very much part of my business. I think – in fact I know now – that you have not told me all of… the truth about your involvement in this."

For the first two kilometres, the only noises in the car were from the engine and tyres. Rose was a closed shop. A clam would have been more open and noisier than her tight mouth. Then she lost the game. Tulloch was not going to speak until she had offered some sort of explanation and she knew it.

The account is not Klevic's – at least not *that* Klevic. He's gone. The account is just mine."

"Rose. I saw the name printed on the cheques. How can you say it's just yours?"

Tight-lipped as she was, Rose managed to emit a hissing noise and scream at the driver of her car. "I can say it because it is! And don't you say it isn't!" The screaming and hissing spread across her face, and her entire body seemed to want to join in. Tulloch was having a problem stopping her from clutching at his throat and another problem understanding the strangled words from hers.

On the basis of it never rains but it pours, such extra problems might have been anticipated to arise following the tensions of the business. Then, another and greater problem manifested itself suddenly and completely unexpectedly. It came from the rain and their fellow travellers of the morning drive. At the bend in the road, where they had met the herd of cattle, Rose's hands hit Tulloch's arms as he tried to steer the car around it. The wheels hit the cow-shit and the shit hit the driver's fan.

The result was disastrous for the car and deadly for its occupants. In a split second, the front wheels crossed the light roadside barrier and the Mercedes rolled over and down the mountainside for twenty rocky metres ending at a very strong tree lodged in very hard rock. The occupants continued their unplanned journey into space for an additional half-metre, stopping only when their heads crashed into the metal door-frame and the glass sun-roof.

Twenty minutes later, a passing motorist had telephoned the emergency services and an ambulance was waiting for the human wreckage to be extracted from the automotive equivalent. The driver shrugged his shoulder to the ambulance paramedic's delicate approach as he passed judgement on the scene.

"It's no use being too gentle with them now. They're both kaput!"

Nevertheless, he resumed his duties when stretchers and bodies had been placed in the ambulance, driving slowly through the remaining cow-shit back to the A & E entrance of the Vaduz general hospital. The stretchers were then moved onto a trolley and wheeled into an examination room. Rose Klevic was first to be examined and, as the ambulance driver had predicted, promptly pronounced dead.

Cocky Lloyd lost any remaining signs of cockiness, when he was informed of the tragedy to his colleagues. His head spun with the memories of events, from his own introduction to the Klevic empire, to the previous evening's meal and conversation with Andrew Tulloch. Dropping the phone from his hands onto the desk surface, he walked from his office to the front door, where a taxi took him to the hospital.

Vaduz hospital services had telephoned the office of P.O. Holdings Inc., without giving full details of the bodies from the crash scene. When Lloyd arrived at the hospital and stated his relationship with the victims, he was conducted to a private ward, where the prone body of Tulloch was laid out on a bed.

Not being an expert in medical matters, Lloyd was surprised to see that the head of the victim was swathed in bandages. Several tubes, which he recognised as having starred in numerous TV programmes, protruded from the deceased's nose and mouth, which also appeared to be inhaling and exhaling.

This was not the sort of corpse to which he had been accustomed – not even in Swansea or Bridgend. He glanced around the room, looking for instruments with a moribund monitor or screeching a long uninterrupted noise to signify to TV viewers that rigor mortis was about to set in. The attendant nurse broke the news gently. "Your friend is very lucky to be here. His lady is not lucky. She is in the mortuary."

It took over a week for Tulloch to recover sufficiently to talk. In that time, Carlsen and his colleagues continued to complete the business sale, but they put any appointment of liquidators on hold. After he signified that he was finally able to discuss anything other than medical needs and comfort, Tulloch was told of Rose's death.

Rather than being completely shocked, he suffered a wave of melancholy, tempered by amazement at his own survival. Whatever she had done in Klevic's company, and whatever truth she had hidden from him, Rose's affection and warmth had now been wrenched from him as if he had lost an arm in the crash.

His recollections of the final moments in the doomed car were fragmented and limited to a few recurring sounds. His questions and accusations. Her angry screams of protest and defiance. It took nearly two more weeks for him to compose a visible sight and sound record of those last events.

Lloyd had visited him on most days, and now Tulloch wanted to ask him to resume the search for any residual loot or evasive imposter. One item was firmly engraved on the walls of his memory cells – the name of the bank account, as printed on Rose's cheques. There had definitely been a 'P' as well as an 'R' Klevic on it. And Klevic had not been the sort of caring husband who would tolerate his wife having access to a standard joint account, unless he intended to use it for his own benefit later.

After describing his sight of the cheque and the printing on it, he explained his recurring theory of Klevic's disappearance, as it might relate to this latest evidence. He then asked Lloyd to visit the only remaining character that he could imagine to be involved or to be witness to the past events. "The son – Rose's son," he whispered to Lloyd. "We must track him down and get whatever information he has about his father.

"Unless we do that, we'll never know whether there is any more to recover or not. I still think there's a chance that Klevic is alive somewhere. It might be with the son in Maracaibo. You're the only one I can trust to do the job properly, Cocky. Sorry to lumber you with it, but can you go out there and see what you can find? He has to be told of his mother's death anyway, if he doesn't know it already."

Lloyd was not entirely surprised at the request. He had heard from Tulloch of the need to leave nothing unquestioned. Due diligence applied to the vendor as well as the purchaser if litigation was to be prevented. He mused a little more.

"Maracaibo, eh? I suppose it would be too much to expect him to live somewhere like Swansea, wouldn't it?"

36

An Inspector calls

To Lloyd's slight surprise, Maracaibo was much larger and nicer than his mental picture of an oil field under a lake. The attractive city was served by several airlines but mainly after flying via Caracas. The better route for him was an American Airlines flight from Miami. That proved to be easier and friendlier than his previous flights to the central Americas, via Atlanta, Georgia, which he had voted to be the most un-welcoming airport in an un-welcoming USA.

Perhaps, he thought, *it's down to the Spanish influence in Miami. Or maybe they're just sympathetic towards me because they know that I'm going to Venezuela.* In the event, Maracaibo was just as welcoming, and even warmer than Miami. With bright sunshine and thirty degrees centigrade, La Chinita Airport was indeed a welcome change from the dark mountains around Vaduz. *I might enjoy this trip,* he thought.

A cheerful taxi driver chatted in a mixture of Spanish and American, as they drifted through the hot streets of the city, towards the InterContinental hotel. He had booked the best hotel in town as a self-presented reward for this work, which was he considered, 'beyond the call of duty'.

Lloyd didn't understand everything that the taxi driver said but he was happy to soak in the sunshine and the attractive sights of Venezuela's second city. The taxi driver didn't understand everything that Lloyd said either, but he did understand the tip he received and seemed happy to grab it, before offering to carry Lloyd's little briefcase, leaving his passenger to lug the heavy suitcase.

Before leaving Vaduz, Tulloch had briefed him again and again about Rose's behaviour before the fatal car crash and his varying suggestions of possible identities that Klevic might have adopted after feigning death. The possibilities seemed endless, as were those possible methods and sources of further embezzlement. Although lucky to be alive, the crash and severe head injuries had taken their toll and exacerbated an already wild imagination.

One detail that had not involved variation was the address given to Lloyd by a search bureau, of Rose Klevic's son. It was a pleasant apartment block near the city centre. Living there, in such an expensive city, would usually require a large income or a large and generous employer to pay the rent. Rose's son was reputed to work for Exxon Mobil, so Lloyd assumed that he benefited from the latter situation. Tulloch would probably assume that he benefited from the proceeds of Klevic's nefarious deals and thefts but Tulloch was still suffering from his head injuries.

As well as being a very expensive hotel in a very expensive city, the InterContinental was very comfortable. Having just survived such a long journey, Lloyd had no intention of scrambling around a foreign city looking for an address that he had just acquired. Besides which, Rose's son was probably working somewhere out on the lake and might be away for ages. He took the straight and simple route and went to bed early, after cooling off with a cool shower and an even cooler beer.

To save further wasted efforts, he rose early the next morning and asked the attractive girl at the reception desk how to enquire about telephone directory enquiries. The first stage of the question obviated the second and third stages. "No further enquiry about enquiries, Señor. I will find the telephone number and call you back in your room." *That's service for you,* thought Cocky, *almost justifies the cost of the room.* Within twenty minutes, the receptionist returned with the number of the phone at the address, which was registered in the name of the Exxon Mobil company.

Telephones are very good at ringing when you cannot reach them but not so good at answering by themselves without an answering machine. For the first three attempts, Lloyd had to conclude that there was no one at home or near enough to answer within five minutes of ringing. By mid-morning, he decided that the only chance of meeting Klevic Jnr. would be to visit the apartment personally. Petrol in Maracaibo, as throughout Venezuela, is extremely cheap, so a taxi ride should be an economic and comfortable way to spend the next half hour.

True to his calculations, the taxi was not expensive, if not all that comfortable. By the time they arrived at the apartment block, Lloyd's linguistic skills had developed a ten-word vocabulary in Spanish. The taxi driver's command of

American-English delivered the remaining ninety-nine percent of required communication. "'Ere we are, Señor sorr. Your frien' ees on the theerd floor. Thangyou verimuch." The tip would buy a whole day's petrol, if only half a loaf of bread.

Elevators in Venezuela require the same basic resources as they do anywhere else – electricity and maintenance. One or other – or both perhaps – were not available. Lloyd climbed three flights of stairs to find himself on floor number four, remembering then that the ground floor would be considered to be the first. As he gently turned to descend the stairs to the third floor, he caught a fleeting glimpse of the back of a figure that looked almost familiar.

Without a frontal view, the only certainty was that, it was male – unless it was a very large woman wearing jacket, trousers and a panama hat. The man was closing the door of one of the apartments before turning away from Lloyd, who was still on the fourth floor stairs and walking quickly to the next flight down. In that time, Lloyd wondered where he had seen him before. He thought he could connect the figure with that of the man who had followed him as he left the Greek island café with Cyrus, the ships' chandler. Could that have been Dmitri Petric, the devoted minder of Patrick Klevic? It might even have been Klevic himself, except that he was dead and buried, wasn't he?

The burly figure disappeared down the stairs. Lloyd emerged from the higher stairwell and carefully trod a thin carpet to the door, which the figure had just closed. Next to the door was a bell-push and the standard card-holder with a business calling card. The name on the card was 'P. Klevic'. At that moment, Lloyd thought back to Tulloch's obsessive conspiracy theory, which he had dismissed so many times as fantasy. *Sorry, Andrew. Looks like you might have been right all along.*

Several firm pushes on the door-bell, brought a similar response to those from his 'phone call attempts. The phrase 'no answer came the firm reply' flashed through his mind. *Now, where did that come from? Edgar Alan Poe perhaps? 'The Raven?'* With no further sight or sound of human habitation, Cocky decided it was time to get back to reality and the InterContinental.

Another taxi. Another lesson in Spanish, bringing his vocabulary up to twelve words. "If anybody tries to sneer at my Spanish, I'll challenge him or her in Welsh." But no sneering from a grateful and cheerful taxi driver or from the polite and helpful hotel staff. Lloyd applied the fully-functional elevator to deliver him back to the floor whereon his room was waiting with freshly changed linen and bath towels.

Although it was almost lunchtime in Maracaibo, Vaduz was by now thinking of dinner. Lloyd had calculated carefully that Tulloch would be eating a bland hospital breakfast. Unfortunately, he adjusted the time difference the wrong way around. Tulloch was actually eating a biscuit with his third cup of tea of the late afternoon, having not been discharged from hospital and still under their force-feed regime.

Lloyd convinced himself that a phone call now would be premature. The fresh towels and clean bathroom suggested shower-time, taking from his skin the outer layer of perspiration, which had surfaced during the stairway efforts in the apartment block. Fifteen minutes later, he was ready for a drink. Perhaps some cold water and fruit juice. Too warm for coffee. Too early for solid food. Just right for a cold cerveza.

By half past siesta time, Lloyd thought he must try to contact Tulloch. He had the number of the hospital and was quickly put through to a ward sister. She asked him to try again in ten minutes while she tried to find Tulloch, who was struggling to get back to his room from the toilet. Lloyd left the hotel phone number with her and asked for a return call as soon as convenient. 'At his convenience' might have sounded amusing to Lloyd but, would have been wasted on a German-speaking nurse in Liechtenstein.

It was a little more than the suggested ten minutes, but less than twenty, when the return call reached Lloyd in his hotel. Unlike hot coffee in cold Vaduz, the effects of cold beer in warm Maracaibo did not induce inconvenience of any variety. Conversation was short and to the point. After brief 'hello, how are you feeling now?' Cocky broke the breaking news. "I reckon you might 'ave been right all along about Klevic, Andrew. I went to see the flat where Rosa's son is supposed to be staying and guess what—"

"Don't tell me. You didn't see him, did you?"

"No. That is, I didn't see the son, but I did see someone who looked awfully like the father. Now, I didn't see his face. Just his back and the side of his head when he left the apartment. But it could 'ave been him and, more importantly, the name on the door – or rather next to it, by the bell, was 'P. Klevic'.

"The only thing that I can't make out is why would he want to masquerade under his own name? Is he being extra clever or am I being extra daft?"

"I don't really know, Cocky. I could call you a lot of things but daft isn't one of them. Can you get back there and stalk him? Or is that too dangerous? We can't be sure until he's been confronted. So far, you've only con-backed him."

"OK, Andrew. I'll go back there this evening and see if I can corner him. Not sure what I'll do if he just admits who he is and tells me to piss off."

"You'll think of something, Cocky. I have every faith in you." He laughed as the gravity of the situation was banished with the joy of possible detection and resolve. The nagging mystery surrounding Klevic's disappearance and apparent death might yet be cleared along with the remains of P.O. Holdings Inc. A more serious tone carried across the Atlantic telephone line. "Have you still got your Smith & Wesson?"

Lloyd did have the handgun. It was carried in a safe compartment of his suitcase. He had still not actually fired it 'in anger, or even in calm', as he was still not completely familiar with the operation of the safety catch. But as long as it didn't fire when he didn't want it to, he felt it might add a certain amount of gravitas to his discussions in an emergency. As far as he could remember, he had definitely inserted the magazine and cartridges into the right slot. At least, he was fairly sure.

"Yes, don't worry. I still have it. Don't expect to have to use it, but don't want to take chances with a chap like Klevic – or one of his old mates." The thought of a gun-fight had not crossed his mind, and memories of the farcical drama and escape from the Congo brought a little shiver to his back. He swallowed hard and said goodbye to Tulloch with a reassuring last, "Don't worry." He would do the worrying.

Daily office work in Maracaibo tends to operate in shifts. Like football, it is a game of two halves. Siesta time lasts rather longer than the traditional half-time break at Stamford Bridge or Old Trafford. It is often four hours long, dividing the early morning half, which usually starts at six or seven a.m., from the late afternoon half, which might end around eight p.m. or later. Lloyd had been advised of this and timed his next visit to the apartments accordingly.

By ten p.m., he thought, anyone returning from work should have returned. The taxi collected him at nine forty-five p.m. and deposited him at the apartment block front doors precisely at ten. This time, he ascended the correct two flights of stairs, before looking for the door with 'P. Klevic' named as the occupant. He was to be disappointed. The door with the name card was still there, but the flat was apparently still unoccupied.

He had calculated the office hours correctly but forgotten that some people like to have a meal after work. Restaurant trade was probably peaking as he tried in vain to get an answer at the door. At the end of the stairs, he heard footsteps. Patting the bulge in his jacket where the automatic lodged, he ducked into the stairwell.

A slim dark clerk or bank manager appeared and was about to open the door to another apartment. Lloyd breathed soft relief and re-emerged from the stairwell.

"*Buenos dias?*" he offered.

The dark man looked quizzically at him. "*Si. Buenos dias – et buona serra, Señor.*" The quizzical look demanded an explanation or a question. Lloyd tried both.

"Uh, *parlo Inglesi, Señor.*"

"Yes, Señor. I expect you do speak English. So do I. Can I help you?"

"Thank you, yes please. Do you know when Mr Klevic will be at home?"

"Mr Klevic? No. I don't know but he is probably eating his dinner at the local café now. He might be there, or somewhere else, for some time – or not. I'm sorry but I don't know more." The man paused, waiting to hear if there were any more questions.

"Oh. I see. Um, do you think he will be at home tomorrow evening, then?"

"Perhaps. Tomorrow is Samedi – you say Saturday? – so I think he might be at home tomorrow – daytime. But, I don't know more." There was a short silence while Lloyd realised that the weekend applied to Venezuela as well as to Britain or Liechtenstein.

"Thank you, Señor. Thank you. I'll try, later. Another time."

"Shall I tell Señor Klevic that you wish to see him?"

"No. That will not be necessary. I'll catch him – see him – when it is – convenient."

37

The last thing Lloyd wanted was for a helpful neighbour to scare Klevic away at this stage. He tried to thank the helpful man again and left the corridor, smiling more thanks as he departed. *A quick bite to eat in a local café,* he thought, *might find Klevic there.* It would be a change from the hotel restaurant, anyway.

Unsure of the location of any decent café, he hailed the next taxi and asked the driver to take him to the local café for 'a good quality meal'. The driver looked blankly at him but obligingly let him into the cab, before driving the few metres across the road to the café on the opposite side. Embarrassment was removed with a tip in excess of the tiny fare.

The café was busy but most of the diners had finished eating by now and a table for one was not a problem. The menu card was displayed to Lloyd's relief and he simply pointed at one line, hoping desperately that it was not the name of the manager. A bowl of soup arrived quickly, at which point Lloyd tried his luck again, recognising the word that looked like 'pork'.

There was no sign of Klevic in the café. By eleven p.m. and a couple of glasses of red wine, he was content to think that he was getting closer and getting fed. Tomorrow would be Saturday, and as they say, it would 'be another day'. The taxi that accepted his hire at eleven thirty p.m. was thankfully, not the same one that had delivered him all the way across the road at ten fifteen. At midnight, with the city still in full Friday night fling, he took a small coffee and retired to bed and a quiet night.

It was fortunate, Lloyd thought, that the next day was Samedi. With a time difference of over five hours between them, which he had finally accepted as Vaduz being hours ahead of Maracaibo instead of the other way, he realised that it was well past his work-time. Tulloch would be expecting a report of unqualified success by now. Time to get moving.

Ducking breakfast, he washed and shaved quickly, dressing while he was still wet from the shower. Another day – another taxi. This one was his driver from La Chinita Airport. Still happy enough to hope for a good tip and a greeting in the strange language that his passenger appeared to speak. Lloyd, however, was too preoccupied to try out his Spanish. The driver was disappointed by his passenger talking briefly in American with an unusual English accent.

Waving a modest fare and tip to the driver, Lloyd stepped smartly to the front doors and up the two flights of stairs. He was becoming more accustomed to the stairs and corridors now. He just hoped that Klevic would be 'at home' and the helpful neighbour would not. Without stopping to think what he would say, he rang the bell of the apartment bearing the business card of P. Klevic.

Just before his bell-ring was answered, he heard two voices from the rooms behind the door. The language was very hard to identify but it was not Spanish or German, and certainly not English. To his untutored ear, it sounded like what he thought could be Russian or Polish. The sort of sounds that he had heard when he was in Kosovo.

His mind immediately turned to the figure seen in the corridor on the previous morning. Perhaps it had been Petric, who was supposed to be of a similar build to Klevic. Perhaps the two former members of FARK were here, hiding in Venezuela like two ex-Nazi fugitives. The second voice was at the door, which was opened as far as the security chain would permit. A young man – perhaps in his early twenties – faced Lloyd, asking now in Spanish: *"Buonas dias, Señor?"*

Lloyd didn't know what to say but he said it anyway. *"Buonas dias.* I'm looking for Mr Klevic. Mr P. Klevic."

The young man's expression didn't change. Nor did the tone of his voice. "Yes. I am Mr P. Klevic. If you please, who are you? And could you tell me your business, please?"

Lloyd was something between taken aback and totally gobsmacked. "Mr P." He emphasised the initial, "Mr P. Klevic?"

The young man nodded and pointed to the name on the card by the bell-push, almost amused at the question. "Yes, that's me. Mr P. Klevic. Now please, I don't wish to appear rude, but would you kindly tell me what you want?"

Lloyd's mind raced. He could tell the young man who and what, but who and what was the other man in the flat. He had to say something more than just 'good morning'.

"My name is Lloyd, Mr Klevic. I am the chief security officer of P.O. Holdings Inc. (in fact, the only one,) "I'm afraid I have some serious news to give to you."

"Oh, yes. Is this about my mother? I have been told of her death in an automobile accident, but please come in. Have you come all the way from Liechtenstein to tell me?" Lloyd entered the flat and they walked into a small lounge, where the second voice was sitting. "Incidentally, my name is Paul – that's what the 'P' stands for."

Lloyd was still wondering what to say next when the second voice turned to face them. It was a man of similar build to Klevic and for that matter also to Petric, all right. But it was not Petric, nor was it the Patrick Klevic of Lloyd's acquaintance and P.O. Holdings Inc. chairman's title. It was more like the man whom Lloyd had seen so briefly in Vaduz and mistaken for Klevic.

The young man spoke again. "Mr Lloyd – this is my father. This is Mr Ostal Klevic."

Lloyd held out a very shaky hand, to shake the firm hand extended by Ostal Klevic. "How d'you do… my name's Llewellyn Lloyd." That was as much as he could think of at this point. He decided to speak of Rose's accident and her position in relation to the company, hoping that Paul or Ostal Klevic would offer more information about themselves and Rose.

"I don't know how much you have heard of your mother's accident, Mr, uh… Paul. It was a car crash, coming down a mountain road near Vaduz. She has coming back from lunch with one of my colleagues in the company. Andrew Tulloch. The car hit a very wet patch of road, on a bend, and slipped over the edge of the road and down the side of the mountain. It hit a tree and they were both thrown up against the roof."

He paused to see if any of this was completely new to the men or if they had anything to ask or add. Both of the Klevic men were impassive. Faces blank, as if they had heard the account before but didn't want to comment. Young Paul spoke first. "Your colleague – Mr Tulloch, I believe? He was injured too, wasn't he? Has he recovered or is he still injured?" Ostal Klevic remained silent. As if he knew the answer but was not unduly concerned.

Lloyd answered. "Yes, it is Andrew Tulloch. He is, as far as I know, still the acting chairman and CEO of the company. He suffered head injuries but not fatal ones. Unlike your poor mother, who I believe was, uh… died instantly. She can't have suffered for any time at all."

He hoped that this would sound sympathetic enough, considering that he had flown there to try to trap their cousin. "Andrew is still in hospital, but he hopes… we hope that he'll be able to recover very soon. We all need him back in the company to complete the clear-up of its financial problems."

Ostal Klevic still stayed silent. Paul nodded, as if to signify his understanding. "I have heard something of that. Not much that I really understand though." He turned to look at his father. "My father may know more. He is… was… Mr Patrick, or Prec, Klevic's cousin. That makes me a second cousin, doesn't it?"

Lloyd shrugged. "I suppose it does, or did." He then turned to the father. "I think I may have bumped into you once before, Mr Klevic. Maybe in the company's offices in Vaduz?"

It was Klevic senior's turn to shrug. "Possibly. I was once involved in the company, when we started it, but I have not been active there for many years. I did call in to Vaduz a few months ago to speak to my former wife. We parted company several years back. We had not spoken since my cousin's funeral and now we won't be able to do so again." He looked genuinely sad, although Lloyd wondered, if that was only to offer silent commiseration to his son.

Lloyd wanted to ask so many questions. Ostal had been at the hurried Klevic funeral. He had known his cousin intimately for ages. He must also have known exactly what happened to Klevic and whether anyone else had taken his place in the coffin. This was not the time or place to ask, however. Somehow, he had to delay any planned departure of the cousin. He needed an excuse to break up the conversation and get back to questioning Ostal Klevic. The pension fund would provide the excuse he needed.

"Paul, I need to check with the company offices about your mother's investment in the company – the group – pension fund. I don't know enough about these things to give you any details, but there may be some money from her fund that is due to you." That sounded important enough to warrant another meeting with Rose's son but what about father?

"Mr, uh, Ostal. I would like to be absolutely sure of that position, in case it affects you too. Will you be in Maracaibo for long?"

He need not have asked. Ostal smiled. "Yes, don't worry. I'm not flying away. I live here too for the time being. Why don't we meet here again tomorrow, if that's not too soon for you?"

Lloyd really wanted to get him on his own. Tomorrow would be Sunday but on Monday Paul should be at work. "I'll try to get the information but it won't be until Monday, as the offices will be closed tomorrow."

Paul looked happy enough with that and so did Ostal. But Ostal had another agenda. He wanted to speak to Lloyd, without the company of his son. "Where are you staying, Mr Lloyd? Hotel... downtown?"

Lloyd picked up the vibes and the inflection, confirming with the name of the InterContinental.

Ostal continued. "If you're not busy tomorrow, why don't we meet for a meal or just for a drink – whichever suits you best. Sunday will be a little dull if you are here on your own. Or perhaps you have another appointment?"

Cocky perked up, thanking him. Glad of the chance to talk again and glad not to have an empty day in a foreign port. "Nothing planned, Mr... Ostal. I'd be very happy to do that. What time would you suggest?"

Paul Klevic looked slightly concerned, if not embarrassed. "I'm afraid I won't be able to join you, Mr Lloyd. But my father knows the city very well. I have... another date. My girlfriend is playing tennis tomorrow and I promised to meet her for

335

lunch afterwards." He made no effort to disguise 'lunch' with his girlfriend. It might have been only lunch after all. Nobody would mind, or worry. He also sensed that his father wanted to talk to Lloyd alone. Father knew best.

Father spoke again.

"How about, if I meet you in the bar at the InterContinental at... about midday? We could eat lunch there or, if you prefer, I suggest a café near the lake. Nice tuna there and not too much oil!" He laughed lightly at his attempted joke.

Cocky was very pleased with his latest progress. He wanted to phone Tulloch as soon as he could. Or as soon as the hospital would accept and connect his phone call. The office in Vaduz might be closed on Sunday but Tulloch's mind and memory – if it hadn't been scrambled by the car crash injuries – should be wide open. As soon as he reached his room in the InterContinental, his telephone burned hot with his revelations to Tulloch of Rose's son and the boy's father.

After such a long period of growing assurance that Patrick Klevic might still be alive and impersonating another murdered man, Tulloch appeared to be stunned and almost disappointed. His shortlist of likely victims of murder and identity theft had admittedly been restricted to the men accompanying the corpse to Klevic's funeral. But there had been so many fragments of information suggesting that someone of Klevic's appearance had been seen that he was fully prepared to hear of Klevic impersonating a complete stranger.

Hearing now of one of the mourners being the real father of Rose's son was something that had escaped his imagination and theories of a 'third man'. Unless the mysterious Ostal was in fact Patrick Klevic and the real Ostal was in the grave. Cocky would have to explore all possibilities, however remote.

The first questions now would be those concerning any transfer of Rose's pension fund and, perhaps more intriguing, those concerning details of the true circumstances of Klevic's death. Tulloch discussed the possibilities and available facts for nearly an hour.

The state of Rose's pension fund would be established with the aid of Goldsmit and his insurance associates. None of the facts concerning the death in the dark island of Lenios could be anything more than conjecture until Cocky Lloyd could meet and persuade Ostal Klevic to divulge what he knew. And that would have to wait until Ostal and Cocky met for their Sunday lunch.

With nothing to do except wait and think, Lloyd opted for the latter. His thoughts turned first to beer and some food. A brisk walk across the road to the local café would be in order, even at the disappointment of the taxi drivers. By the time that he walked out from the hotel over the hot road and into the café, his thirst exceeded his interest in pensions by a factor of ten thousand.

A large glass of cerveza regional draft was followed by a smaller glass of Cardenal premium lager, and that was followed by another. By the time that he had consumed those three, he was ready for some hot food. The menu was not a familiar picture of mealtime grub in Mumbles. He had to be adventurous. Pointing at 'polvoroso de pollo' and 'caraotas negras', before crossing his fingers, he became nervous until relief arrived on a plate of chicken hot-pot with black beans on the side.

The inner man was soon fed, watered and comfortable. Approaching the pavement, he saw an eager taxi driver optimistically looking for the eccentric gringo who needed a taxi to cross the road. Disappointment for one was balanced by satisfaction for the other. Sleep came to Cocky Lloyd with the strains of distant Latin American music drifting around the InterContinental from a loud radio as the Simon Bolivar Orchestra lulled him to his slumbers. 'A slumber with a rumba' drifted through his mind as he dozed off between crisp, cool sheets.

Sunday breakfast was limited to fruit juice and a small plate of perico – the local dish of scrambled eggs with tomato and onions. Coffee was surplus to requirements until Ostal Klevic would arrive, when he would offer it as his contribution to hospitality. The flavours of Saturday evening's dinner and bed-time music were still pleasant memories, and he would accept any offer of a visit to a local café for a light lunch and some serious talking.

True to his promise, Ostal Klevic entered the InterContinental, at precisely midday. The offer of coffee was politely declined, as the café that he had in mind would get busy soon and they should move there promptly to get a good table and then order refreshments. A waiting car on the forecourt was driven gently away to provide maximum comfort to the visiting Welshman and, faster on the dual carriageway, arriving at a small café by the lakeshore within twenty minutes.

Noonday sun in Venezuela could be uncomfortably hot. The café benefited from a cooling breeze coming off the lake and ceiling fans inside the dining area. Ostal offered to order for both of them. An offer that Lloyd accepted, although he did mention his pleasant dining experience of the previous evening. After receipt of antipasto and two glasses of Cardenal lager – Lloyd having impressed Klevic with his familiarity of local beers – several small portions of lunchtime dishes were ordered by Ostal. The two men were then prepared to discuss Lloyd's mission.

As an opening gambit, the request to Tulloch for details of Rose's financial entitlements were explained to Ostal. Whatever it would be, Lloyd said, would depend on the valuation from the insurance company handling what had been salvaged from the former group pension fund. As the details would come from Tulloch and would be only applicable to young Paul Klevic, there was little or nothing that the two in the café could add.

Having passed on all that he could offer in the way of information, Lloyd then turned to – what for him – would be so much more interesting. The relationships within the Klevic clan and the events in Lenios surrounding the death of the P.O. Holdings Inc.'s chairman and C.E.O. The first item on his agenda was to express surprise at Rose's marriage to Ostal. Lloyd, Tulloch and, as far as he knew, all of the directors and staff at P.O. Holdings Inc. had assumed that Madam Klevic was the wife of the chairman.

A smile appeared on Ostal's face. "And you also assumed, I expect, that my son Paul would be his son and perhaps in collusion with whoever had taken money from the company. Is that right?" Lloyd shrugged without confirming or denying it. Ostal continued. "Well, I can understand your concern. To explain properly, I should tell you about our – my cousin's and my own – relationship."

38

THE BALKANS SETTLEMENT

"Prek – Patrick, he called himself later – was a close cousin to me. By which I mean that his father and mine were brothers and we were born about the same time in the same village. That is now in what is called Kosovo. I think you know that. Prek was always what we would say brave, but some would say dangerous. It's hard to tell the difference sometimes, is it not? We worked together with our fathers. Doing anything that could earn money or food or fuel.

"There was always a lot of trouble and tension between us and the Serbians. As you also know, I expect, that developed into open civil war. A war in which we were forced to defend ourselves, and that involved getting weapons to fight the Serbs. Our business before then was doing well, as long as I could handle the money side of the business and hold Prek back from some of his wild ideas. That was the start of what became the P.O. – Prek and Ostal – company, which became P.O. Holdings Inc.

"Two things happened to break our partnership; first – he started trying to take my wife from me, and secondly, he joined the Kosovo Liberation Army – KLA – and later, a splinter group called FARK. These were desperate men using desperate methods and heavy weapons. I didn't want to join them although I wanted to help the KLA if I could. And I did. But not the way that FARK operated."

Ostal paused and took a long sip of the Cardenal beer, before resuming. "Prek was in league with other men outside Kosovo. Russians and Chetyans who could get heavy weapons for money. I arranged to get the money for the weapons – don't ask me where – and Prek was to deliver them. Somehow, the money went out but the weapons didn't come in. Our people were defenceless against the Serbs and were slaughtered.

I had to face the KLA and explain what happened to the money and the weapons, but I couldn't. It looked as though Prek had double-crossed them. I talked to him and said that he had to either come up with the money or we would both be killed. His answer was not nice. He said that he would return the money and explain why the weapons could not be delivered, but I would have to divorce Rosa – my wife – and let her live with him. He called her 'Pandora' after the girl with the box of secrets and troubles.

You can imagine that this was outrageous to me. It was true that she had fallen for him in a big way. He was more adventurous than me and she probably thought that I was a bit boring, but she was the mother of my son and I didn't want to lose her. On the other hand, if I couldn't get the money back to the KLA or FARK, we would probably all have been killed – including Rosa and Paul.

I think there is a famous story by your Robert Louis Stevenson, called 'The Master of Ballantrae' which has a similar situation. Well, in the end, I agreed, in order to save

Rosa and Paul as well as myself and Prek. He returned some – not all – of the money and said that the Chetyans had taken the rest and kept the weapons. Whether the KLA believed him or not, it didn't matter, because there was another massacre that didn't involve us and most of them were killed or scared away.

That's not a very nice story but it's what happened. I gave the money from Prek to the remains of the KLA and took Paul away to school in Germany. Rosa went to live with Prek and he carried on his dealings in the company name of P.O. Holdings Inc."

Ostal looked tired from unburdening himself of the horrors of the Kosovo War and the break-up of his family and home. He took another long sip of beer and some of the antipasto. A waitress approached their table, laden with tuna steaks and vegetables, including some dark beans. *"Caraotas negras?"* ventured Lloyd. The waitress, olive-skinned and slim, smiled at his attempted Spanish.

"Si, Señor, "caraotas negras." But somehow, her pronunciation allowed the description to join forces with the dish of beans, without appearing to contradict that of Lloyd's.

Ostal smiled again, happier now that his guest was making the effort to assimilate himself with the surroundings and atmosphere of Sunday at the lake. He pushed the bean dish towards Lloyd, still smiling. "You didn't tell me that you spoke Spanish," he laughed.

"No. I didn't. And of course, I don't." Cocky returned the laugh as he piled the beans next to the tuna. "And, as you said yesterday, they have kept the oil from spoiling the tuna."

Ostal was impressed at his memory and appreciation of the little joke. Before he could digress from the subject of his family history, Lloyd resumed probing. "What happened to Rosa and your cousin, then?"

A forkful of tuna and beans obstructed an answer for a few moments. Carefully chewing the food for a few moments whilst considering where or how to start, Ostal thought back to the civil war that he and his country had suffered. "I cannot be certain of the details. I took Paul to Germany, staying with relatives of some Albanian friends in Bremen. Far away from the fighting. Prek and Rosa stayed in Kosovo for a very short time too. It would have been very risky to stay there for long.

"Some years later, I heard that they had moved to various places like Andorra and Liechtenstein. Partly to develop the business – or businesses – and keep away from death and taxation for as long as possible. Those are the two certainties in life, aren't they?" Lloyd was again impressed at the Kosovan's knowledge of English literature but didn't dare to interrupt.

"That was, I think, a quote from Mark Twain. Whoever it was, Prek subscribed to the same philosophy but tried his best to avoid both eventualities. I also heard, or rather Paul heard from his mother, that they rented an apartment in Monaco but then, moved from there to a strange place on an island in Greece. A very strange place. Used to be a leper colony but had been almost unoccupied for some years.

"Some of Prek's old friends bought it as a possible holiday development, but he just developed the main house as his personal villa. Typical of him to use his friends and their

344

money for his own benefit." There was, for the first time, a hint of bitterness in Ostal's voice. "Once he had gotten" – Lloyd noticed the American influence creeping in – "rid of me, he had no restricting hand on the company finances. It must have been like – how do you put it? – an alcoholic in charge of the wine shop."

Most of the history now unfolding was not entirely new to Lloyd. He had picked up so many anecdotes from other staff at P.O. Holdings Inc. and second-hand reports from Rose, via Tulloch, that he already had a strong impression of the Klevic grasp of other people's wealth. A candidate for political power would have suited him. Probably next on his wish list. He thought it timely to interrupt, if only to maintain the momentum.

"I had heard of some of his, uh, investment practices. But I didn't know him too well. Only met him a few times before he was… before his death. Seems very strange to me though that a man like that would have a fatal accident in his holiday home. How did that happen?" Lloyd knew too well that Ostal had been one of the mourners at the funeral. Perhaps 'mourner' was stretching the description but he was at least in attendance.

Ostal knew just as surely that Lloyd had been poking around on the main island, including a visit to the airfield and its ship's chandler-cum-air traffic controller. No attempt was going to be made at pretence.

"As I expect you know, I was on the island – Lenios – when Prek died. And you will also know that Rosa and I flew his body to Albania for burial." Cocky raised one palm with a half-shrug and nodded. He made sure that his mouth was occupied with beans before nodding, as Ostal's had been earlier.

"I know that because I visited it again a few weeks later, when I heard from one of the staff there – Athos Carolides – that you were there and interested in Prek's funeral cortege. It was a very small cortege, considering the size of Prek's reputation. Just Rosa and me, with Petric and Carolides to carry the stretcher with his body. Not even a coffin until we landed in Albania.

"After the funeral, Rosa and I, with Carolides, flew back to the island and over to Lenios on the boat. The other man – Petric – was Prek's old second-in-command from Kosovo, Dmitri Petric. Similar name, similar build and, originally, Prek's devoted protector. That was all. No other similarities. A strong and very brave fighter but no attempt to cheat or double cross anyone at all. We were not friends but I had respect for him."

It was time for Lloyd to cut to the chase. He might never again have the opportunity to ask directly. "It really was Prek in the coffin when it went into the ground, wasn't it? Not Petric?" He knew that Adrian Bogdani had reported a meeting with Petric, but that might well have been said to put him off the scent.

Ostal was amused at the thought of his cousin escaping death when it really arrived to catch him. He shook his head with another apologetic smile. "No. No chance of that. He was very dead. Very. Petric did stay in Albania and I think he went on to Kosovo, but he had his reasons and he was quite, quite alive."

Lloyd jumped in, still careful to avoid diverting Ostal from the account of death. "What were Petric's reasons, then? Didn't he want to come back and help to take care of Madam Klevic? – Rosa?"

Ostal resigned himself to giving a full account. He felt he could trust the visitor and there was no extradition treaty in Venezuela to threaten him if his trust was misplaced.

"Dmitri Petric had two reasons to leave Lenios and stay in Kosovo. The first was to avoid major trouble in Greece following his boss's death. The second was to re-visit some of the places which had suffered very badly during the war. To find out if and how his master really had cheated their own people."

Lloyd was not going to let go now. "What sort of trouble would he have? Klevic – Prek, sorry – had an accident, didn't he?"

Ostal's voice deepened, the tone stronger but the volume much lower. "Yes, an accident. But not the sort of accident that you might expect. When they were getting ready to leave Lenios and return to Liechtenstein, there was some sort of leaving party. I had been in Europe on my own business for a week or so and had gone there to pass some gifts to Rosa from Paul. So I became involved in the party, although it was a little awkward, as you might imagine.

"We were on a stone terrace, by the side of the swimming pool. Not that anyone was swimming – unless they were swimming in drink. There were plenty of drinks being swallowed then and perhaps everyone was talking much more than they might have considered… uh… sensible.

"Prek was not a fierce drinker but he had drunk more than usual. He had been talking to some of his old associates in Russia and Chechnya – they owned the villa – about money and some more dangerous sorts of business. Not altogether completely legal, I think. I don't know if they had been threatening him, but he seemed to be on edge – worried about something very serious.

"The drink made him shout a little – shouting at Rosa and shouting even at Petric. Not at me – he kept quiet when I was near. I heard him screaming at Rosa. He was almost unbalanced. He said something about what he was doing and that it was none of her business. Something about secrets and the other Pandora. Whatever that meant. I thought he was talking about a new mistress.

"Then, he started shouting at Petric. Saying that Petric had avoided all of the trouble when he – Prek – had risked his life with the Cechens and FARK. All sorts of nasty details came out, including some of the double-crossings. Petric and I could hardly believe what he was saying. Nor could Rosa. We had all lost many friends and family members due to that. And now he was almost bragging about it.

"Finally, he started to try to hit them. Petric just let him strike him. It wouldn't hurt him much but Rosa fell down, weeping. Prek had waved a bottle, as if to hit them with it. And then Rosa actually tried to hit back. She grabbed hold of the metal pole with a net on the end. You know? The one used to clean the insects from the water? She hit him on the head from behind him and pushed him with it.

"Prek roared but lost his balance and slipped. His foot slipped over the edge and he fell down – first onto the stone edge of the pool and then into the water. Although his head was cut from the fall and he was stunned, he tried to push himself up and out of the water. But Rosa was frightened that he would kill her. She pushed him back under the water with the pole until he seemed to have drowned. She should have known better. Prek scratched at the side of the pool to get out before he drowned. He was so frantic, his fingernails broke and nearly came off completely.

"As soon as she loosened her grip on the pole, he wrenched it from her and pulled himself out from the far side of the pool. At first he seemed calm. Just walking slowly back up the stairs to his room. We were all worried but hoped that the water had cooled him down, so we followed him up the stairs. I went to the toilet but could hear him talking – normally at first. But then, Petric told me, he really went quite berserk. He walked over to a desk, took out a gun and tried to point it at Rosa. Petric grabbed his arm to get the gun from him.

"Before anyone could get it, he tried to hit Rosa with it. She was struck on the side of her arm and on her back. Then, he said he was 'going to end her existence'. And he waved the gun towards her and pulled himself away from Petric. He knocked Rosa down onto the floor with his right arm and tried to hold the gun with his torn fingers on his left hand. But he couldn't hold it properly. It fell from his hand onto the carpet. As he came back to kick Rosa, she grabbed the gun before he could reach it.

I don't know whether she tried to fire it, but it fired anyway. Straight up into Prek's throat and out from the back of his eyes. He must have died instantly. There was blood and mess all over his face and a bullet in the ceiling."

Lloyd was silent and still. The disintegrating African ceiling in Matadi, with bullets in it, flashed back through his mind. There had to be more to come. Ostal took another sip of Cardenal lager. He wiped his mouth, which had become very dry, and then he resumed, slowly.

"Petric was more concerned for Rosa than for his boss. The truth about Kosovo had stunned him. He jumped down to the floor and took the gun from Rosa. Then he looked around and said, "Let me clear this mess – if I can." He was almost in tears. His boss was dead and, worse still, he knew that the man he had protected and followed for so long had cheated all of them and caused the death of many of their friends.

"Some of the staff had heard the shot and the shouting. They came banging at the door and we helped Rosa out of the room and into hers. Petric stayed with Prek's body. Then we heard the window opening and a thump from the stones around the pool outside. Petric went back down and out to where Prek's body had landed. He picked up a big stone, turned the body over, and smashed the remains of the head and face with it – again and again. I don't think it was any sort of revenge for what he had just heard. I think he just wanted to disguise the wounds where the bullet had hit Prek's jaw and exited out through his eye socket.

"One of Prek's arms had been broken in the fall, but he still smashed that too. Prek had been wearing a very expensive watch. Petric could have taken it but he preferred to smash it. All you could recognise on his upper body was one broken arm and the red star and crescent tattoo – the FARK motif – on the other arm. It was as if Petric wanted to destroy Prek's past as well as to disguise the gunshot wounds.

"After that, I suggested that we should get the body away from Greece as soon as possible. They would understand the need for a Muslim – even a lapsed one – to be buried quickly and in his home soil. When Rosa recovered from the shock, she really did recover – completely. She organised a doctor to meet us and to sign a death certificate, and an aircraft to fly us with Prek's corpse to Albania for burial.

"As I said, Petric felt compelled to stay in Albania so that he might unearth more details from whoever survived the massacres in Kosovo – to confirm or deny Prek's confessions. Or they might have been boasts. Hard to imagine what had been going on in his mind then – or in Petric's mind either, after he heard them.

"The rest of us came back with the aircraft, and we cleared up what we could before there could be an investigation. The Greeks didn't seem to worry once they had a signed death certificate. Just one more crazy Albanian Muslim out of the way.

"I think you know what happened after that. Much more than I do. Come on. This is quite depressing. Let's get some more beer and beans. You seem to like those."

Cocky Lloyd was indeed enjoying the beans and tuna. They harmonised well with the beer and the lakeside vista. He was also beginning to like his companion, particularly as he had related more of the mystery surrounding Klevic's death than he or Tulloch could ever have expected. It would be a consolation for Tulloch, who was probably disappointed at the evaporation of his nagging conspiracy theory – even though it had only originated from an old film on his hotel TV.

There were a few remaining loose ends for Lloyd to connect concerning the young man in Maracaibo, the son of the late Rose Klevic and of his host at the café table. Provided that Tulloch and Goldsmit between them could provide some advice of any residual benefit from Rose's personal pension fund, that could be settled tomorrow. In the meantime, he would soak up the local atmosphere and Ostal Klevic's hospitality, with a view to a return match, before departure for Vaduz and whatever future remained for him in P.O. Holdings Inc.

Evening arrives early and swiftly in Venezuela, by European standards. By the time that the two customers left the long lakeside lunch, it was approaching at high speed. At the hotel, Cocky thanked his host sincerely, assuring him of whatever help he could offer him or his son in future. That would commence the next day.

Tulloch's news, after discussions with Goldsmit, was encouraging. As Rose's only known relative, her investment in what was now her personal fund, plus the death in service insurance benefit, would be payable to her son Paul. It should total well over a quarter of a million US dollars, which for a young man working his pants off, would be a little gold mine. Significantly, it would be legitimate and obtained perfectly legally and honestly, albeit under the most distressing circumstances.

Details of the legacy from his mother were passed to an appreciative Paul, in the company of an equally appreciative Ostal Klevic. As they expressed their thanks and surprise to Cocky, his imagined alter ego of James Bond films couldn't resist returning some of Ostal's humour to his host of the previous day's lakeside meal.

"No such thing as a free lunch," he quipped.

39

CLOSING THE BOX

Lloyd returned to Vaduz on the next day's flight. All of the harrowing details of the Kosovo wars and of Patrick Klevic's violent death were then relayed to Tulloch, who was still in hospital. Over the next three months, the former trading assets and affairs of P.O. Holdings Inc. were passed to the new owners of the trading business.

Under Tulloch's helpful control, the residual shell of the company was then put into the loving hands and enormous professional fee income of a major firm of certified public accountants in Delaware.

'Liquidation', they realised, was the inevitable fate of unwanted companies, as surely as it had been to unwanted aides of Enver Hoxa, or those of Stalin and Hitler and many other ruthless dictators.

Rosa Klevic was buried in the municipal cemetery in Vaduz. The funeral was attended by Ostal and Paul Klevic, as well as Tulloch, Lloyd, Goldsmit and Carlsen, plus, some other former staff of P.O. Holdings Inc. With her burial, Ostal observed dryly, Pandora's box was finally closed. Nobody laughed. Tulloch shed a tear silently.

Rudolph Goldsmit continued full-time work as a consultant actuary. His standing in the insurance community was enhanced by his success in disposal of the higher-risk investments in the pension fund and converting the employees' contributions to individual personal pensions.

Jacob Carlsen remained semi-retired, working part-time as a non-exec. director of his bank in Zurich. He maintained business contacts with Tulloch and Goldsmit after P.O. Holdings Inc. had been liquidated.

Andrew Tulloch recovered after four more weeks in hospital. He was appointed by the court in Delaware, to assist the insolvency department of the certified public accountants, appointed to liquidate the shell of P.O. Holdings Inc. after the sale of its trading business. Liquidation was completed in ten months, which was something of a record for such operations.

Later, he was recruited by a large company of commodity traders based in Geneva. The appointment was recommended by Carlsen and Goldsmit. It carried a substantial salary to him and a large head-hunters' fee to the firm of Bastarde & Co.

After two years of very successful trading in his new company, Tulloch became the chief executive officer. His company then acquired that of his old employers in London, where he made sure that his former manager was retained as assistant treasurer with responsibility for risk management. The Grim Reaper suffered a nervous breakdown and retired after two months on half-pension.

Tulloch kept in touch with his lady lawyer in London. They were frequently seen dining together. He avoided driving as much as possible and preferred to visit restaurants by taxi and to pay the bills in cash.

George Armstrong retired briefly to Bradford, where he complained that 'there were too many foreigners'. After three months, he returned to Grand Cayman where he was employed as an hotel barman. His customers complained of the excessive loud operatic music, which killed their conversation, and he was retired again – without compensation.

James 'Elementary' Watson retired from the Hong Kong Police two years after the colony was returned to the PRC. Before returning to England, he enquired about the company of precious metal importers in Guangzhou. He was assured of their commercial success and of their high standing in the local business community and with the Communist Party.

Chou Li Chan (Joseph) was not seen again in Hong Kong, or in Macau or Guangzhou. His tailor's bill remains unpaid.

Llewellyn Lancelot 'Cocky' Lloyd returned to Hong Kong, but was unable to find suitable employment there. After three months, he received an offer of a job with a firm of insurance loss adjusters at his namesakes – Lloyds of London. He worked as an investigator, specialising in claims for kidnapping and fraudulent losses. The Smith & Wesson handgun remained unused.

Lloyd's office was based in London but he travelled extensively. He visited Swansea and Mumbles to see Gladys Watkins again. By then, she had been engaged to the insurance salesman for some time.

Cocky attended their wedding and the reception in the Langland Bay Hotel. He gave the couple a wedding present of matching nightshirts in Welsh international colours.

T'sang Xi Lao (Betty) left Hong Kong and was taken to live with her parents in Shanghai, still suffering badly from brain damage resulting from her drug-induced abduction. Cocky visited her several times before he too left the former colony, but she did not recognise him.

She never recovered and died two years later.

Pathos Paramides developed cirrhosis of the liver but continued to drink more raki than he caught fish. He was obliged to resign from any official post in his village council, after vomiting on the shoes of the retiring mayor at a council meeting.

Cyrus Constantiou developed his ships' chandlers business with his son. He was also given full executive charge of the airport on the island and later became mayor of the harbour town, after his predecessor was involved in a fight with the drunken Pathos and also had to resign.

Doctor Aristotle Panalides gave up his post as coroner but continued in general medical practice on the mainland. He said that he always preferred live patients to dead ones anyway.

Athos Carolides and the sailors on Lenios were retained by the registered owners of the villa. It was reclaimed by a syndicate of Russian and Albanian business associates, together with the furniture and the launch, in part settlement of debts owed by Patrick Klevic. Nobody disputed the claims. Carolides maintained the villa and his contacts with Ostal Klevic and his son Paul.

Arian Bogdani really did meet Dmitri Petric, as he had claimed. They worked together to reconstruct an account of the massacres in Western Kosovo. Most of the details were never released. The bodies of a Serbian and a visiting Chechen who were reputed to have supplied arms in several countries were found later near Bela Crkva. Nobody was charged with the murders.

Dmitri Petric after working in Kosovo with Bogdani moved suddenly to Albania. The headstone over Prek Klevic's grave was badly damaged and the earth and coffin disturbed. Petric was arrested. After a brief interrogation, he too was released without charge. He returned to Bela Crkva.

During the restoration of the grave, the damaged coffin was opened.

It contained only stones.